New Year's Eve

New Year's Eve

A Novel

Lisa Grunwald

Crown Publishers, Inc.
New York

Grateful acknowledgment is made for permission to reprint lyrics from:
"What Are You Doing New Year's Eve?"
By Frank Loesser
© 1947 (Renewed) FRANK MUSIC CORP.
All Rights Reserved

Published by Crown Publishers, Inc., 201 East 50th Street, New York,
New York 10022. Member of the Crown Publishing Group.

Random House, Inc. New York, Toronto, London, Sydney, Auckland
http://www.randomhouse.com/

CROWN is a trademark of Crown Publishers, Inc.

Printed in the United States of America

Library of Congress Cataloging-in-Publication Data is available upon request.

ISBN 0-517-70491-9

10 9 8 7 6 5 4 3 2 1

First Edition

For my family—past, present, and future.

I can guess about the past and
what you mean about the future;
But a present is missing,
needed to connect them.

T. S. Eliot
The Family Reunion

New Year's Eve

New Year's Eve, 1985

"Who Cares Whether Guy Lombardo's Brother Is Dead?"

We were pregnant together on New Year's Eve: my sister and I, twins in our thirties, brown-haired, mammoth, rivals in waiting. Heather, of course, felt better than I did. Looked better, too. Worried less. Talked more. This was to be her second child, and my first, and so she knew everything I was heading for, or at least everything she was heading for, and she made sure that I knew she knew, and that our father knew, and that our husbands knew. Her air of certainty, always brisk, was, that night, sublime.

New Year's Eve was our family ritual, our Christmas morning, our Fourth of July. It was the night on which we gathered, no matter where else we might have been tempted to go, to discover anew both how safe and how costly it was to be together. It was the night on which we brooded and smiled, ate too much and drank too little, and waltzed with each other at midnight. It was also the night that was never the way I hoped it would turn out to be.

"Stomach to stomach, girls!" my father said brightly, camera gleaming in his hands.

"No, Dad," I begged him. "Please. Not now."

"This is going to be great!" Heather said, and sprang to her unswollen feet.

I looked to my husband, Edgar, for help, but he was off in a corner, feigning interest in Richard, my brother-in-law.

Dad told us just how he wanted us standing: our arms at our sides, our stomachs just touching.

"Look at your sister," Dad told Heather.

Instead, she reached out to tug at my shirt.

"Leave it," I said.

"It's—"

"It's what?"

"You'll see."

"Cheese!" my father said merrily.

I grimaced. Heather grinned. The camera flashed and whirred. Dad smiled. "You'll be happy to have this someday," he said, and he was wrong, though no one then could have possibly known how wrong he would turn out to be.

———

I watched the picture develop as if I were watching the future unfold. I marveled, as I often had, at the differences between Heather and me. We looked like sisters, but not like twins. She was tall; I was not. She was lithe; I was not. Her hair was curly; mine was straight. Neither of us was quite beautiful, but she did more with what she had: tweezed her eyebrows, did her makeup. When we were children, our mother had dressed us alike, despite our impassioned protests and the bother of changing two sets of clothes when either one of us got a spot.

Now only our eyes were the same, as if we'd been given exactly equal power to witness each other's lives.

"Told you so," Heather said gaily. She leaned over my shoulder to point at the photograph of my too-small shirt, the proof of my huge and hated weight gain.

When she walked away, I used my thumbnail to measure whose belly was bigger. Mine. And hers should have been bigger, because her due date was four weeks ahead of mine.

She had always gone first. She had been born only twenty-two minutes before me, but I believed that in those twenty-two minutes resided her power and her control. She thought of herself as older. She had, subtly, always been treated as older. She had been named for our father's mother, who had died the year before. I wasn't named for anyone. Erica was just a name that had seemed to my parents to go well with Heather.

She had been the first one to smoke a cigarette, try marijuana, get her period, kiss a boy, lose her virginity, marry, have a child. She'd known that she wanted to be a doctor before I'd known I wanted to teach. She had been my protector, my lookout, my voice at the drugstore counter when I'd been too shy to ask for help. She had killed the spiders, led the way home, rung the doorbells for trick or treat.

Often I had wondered: If I had been born twenty-two minutes before Heather, would I have gotten the name? If they had given me the name, would I have had the power? If I had come out before Heather, would I have learned in those first, free minutes that I didn't have to look back?

———·———

Dad checked his gold pocket watch and turned on the TV at 11:35.

"What channel is Guy Lombardo on?" he asked.

"Guy Lombardo's dead," Heather said.

"His orchestra," Dad said.

"His orchestra's dead too," Heather said.

"His brother," Dad said. "His brother took over the orchestra."

"His brother's dead," Richard said.

Heather laughed.

"You made that up," Dad told him.

"Who cares whether Guy Lombardo's brother is dead?" Heather said.

"*I* care," Dad said, eyes merry. "How can you not care?" he asked her. His face, square and handsome but deeply furrowed, hovered above Heather's antically. But I sensed in him more rage and distraction than he wanted to show.

"Because," Heather said to him blithely, "it isn't 1932 anymore."

She and Richard laughed again. She settled back on the couch, beside him, content to enjoy the joke she'd made, just as, often, she was content to enjoy the confusion she made, or the sorrow. I didn't laugh with them. I couldn't. I felt awful for Dad. For years, he'd been growing old gracefully, but now he was facing retirement, he seemed beset by a roving obsession with time. He was sixty-eight and hypnotized by the specter of seventy.

———

Jeffrey, Heather's two-year-old, had been shredding sheets of red paper and collecting them in a pile. Now he gathered the pieces, stood up slowly, and tossed them skyward. Studiously, he watched them settle—mostly on Richard's and Edgar's shoes—and then started singing while dancing around them: "Ring around the rosy, pocketful of posies . . ."

"Have you ever listened to the words of that thing?" Dad asked Heather.

"Ashes, ashes," sang Jeffrey.

"What?" Heather asked Dad.

"All fall down!" Jeffrey shouted.

"Sweetheart," Heather told Jeffrey.

" 'Ashes, ashes,' " said Dad, " 'we all fall down.' What kind of a message is that for a child? Don't you know that this song was about the Plague?"

"Down!" Jeffrey shouted for emphasis.

———

There was not a Lombardo to be found. On Channel 4, a nondescript interviewer was asking the cold, foolhardy celebrants in Times Square for their New Year's resolutions.

The dreaded subject had been broached.

"Revolution?" Jeffrey said.

The grown-ups looked around nervously. My father was out of the room just then, but we knew that he would be back.

"*Re*solution," Heather and I said at exactly the same instant. We laughed. Even in our worst phases, we had often spoken in stereo, or answered each other's unasked questions, or started to sing in unison the same song, in the same key.

"Resolution?" Jeffrey asked, too young to know he was playing with fire.

"It's a promise," I told him.

"What's a promise?" my father asked, returning.

No one said a word.

"Cookie, do you have your noisemaker ready?" Heather asked Jeffrey.

"What's a promise?" my father asked again.

"Revolution. *Re*solution," Jeffrey said.

"Well, well," my father said, perking up.

We—his twin daughters—looked at each other, our eyebrows raised, our words unneeded. The look excluded the rest of the room. It jumped through time.

"A resolution," said Richard, "is like a deal you make."

Heather laughed and rumpled his hair.

"Richard thinks that everything is like a deal you make," she said.

He ducked his head out from under her hand.

"What deal?" Jeffrey asked suspiciously.

"Well, let's see," my father said, warming to the subject. "You choose a way that you are going to be better. Then you tell us what it is."

"For God's sake, Dad," Heather said. "He's only two."

Of all our New Year's rituals, by far the most treacherous was our father's insistence on the round-robin public naming of our New Year's resolutions. It was his version of the Quaker meeting or, for that matter, the twelve-step program, extremely bizarre for a man whose career as a doctor and whose outlook on life had left him not a whisper of room for any spirituality. But not a New Year's of my life had passed without his mandate that we own up to our sins. It was the part of New Year's that he'd always liked best: the chance to invoke the future he loved, and to banish the useless past. When our mother had been alive, she'd always managed to tease him about it. But she had been gone for nearly three years, and, with her, not only a source of forgiveness but also a sense of proportion.

"What do I get for the promise?" Jeffrey asked.

"You get to know that you're being a good boy," Dad said.

Jeffrey lost interest. "Juice," he said.

My father had other fish to fry.

"Let's gather round," he told his family.

"It's nearly midnight," I said to him.

"Heather first," Dad went on, unperturbed. "It's always Heather first, isn't it?"

Edgar gave me a brilliant squeeze.

"Heather?" Richard asked his wife. "What's it going to be this year?"

"Let's see," Heather said. She smoothed her hair with the side of her hand, a mannerism of Dad's that she would have hated to know she'd inherited. "I resolve—" she began, then looked around the room as if she was looking for a target. "I resolve to take a lengthy sabbatical, and spend the next three New Year's Eves in Paris, London, and Rome."

"I don't think that's funny," Dad said.

"I don't think it's possible," Richard said. He knew that she'd never be able to step off the wild, glad ride of her booming career for more than the briefest maternity leave.

"Lighten up," she told Dad and Richard. "What would be so bad about me taking a little time off?"

"You've got to take care of your practice," Dad told her.

"Dad," Heather said with a marksman's precision, "I've got plenty of time."

My father's eyes filled with rage and self-pity, and also the guilty knowledge that he was jealous of his own child.

———

For years, I've begun my classes by talking about all the ways that Greek myths show up in our lives. I tell my students about Achilles' heel and I tell them about Midas' touch. I tell them about Nike, and I tell them about Nemesis. I tell them how lethargy came from Lethe. And I tell them about Kronos, the god who in legend became Father Time, that wizened figure with sickle and hourglass who's haunted so many New Year's Eves.

Kronos was a Titan, one of the seven children of the Earth and the Sky. He was told that one of his children would someday usurp him, so he developed the nasty habit of devouring them at birth.

I thought of my father as Kronos. He was bitter as hell about getting old, and now, as the time sped on, he sized up his children hungrily but seemed to fear he had missed his chance.

———

"My resolution is next," I said as I shook my head at Heather and turned to bend over the caviar.

"Yes, Erica's next," Edgar said.

"Maybe I wasn't finished yet," Heather said.

"It's my turn," I said, trying to meet her eyes. I loathed his game as much as she did, but I loved him, and hated her cruelty.

"I resolve," I said, "not to let Heather be mean."

Heather looked at me arctically. But Dad hadn't even heard me. He was still lurking in his own feelings.

"More juice, Mom," Jeffrey said, and Heather went to get it.

The husbands, as always, were spared. It was probably just as well. Richard was fifteen years older than Heather, a tax lawyer on Wall Street who was stern enough with his own rituals to resent taking part in others'. Edgar, who was a teacher, like me, had a professorial openness to all question-and-answer sessions, and he would have been a good sport. But when the Marks family assembled, the spouses were seconds, not players themselves.

My father's own turn came, blessedly, just moments before it was midnight.

"My resolution is to rewrite my will," he said.

"Again?" we all asked him in unison. That was, I knew, what Mom would have said, and it made me happy to hear it.

Then the sounds of car horns and of revelers in the street drifted up toward Dad's apartment. Heather flashed the lights off and on. Jeffrey blew on his noisemaker, then sucked it back in so hard that he began to cough.

"Hey!" my father said festively, and kissed Heather and me, and lifted his glass.

Heather came over and hugged me. Belly-to-belly, we had to laugh.

"Happy New Year," she said.

I kissed her.

"It's going to be great, isn't it?" she said.

"What is?"

"To have the babies together."

"Is it?" I asked her, both moved and surprised.

Edgar came over and parted us. He put one hand on my belly and the other at the back of my neck.

"To us, darling," he said, and kissed me.

I felt the baby kick and stir.

"Next year," he said somewhat pointedly, "maybe we'll celebrate New Year's Eve with our own family."

From the mantel above the fireplace came the chimes of my father's favorite clock. The clock was French and antique and had four glass sides and a globe on top that showed the progress of the year.

"Ring ring!" Jeffrey said. "Ring ring! Ring ring!"

"It's off by at least a minute," Dad said, and then set about fixing the time.

What I wanted, washing the glasses and stacking the plates in Dad's dishwasher, was for him to stop acting so tragic, or at least make some minimal effort at grace. And I wanted Heather to fail, or to be fat, or to admit she liked one thing about me, or had one fond memory of our past.

But here is what I really wanted: I wanted to have these people around me always. I wanted our fights and our speculations, our triangles, duels, and solitary pouts. I wanted us to live under the same large, actual roof, attending our various joys and pains, and not being forced, as we always were, into the fragmented future.

New Year's Eve, 1958

"This Is a Waltz by Strauss"

Heather and I wear our new nightgowns. They are orange, with matching white daisies, and lace, and they reach all the way to the floor.

We are five. It's the first New Year's Eve I'll remember, the one that I'll long for and try to retrieve.

We tiptoe into the living room, the room where we're never allowed to play. Balloons hang in clusters like chandeliers; our stuffed bears and bunnies are sitting like guests on the couch and the velvet chairs.

The crystal champagne glasses catch the light. Inside them, bubbles shoot up to the surface in straight, magical lines.

"Happy New Year, girls," Dad says, and we run into his strong, sure arms.

Heather goes into the kitchen with Mom to help her toast bread for the caviar.

The TV is on with the sound turned off. Dad stands by his new hi-fi and watches with satisfaction as the thick arm drops a record down.

I'm sleepy. I look up to see Dad's clock. The small hand has almost caught up to the twelve. The big hand is halfway between eight and nine.

"This is a waltz by Strauss," Dad tells me. When he tells me facts, I think they are secrets.

He's happy. He calls out to Mom, who glides in carrying caviar, smiling, Heather beside her. Mom looks so pretty. Her face is wide open, her eyes are dark brown, and her hair short and shiny.

"The Strauss," she tells Dad contentedly.

She puts the caviar down, and then he draws her into his arms, and they start waltzing around the living room.

Dad takes out his movie camera and films Mom dancing with Heather, Heather dancing with her bear, Heather and me dancing together, holding hands, tripping over our new nightgowns.

We get to dance with him too, taking turns. When it's my turn, I want to look into his eyes the way Mom did, but I need to look down at my feet so they won't slide off his shoes. They slide off anyway, but he lifts me up, puts me back on, and kisses the top of my head.

He is always coming and going from us. He is always tired and insistent, but Mom is always telling us why, always describing the strangers he's treated and saved, the families he's rescued, the hero he's been. He's the largest thing in our little lives. He is here tonight. He has put us first. We are able to be his hero's welcome, the place he returns to, never unsung.

When the dancing is over, Heather and I lean close and whisper, and we run to our rooms to get our costumes from the closets. The costumes are cardboard butterfly wings. Heather's are orange, and mine are green. Dad smiles, as we've hoped all week that he would. He films us flapping our arms as we fly in twin circles around Mom's skirt.

He lets us taste the champagne, and we get to eat all the cookies we want.

Heather lies next to me on the couch, the fabric of my night-gown sleeve indistinguishable from the fabric of hers.

On the TV, the screen fills with bits of confetti, and bright new balloons, to drift down through the years.

New Year's Day, 1986

"The Right Note Would Sound Wrong"

It turned out it had been a guy named Jerry Kravat leading the orchestra at the Waldorf-Astoria the night before. Heather called New Year's morning to read me an article from the *New York Times,* in which Kravat explained that he deliberately had his musicians play the wrong note in the second bar of "Auld Lang Syne"—F sharp instead of F natural. "People," he was quoted as saying, "are accustomed to hearing the wrong note. The right note would sound wrong."

"Funny," I told Heather.

"This is an unmistakable reference to Guy Lombardo," she said.

"I guess so," I said.

"All those years," she said, cackling, "Lombardo was screwing up 'Auld Lang Syne.' "

"I guess so," I said again.

"Think I should call Dad and tell him?" Heather asked me.

"What a great way to start the new year," I said.

"You're losing your sense of humor," she told me.

"Do what you want," I said, and hung up.

"Heather?" Edgar asked me. We were still lying in bed.

"Of course."

"What did she want?"

"What she always wants."

"To make you crazy," Edgar said.

My sister knew every weakness in me. She was like a china collector, with an acute awareness of each chip and flaw.

Edgar nestled against my shoulder. "How did you sleep?" he asked me.

"The baby was kicking."

"I love it," he said.

"I know," I told him.

He lifted the sheet and covers and the T-shirt of his I'd been wearing to sleep in since everything I owned had gotten too small.

"What day?" I asked him, a ritual by now.

"April first."

"No. Please. Can you imagine?"

"April Fools' Day."

"Don't let it happen."

"Okay."

He put a hand on my belly.

"Maybe ours will be born before Heather's," I told him.

"Maybe by twenty-two minutes," he said.

Spring, 1986

"They're Still Adjusting to Life on Land"

Heather called me from her labor room on the morning of March first. Her fellow doctors at the hospital had arranged to get her a portable phone.

"Hi," she said.

"Heather?"

"Hi."

"Where are you?"

"The hospital," she said breezily.

"Are you okay? Is Richard okay? Did you have a false alarm or something?"

"No. I'm in labor."

"You're what?"

"I'm in labor."

"You're kidding," I said.

"No, I'm not," she said. "Wait." She covered the phone. I could hear her giving some muffled instructions.

"I'm four centimeters," she said.

"Already?"

"It's been a breeze."

"Of course," I said.

"What?"

"Did you get Demerol?"

"No way."

"Anything?"

"No way. I told you. It's bad for the kid. Wait." There was a longish silence.

"That was a big one," she said.

"Did it hurt?"

"Not too bad," she said.

"That's good," I said.

"Well, I guess I'd better go."

"Okay."

And she hung up to have her child.

———

I held David for the first time the next day. It had been just a few years since Jeffrey's birth, but nothing I remembered had prepared me for David's size.

He was smaller than the blue teddy bear that someone had sent as a birthday gift. He was smaller than my pregnant belly. His face was pinched and mottled, and the skin on his feet seemed loose. Holding him scared the hell out of me. Every breath he took came with a different, tortured sound.

"It's perfectly normal," Heather said, reading either my face or my thoughts.

"Why do they do this?" I asked her.

"They're still adjusting to life on land."

He wriggled a little and let out a cry, his face the shade of a tropical sunset, his tiny mouth an impossible O.

Heather scooped him up in one expert arm and settled back into her hospital bed. She opened her robe to nurse him.

"I'm not ready for this," I told her.

"You'll do fine," she said rather kindly, and I was touched, but no less terrified.

———

Sarah arrived six weeks later, on a massive cloud of Demerol and deep, deep joy.

I was in labor for only eight hours, and after the first dozen bad contractions, I never felt a thing. As I pushed, a nurse held one of my legs up. Wilma, my doctor, held the other. At my back, Edgar held my shoulders and rolled them forward and whispered to me and exhorted. I was the center of the world.

There was a small framed print in the labor room, of a mother standing next to her child, and for me, the business of that long, deep night was trying to picture myself as the larger figure instead of the smaller one. Through clenched, closed eyes, I saw nothing and imagined the baby and me. Feeding into us were the voices. The nurse, Julia, like an auctioneer: "Come on, Erica, come on, come on, come on, sweetheart, you can do it, hold it, hold it, hold it, don't let up, don't let up." And Wilma, from the other side: "That's a good one, that's a good one, hold it for ten seconds now, one, two, three . . ." And Edgar: "Come on baby, come on darling, tuck your chin in, don't let up."

And then, from Wilma: "I see her."

And from Julia: "She's got her mommy's hair."

I thought she was talking about my mother. I thought she meant that somehow I was bringing her back into the world.

Then I realized she was talking about me. I was going to be Mommy. I was going to be Mother, the word with the most freight in any language.

Her eyes were wide open when she was born, and Edgar and I were sobbing.

We called Dad. Dad called Heather. Heather called Richard. Heather called us.

"So how was it?" she asked me.

"Amazing," I said.

"Did you get drugs?"

"Yes."

"Wimp."

I laughed.

"Who does she look like?"

"Frank Sinatra. When are you coming to see her?" I asked.

"I'll see her when you get home," she said.

In the background, I heard a faint, brittle cry.

"David's hungry again," she said.

"How can you tell?"

"You'll figure it out."

The first two weeks were lovely. Edgar had taken time off from his classes, so we were a team, and we were humming. When friends from the university came to visit, Edgar greeted them giddily at the door, then ushered them into Sarah's room, where I sat like Mother Earth, dispensing milk and maternal gazes.

Edgar woke me for the feedings, bringing me water to drink, a pillow to rest on, a cloth diaper for my shoulder.

He emptied the diaper pail unasked.

He swaddled her with precision.

He burped her with gusto.

He came with Sarah and me to the two-week checkup with Joe Worth, one of the three doctors who shared Heather's practice.

Joe moved his enormous hands over Sarah's tiny body and pronounced her fit.

"You'll probably want to call Heather if you have any questions," he said, "but don't. She needs her time off. And it'll be better for you and Sarah in the long run if you learn how to trust the rest of us."

I smiled. "Absolutely," I said.

"And trust yourself," he said.

I stopped smiling.

"She's great," he said, handing Sarah to me and waving a hearty good-bye.

Edgar picked up Sarah's booties and hat.

We looked at each other and started to laugh.

"What the hell do we do now?" I asked him.

"Beats the hell out of me," he said, and tossed Sarah's hat in the air.

———

Then he went back to work, and a single day seemed longer than my whole life had been. I nursed Sarah every three or four hours, weighed myself almost as often, and was so amazed by the sight of her sleeping that I couldn't sleep myself. At five in the afternoon, I finally managed to take the shower that I'd been wanting to take all day. I left the door to the bathroom wide open. I put Sarah's basket three feet away. And even so, when I rinsed my hair, I felt as if I were risking her life.

I called Dad, who seemed amused by me but didn't offer a visit.

If I didn't feel quite prepared to take on the hazards of being a mother, I felt even less prepared to give up the shelter of being a child.

———

"Are you ever coming over?" I asked Heather at seven o'clock on the morning of my second day alone.

"Sure," she said. "Okay."

"When?"

"How about tomorrow?" she asked me.

"Now."

"I can't today," she said.

"Now," I said.

She laughed. "Why don't you take her to the park?"

"*Outside?*" I asked.

"She's two and a half weeks old," Heather said. "She'll be fine."

But I didn't take her out. By the time I had packed a bag for her and changed her three times and fed her twice, it had started to rain. It rained all day. I sang to her and rocked her. I couldn't stop watching her sleep. After nine months of waiting for time to pass, it seemed that I was still waiting. What I was waiting for was a time when I would feel that she was safe.

I did not know how to love her. But the sweet powdery softness of her skin overwhelmed me.

I was beginning to understand that there might be a difference between happiness and peace. I had never felt so much of
the first, so little of the second. How could I be peaceful when
a life was in my hands?

———

Two days later, Heather still hadn't seen Sarah.

"She's probably just busy," Dad said when I'd stopped feeling
hurt by his absence long enough to tell him how hurt I was by
hers.

"I know she's busy," I said. "She's always busy. That's not the
point."

"What's the point?"

"The point is that she could find a minute to call me if she
wanted to."

"She never calls me either," he said.

"You didn't just have your first baby," I said.

"Exactly," he said.

"And what does that mean?"

"It means that you just had your first baby. You've got your
whole life in front of you."

"I've got *Sarah's* whole life in front of me," I said.

"You're young," he said.

"Sarah's younger than I am."

"You're younger than I am."

"Okay, Dad, you win."

Who was busier than thou? The question was just one legacy
of my father's once-driving career. Time in our childhood had
not been a river. It had been a tiny slip of a stream, flowing
meagerly but predictably, and we had been trained to perch on

its banks and jump in on every single occasion when our father floated by.

We'd had four hours every Sunday morning with him, and a winter vacation each year of one week, and the fixed ritual of New Year's Eve, and the flexible rituals like our birthdays. Beyond that, he had been home for dinner perhaps two nights a week, and we'd grown up waiting for him to arrive, running into the living room to look at the clock on the mantel shelf. We'd used up time waiting for time.

He had always come promptly at eight o'clock, checking the watch in his vest pocket, even as we clamored to kiss him.

Even after my father stopped practicing, he continued to consult this watch, as if he were always late for something, or worried about falling behind. His vest pocket was a horizon, his gold watch an always-setting sun. Now that he had time, he seemed to spend it mainly thinking about the time he didn't have.

"When are you going to see my child?" I asked Heather on the phone the next morning.

"How about tomorrow?"

"That's what you always say."

The phone rang once all day. It was Edgar.

"I never even had turtles," I told him.

"What?"

"No pets. No dog. No cat. No turtles."

"You must have had goldfish," he said.

"I'm serious, Edgar," I said. "I've never cared for another living thing."

"How about plants?" he said.

"When are you coming home?"

"The usual time," he said. "Okay?"

"No."

"I've got students backed up in the hallway," he said.

"I've got five more hours alone."

"You'll be fine."

I hung up and burst into tears.

———

Edgar and I met on the crest of a wave at Jones Beach in 1984. That is not a metaphor. I dove into a breaker, and when I surfaced, he was there.

It was the end of the school term, and we had both gone on a faculty outing set up to foster esprit de corps. Neither of us could remember having seen the other on campus before. There was no reason why we should have. He taught history. I taught myth, and though our disciplines intertwined, the buildings we taught them in stood blocks apart.

"I'm sorry," he said as the wave bumped him toward me.

"I'm Erica," I said when I saw his face.

We went home together that night.

I reread the water myths. Poseidon ruled the ocean, having helped overthrow his father, Kronos. But Poseidon was also vengeful, combative, and liked to fool around, and that wasn't exactly the kind of person I hoped Edgar would turn out to be.

I decided he might be Nereus, the original Old Man of the

Sea. Edgar was my age, just thirty then, but he possessed the kind of calm that, I felt, only came with wisdom.

Nereus was the father of fifty mermaids. Edgar talked about the children we'd have even before he talked about the marriage we'd have, but he talked about both a lot.

He asked me to marry him exactly three months after our day at Jones Beach, and I said yes immediately. Later I saw, beneath my family's apparent enthusiasm, the slightly sneering suggestion that I was just playing catch-up with Heather.

But I loved Edgar. I loved his steadiness and his strength, his shocking lack of confusion, and the way that he loved me.

He was an only child, and his parents lived in Boston, which they made seem remote. He had been raised with money and nannies, by people who'd traveled as much as they'd been home and who'd believed that eighteen years was the extent of their true responsibility toward their son.

My family was as exotic to him as his was to me, but mine was deeply appealing to him, part of an old fantasy.

He understood my nostalgia, and, unlike my sister, he usually forgave it.

We were married at the Plaza, by a rabbi with a hilarious lisp. Then, after the ceremony, we were ushered into a tiny room, where we kissed, and stopped time. It was a kiss with no mental audience, no inner judgment, no thoughts of the next moment, or the last. Then, like an accident, it carted my life before me. I was kissing last lovers, first boyfriends. I was on a beach in summer, under a blanket in winter. I was twelve and twenty. I was seventy. I saw a sunlit patch of pavement I had played hopscotch on when I was six. Then Edgar brushed his hand against the garland in my hair and managed to pluck out a single flower that he nearly crushed between our hands when he took my hand in his.

———

A year and a half later, Edgar asked me for a kiss. He had come home half an hour earlier than usual, but I hadn't exactly hung out a flag. I had just put Sarah down to sleep.

I kissed Edgar's lips perfunctorily, then fought a startling urge to touch the corner of his mouth the way I did to start Sarah nursing.

I looked down at the bed.

"Tired?" he asked, as if it was a question.

"Exhausted," I said, as if answering him.

What he'd really said was: What about me?

What I'd really said was: What about me?

I was not used to being his nemesis, let alone his scold.

But I was also not used to feeling that he was the Other—the foreign, male, presence—that Heather had always said Richard was.

It was May. The trees in Central Park billowed and shimmered in pink and white. The next morning, I wheeled Sarah's stroller to a bench beneath them and looked out at the future: There were children on bicycles, children on skates, children in trees, children in tears.

And there were the white mothers, and there were the black baby-sitters, each gathered in separate clusters on the benches in the playground, each dispensing various amounts of apple juice, graham crackers, comfort, and clothing as children came and went from them in overlapping circles. And apart from a park custodian, there was not a man in sight.

It was twenty minutes past ten, and Heather at last appeared, half an hour late.

"You're late," I said, though the mere sight of her had calmed me and made me feel more complete.

"I know," she said, and deftly steered David's stroller next to Sarah's. Finally then, she looked down at her niece.

"She's teeny," she said.

"I know," I said.

"She's cute, though," she said.

"Thanks."

"Like Edgar."

I let this comment roll over me as Heather stood up to tie her hair back. Her body seemed depressingly fit.

"Are those your real jeans?" I asked, awestruck.

"I just fit back into them. Yeah," she said.

"Incredible," I said. "I hate you."

"You'll get there."

"I'm sick of maternity clothes," I said.

"Well, *you're* in a wonderful mood," she said.

"She was up at one, three, and six," I said, not wanting to tell her that what really bothered me was Edgar, who'd slept through each one of those feedings. On the scorecard of Heather's and my relentless competition, having a glorious marriage had always been one major point for me.

"It gets better," Heather said.

"When?"

She shrugged.

We both looked down at Sarah, who chose the moment to open her eyes, and then her mouth, into a wide crescent.

"She's hungry," Heather said.

"I know that," I snapped.

I reached into the stroller and lifted her out and put her to my breast.

I said: "They're close enough in age to be—"

"Twins?" Heather said.

I shrugged.

She smiled. She reached into David's stroller bag and pulled out a gift-wrapped box.

"You already gave me a shower," I said. She had. She'd invited my colleagues from school and had even tracked down my best friend from college.

"Open it," she said, grinning at me.

But I was still nursing.

"I'll open it," she said.

In the box were two sets of identical and adorable baby clothes.

We started laughing together. Mothers on neighboring benches looked over.

"I can't believe you did this," I told her. "I thought you were going to kill me if I ever tried to dress them alike."

She smiled and reached out, still laughing, to hold her niece for the first time.

———

In the afternoon, Sarah slept for three hours. I tried, again, to take a nap. I turned the TV on and changed channels, stopping, transfixed, at a Spanish-language station that was showing a program on infant CPR. I didn't know a word of Spanish. I watched the entire thing, utterly rapt, then brought Sarah's basket back into my room.

I dozed. I heard the baby's cry in the sound of a car on the street, in the curtain pull bumping against the window.

———

"Did you love them right from the start?" I asked Heather when I called her on the phone that night.

"Give yourself some time," she said.

"Did you miss Mom?" I asked her.

"You're going to be fine."

———

A Tiffany rattle arrived for Sarah, a gift from Bruno Lyons, who was head of my department and a famously distant attraction for both his students and his staff. He was in his early sixties now, but I had harbored a crush on him ever since I had taken his courses at Princeton. I called, nervously, to thank him.

"We miss you already," he said, and I watched two grins gleam in the rattle's twin barbells. "Are you sure you won't come back before summer?"

"I've got to get used to this," I told him.

"Do you remember Estanatlehi?" he asked.

I racked my memory violently, but it didn't seem to be working.

"Estanatlehi?" I asked him.

" 'The woman who changes,' " he said.

"Navajo?"

"That's right. She never remains the same. She lives countless lives in succession, grows old, grows young, has children, greets the seasons."

"What's your point, Bruno?"

"Things change."

"Oh. Well, thanks."

I hung up, still clutching the rattle.

———

At night, Edgar held Sarah while I took a shower. It was the first moment all day when I'd been alone, the first moment when I hadn't had to worry about her. I worried anyway. Through the water, the steam, the shower door, the bathroom door, I heard the staccato overture to her crying. *Eh. Eh eh eh. Eh eh eh eh eh.* My hair was full of lather.

I flung open the door.

Edgar was sitting with her on the bed. He was watching the basketball play-offs while trying to rock her into silence. He wasn't looking at her.

"She's crying," I said.

"I think she's hungry," he said, still looking at the TV screen.

"She's not hungry. I just fed her," I said.

I took her from him and put her over my shoulder. She stopped crying instantly.

He turned off the game and looked at me.

"Didn't you see me feed her?" I asked.

"I guess," he said. "It's all kind of a blur."

"What's a blur?"

"I'm tired too, you know."

"You got seven hours of sleep last night."

"I played basketball at lunchtime. I'm beat. Why don't you give her to me and dry yourself off?"

I stood in a small pool of water.

I went back into the bathroom and wrapped a large towel

around my large body. I wondered if I would ever be able to wrap the small towels around me again. I wondered if there was a single thing that I'd ever liked about Edgar, or that he'd ever liked about me.

I was impossible with him. I accused, apologized, wept, explained, exhorted, admonished, instructed, withdrew. I wanted him to find his own rhythm with Sarah, but all I perceived was a lack of rhythm, a failure of timing on his part. He would cheerfully thaw out a bottle for her, but then he'd withhold it from her lips for just a second or two while he finished telling me some story. He was better at swaddling her than I was, but after a diaper change, he'd leave her unwrapped for just a second or two while putting a cap back on her head. In those just-a-second-or-twos lay the difference between her not crying and her crying, and in that difference lay my rage and contempt. He knew how to react to her crying; I knew how to anticipate it and, more often than he did, prevent it.

"What's the big deal if she cries?" he asked me.

The fact that he had to ask seemed further proof of his perfidy. How could I explain to him a situation so far beyond reason? How could I explain that when she was sleeping, I wanted to wake her up, and that when she was up, I wanted her sleeping? How could I explain the emotional imperative, let alone the physical one: the milk coming to my breasts at the sound of her cry, or of any baby's? What would he feel like, I wondered, if milk started dripping from some part of him?

I decided I couldn't explain it.

"He doesn't even hear her," I whispered to Heather that night on the telephone. It was midnight, and we were both nursing our babies, in separate apartments, by separate lamps.

"You mean the perfect man isn't perfect?" she said.

"Don't be mean. I'm *confiding* in you," I said. "Sarah cries, and he just keeps on talking as if she's on some TV show."

"Oh, God, Erica," Heather said, laughing nicely. "I don't know what to tell you. Welcome to motherhood."

"Men are useless," she said the next day.

We were sitting on the park benches, though it had rained the night before, and the sky was gray, and the air was cool.

What Heather said wasn't a statement. It was a challenge, a dare, a temptation.

I'd never thought Edgar was useless. I'd thought he was marvelous.

"Totally useless," I said.

Heather and I had chased each other for years, like hands on a clock. Now, with Sarah just five weeks old, we were talking almost daily for the first time since our childhood.

We spent the mornings together, rain or shine, colic or cooing. In the afternoons, she strolled David home from the park to be with Jeffrey, and I strolled Sarah home, and she napped, and she woke, and I called Heather two or three more times with the latest reports on her progress. I would sneak in the little questions that I'd never ask Sarah's own doctor, Joe Worth. Heather answered them all with astonishing grace, never once making me feel stupid. She even told me, once, that I was much calmer than most of the parents she saw. That buoyed me for several days.

Occasionally, I would wonder if her tolerance came from loyalty or simply from the fact that she hated to be alone with her children even more than she hated to be with me.

I knew she missed her work. She laced our talks with coy complaints about her colleagues and how they kept calling.

"I've still got a month left, for God's sake," she'd say, but I knew she was counting the days till she could reclaim her white doctor's coat, her armor.

In the meantime, she seemed to want to be with me. Some afternoons, she'd even leave Jeffrey with his sitter, Debbie, just to meet me with David to do errands. We lived just five blocks away from each other, so her shops and stores were the same as mine.

On a Thursday afternoon, we put Sarah and David in their carriers and met at a neighborhood take-out place where chickens turned in the steamy windows and smelled sumptuous inside. We each ordered dinners for our families, then bought two potato pancakes to eat while we were waiting.

Heather took the first bite.

"Oh my God," she said.

"What is it?"

"Oh my God."

"What?"

"My milk came in."

"For a latke?" I said, and we started to laugh. We laughed so hard that we woke the babies. They started crying. My milk came in. We were stranded in the store, surrounded by men with greasy fingers who were watching us leak and giggle as we ate latkes and bounced our babies in our arms.

On a Tuesday morning, I knelt at Heather's feet while she breast-fed David, and I trimmed his nails for her.

I stepped on a scale at her place once a week. She bought me a smaller pair of jeans.

"I'm done making babies," she told me one day. She decided to have a tubal ligation. I baby-sat David while she was away. I was awed by the fact that I had it in me to take care of two children.

But I could comfort David. Heather could comfort Sarah. We knew more about each other's babies than our husbands did.

The first time Sarah smiled—an unmistakable moment of communication with the black-and-white bunny that shared her crib—it was Heather I told first, not Edgar.

We were comrades in a milky war, trenched down with babies, bottles, blankets, pacifiers, diapers, creams. The sounds of this war were cries, gurgles, and the repetitive tinkle of crib mobiles. The smells were noxious. The sights were mild. But the enemies were the allies: our children and ourselves. In short, we needed each other to survive the monotony and the fatigue and the way we'd lost track of our lives.

Side by side in their matching strollers, the babies were starting to look alike.

New Year's Eve, 1989

"Class, Please Turn Now to Page Fourteen of
The Cat in the Hat Comes Back!"

It was the eve not only of another new year but also of a new decade. The newspapers and magazines were fat with predictions. The future was going to be sober and earthy; the past was a ten-year revel.

For a month now, Dad had been talking expectantly about this night, seeing it not only as the chance to extract the usual New Year's resolutions but also as the occasion to address more global woes and weaknesses. "Auld Lang Syne," his customary incantation for invoking the future and exorcising the past, could now negate ten years instead of just one. He was giddy with anticipation.

I was too, but for different reasons. Sarah and David, now three and a half, had moved the entire family toward a shorter, but sturdier, center of gravity. Watching them play on New Year's Eve had transformed the night into a milestone that had not yet disappointed me.

But it seemed as if we might miss our chance. In a medical fluke for December, chicken pox had hit Sarah with particularly, itchy force. This morning was the fifth day of the siege, and it showed little signs of abating. A host of child-centered vacation plans had dissolved in a haze of Benadryl, calamine lotion, and oatmeal baths.

I racked my brain for diversions. Mentally, I consulted the beautifully hand-lettered List of Reasons that Edgar had made me before Sarah's birth. Most of them were familiar by now. We had had the sensuous mess of finger painting; the little-girl glamour of glitter; the gorgeous precision of Lego. We had had the joy of opening a new box of sixty-four crayons, and the eventual sadness of realizing that the built-in sharpener never quite worked. We had faced and fought the temptations to eat both Play-Doh and paste. We had even struggled through the saccharine hills and winding roads of Candy Land.

None of the usual amusements was working. She was itchy and miserable, and so was I.

"I miss David," she said hourly. I knew that she meant it. They'd seen each other almost daily since birth: mornings at nursery school, afternoons with their sitters, even weekends and some Friday afternoons together with Heather and me. The photographs adorning my office were inevitably snapshots of both children. They had favorite games and private jokes, specific and utterly obscure routines. Sarah took David's hand. She smoothed his hair. "David's my best friend," she loved to say. She gave him her grapes and cookies, both the real ones and the make-believe. He hid the playthings that scared her. They shared twin passions for *Mary Poppins,* Playmobil dolls, Mickey Mouse, and ketchup.

Heather's and my closeness now came from theirs, and from the shared desire to keep them close. On the bank of a hundred arguments, we had taken turns stopping and turning around.

We were bound together by them the way we'd once been bound by our parents, the way we were still—when we saw him—bound by Dad. It seemed their twoness had rescued ours. A host of forgotten rituals had come inanely back into our lives. We ended our talks saying "Budweiser," a throwback to the seventies, when a TV ad had once told us that "Budweiser" meant we'd said it all. With occasional hours off from her work or mine, we shopped together, by far our best sport. "Contrari-wise," she said sometimes, or "Nohow," both holdovers from the days when Tweedledum and Tweedledee had been our fa-vorite characters. Sometimes our nicknames even returned. I called her Dee. She called me Dum.

Still, of course, she was Heather, so when, by noon, I had concluded that there was no way we could go to Dad's, I braced myself for the call to her. I suspected that my wealth of senti-ment still far outweighed her own.

———•———

As I'd feared, my news was received without surprise or partic-ular sympathy. Heather and Dad, the doctors, had known all along that this would happen and that Sarah would not be up to coming.

"Bummer," Heather said simply.

"What if we did it here?" I asked her.

"There?" she said.

"Come on. It'll be great. We'll give you some petits fours, and David can get the chicken pox."

"Very funny."

"You're always saying it's better if they get this stuff over with when they're young."

"Do it there?" she asked again.

"Yes, *here*," I said. "That way, if Sarah is sleeping, we can still be together on New Year's Eve."

"I don't think Dad will want to," she said. "I already sent the food over," she added.

"If he said yes, would you do it?"

"Maybe."

I hung up and called Dad.

"Do it there?" he asked, as if I was suggesting a voyage to Zanzibar.

"Yes, *here*," I said. "That way, if Sarah is sleeping, we can still be together tonight."

"Oh, I don't know, sweetheart," he said. "I don't think Heather will want to."

I sighed.

"If she says yes, would you do it?" I asked him.

"Maybe," he said.

I called Heather back.

"You know," she said, "I really don't think I want David to be exposed to chicken pox right now."

"Oh, Dee," I said, feeling close to tears.

"I'll talk to you later."

"Are you coming or not?"

"I'll think about it," she said, by which I knew I was on my own.

———·—·———

I sensed in Edgar a quiet thrill.

"You could at least pretend to be disappointed," I said.

He smiled at me. "Could I?" he asked.

"It'll be the first time that we won't be spending New Year's Eve all together."

"I know."

"It means a lot to me."

"I know."

"It always has," I said, feeling teary. I thought of my parents dancing.

"Want to go, and let me stay home with Sarah?"

"Of course not," I said, though I was more tempted than I wanted to admit. I was not just sentimental but religious about this night.

———•———

I had read, over the years, about New Year's superstitions. Sarah's baby-sitter, Rosie, had told me that in Jamaica people bathed in the ocean. In Trinidad, houses were given fresh coats of paint. I knew that in Vienna people ate marzipan pigs, which were supposed to bring them wealth and fame. In Italy, I had read, people ate twelve grapes at midnight, one for each month of the coming year. In England, doors were left open to allow the old year to exit and the new one to enter; chimneys were swept, and shaking hands with a chimney sweep (as I knew, anyway, from *Mary Poppins*) brought fresh luck. Americans ate black-eyed peas, threw cracked china from their windows and old food from their freezers.

My superstition was a relatively modest one. It was simply to spend the last night of each year with the people I'd known since I was born. If I could carry them through each midnight and into the small, still hours of each new year, I felt I could carry them with me always.

I wanted my family to be like passengers on a train that could move through all the landscapes of time. The weather outside could change; the train could slow down or speed up; the nights could fall, and the mornings could dawn, but there we would be, together, chugging along past who knows what scenery. Instead, I had reluctantly learned, some people were going to be taken off the train. And, somehow even more painful than that, others might just calmly put down the newspapers they were reading, stand up, stretch their legs, and casually move to another car.

———

Sarah and I curled up on the sofa. Edgar put Mozart on the stereo. Winter light bleached the walls.

I read her *Stuart Little.* She delighted in the mouse's exploits, and I marveled at the fact that, unlike me, she seemed to share his adventurous, traveling soul. I had known, from my earliest childhood, that whatever adventures I'd have in my life would take place close to home, in my uncareless heart. I loved home too much to risk losing it, as I believed true adventurers always did.

I read her *Madeline and the Gypsies,* in which Madeline runs away to join a circus with Pepito.

I read her my favorite lines: "The best part of a journey, by plane, by car, or train, is when the journey is over, and you are home again."

I choked up on the word *home,* realizing how much of me still thought that home was the place four blocks away where Dad was, even now, probably taking the good crystal glasses down.

"What's a journey?" Sarah asked me.

"A trip," I said.

"Why is home the best part?" she asked.

Furtively, I kissed her neck. "Because," I said, "home is where you are always safe."

"But if it's the best part," she said, "then why do you take the trip?"

Good question, I thought. I might stay landlocked forever if merely left to my own devices. I stared at Ludwig Bemelmans's portrait of Paris's Gare Saint-Lazare. Even my mythical train, I mused, seemed a hazardous conveyance.

———•———

Mercifully, she was asleep before dinner, another day's itching over, until the now-routine midnight oatmeal bath.

Edgar and I sat down to steaks, baked potatoes, and salad. I was not a noble sight. In the mirror that hung over the wooden sideboard, I saw my mother on a bad day. Except that my mother had never looked this bad. True, my nose and teeth had grown larger, and my eyes and chin had grown smaller. But it was not only age that I saw in the mirror. It was a general spirit of madcap disarray. Makeup had not touched my lips or cheeks, and the ragged horizon of my bangs told the story of a dozen harried self-trimmings. My once-crisp, once-white T-shirt held a harrowing spectrum of colors: the fleshy pink of calamine lotion, the beige of crusted oatmeal, two bright orange dots of children's Tylenol, a few specks of dried green Play-Doh, and some random patches of chalk markings in a variety of dusty hues. There was considerably more color on my T-shirt than there was on my face. I looked as if I'd been coated with paste and rolled through a nursery school trash bin.

My mother would have taken a shower, washed her otherwise-

manageable hair, darkened the lines of her eyebrows, and concealed the lines of her worry. And I knew that I would have
done the same if my family were coming over.

I looked from the mirror to Edgar, who was looking at me
with love in his eyes. It had taken some time, and some serious
sex; it had taken his falling in love with Sarah, and my learning that she'd survive infancy, and now we were finally back on
track. I could swear from this glance that he had the illusion
that I was an authentic woman.

"What are you looking at?" I snapped at him.

"You," he said.

"Don't look at me."

"Why not?"

It bewildered me that at thirty-six, I was not yet the person
I wanted to be. When would the three of us be enough, feel
complete, feel sufficient, feel unabridged?

So we rode on into the new year, in our separate compartment, with me straining to see into the next cars.

———

At a little past eleven, Edgar and I knelt together beside the
tub, giving Sarah another oatmeal bath, when the doorbell
rang, and I leapt up so fast that I splashed Edgar's shirt with
oatmeal water.

"Wonder who that is," he said wryly.

"Oh come on," I said, wiping my arms with a towel and running into the bedroom to change.

"Is it David, Daddy?" I heard Sarah ask in a happier voice
than I'd heard all week.

"You bet," he said.

"I'm happy!" she shouted.

"Me too!" I called.

I wrapped her in a towel, a small spotted papoose, and ran, grinning, with her to the front door.

———

"Happy New Year, Cookie," Heather said to Sarah.

They stood in the foyer of our apartment: Heather, David, Jeffrey, and Dad.

"I can't believe you came," I said, nearly smothering Sarah inside our embrace. "What was it, the petits fours?"

Heather smiled. "No, the chicken pox," she said, and she bent over to unzip David's snowsuit.

Sarah scrambled down out of my arms. Her towel fell to the floor. Freed from his snowsuit, David ran forward and threw both his arms around Sarah, who fell. All the grown-ups said, "Aw."

Then David reached out to help Sarah up. They stood toe-to-toe and face-to-face, beholding each other longingly. David took out the blue Playmobil man that he always kept in his pants pocket. Sarah, completely naked, tore into her bedroom and raced back out with the red Playmobil woman that she put under her pillow each night.

They held up the dolls and made them kiss.

The grown-ups all said, "Aw" again.

"Can we play?" David asked us.

"Can we?" Sarah said.

"You've got to get some clothes on," I told her.

They ran off to Sarah's bedroom. Twenty seconds later, with Sarah clothed, albeit haphazardly, they dashed into the living room, and we heard the shrieks and giggles that always ascended from them when they got to play together.

"Hi, Jeffrey," I said, feeling sorry for him, and for all of us who were left out of their love.

Jeffrey waved a hello to me.

"He's not talking," Heather told us.

"Why not?" I asked.

"I think it has something to do with cheese."

"Why cheese?" Edgar asked her.

"Beats me," Heather said.

"Why aren't you talking, Jeffrey?" Edgar asked.

"I can't tell you," he said. "I'm not talking."

Heather steered him into the living room.

"Where's Richard?" I asked Dad as I hung up the coats.

He raised an eyebrow. "L.A.," he said.

"On New Year's Eve?"

"On New Year's Eve."

"What kind of deal closes on New Year's Eve?"

"She's screwing her marriage up," Dad said.

"He's not easy," I told him.

"She's cold. She's not cozy."

"She's loyal," I said, and I felt it. I would have defended her merrily, if I'd had to, all night long.

———

Our living room had French doors that opened onto the dining room, and the dining room had a door to the kitchen, which led to the hallway and back to the living room. In three and a half years of crawling, cruising, learning to walk and then run, Sarah and David had worn a path connecting this circuit, inventing games that circled around whatever grown-ups were watching them.

So as Dad and I settled onto the couch, we found David and Sarah debating which one of them would lead the way around the course.

"I want to follow," David said.

"No, *I* want to follow," Sarah said.

"No, me."

"No, me!"

"Kids, kids," Dad said.

"I want to go second," David said.

"No, you go first," Sarah told him.

"Can you imagine us arguing over who should *follow?*" I asked Heather.

"David, you be the leader," she told him.

"Sarah, why don't you try?" I said.

"They'll work it out," Edgar said sensibly, and Heather said, "I'm going to get the champagne."

I followed her back to the kitchen.

"What did he say about Richard?" she asked me.

"Not much."

"Well, it's none of his goddamned business," she said.

"You know him. He loves to worry about you."

"Why doesn't he pick on you for a change?"

"You'll see," I told her. "He will. Just wait. 'Do we hear the pitter-patter of feet?' Why does he care if I have another? He barely knows Sarah's name."

She laughed.

"How *are* things with Richard?" I asked her.

"Lousy."

"Why?"

"He says he wants to move out of the city."

I froze. "You wouldn't," I told her.

She shrugged.

"Would you?" I said.

Then the kids tore by, side by side, waving their arms and trying to skip.

"We're skipping!" they shouted. "We're skipping! We're skipping! We're skipping! We're skipping! We're skipping! We're skipping! We're skipping!"

"I guess they're skipping," Heather said.

———·———

For nearly fifteen minutes, Jeffrey had maintained his silence stoically, but now he seized the fireplace poker and lunged toward his uncle joyfully.

"Well, this is very jolly," Dad said, and I watched Heather roll her eyes skyward.

Over the years, I had seen grandparents playing with their grandchildren in the park. I had seen one change a diaper once. Even more exotically, I had heard that some kept cribs, high chairs, and toys in their own apartments. My father now had three grandchildren, but his apartment remained untouched by them, except for the framed photographs on the mantel, which buttressed his favorite antique clock. If Dad had ever known how to play, he'd long since forgotten the games or their point. Occasionally, he would look at one of his grandchildren intently, as if expecting them to draw him out. He seemed to possess a unique talent for missing their moments of special grace.

———

With Jeffrey's help, Sarah and David piled up the pillows on the living room floor. The pillows, they said, were their swimming pool. They took turns diving into them, pretending to float and swim.

"We're swimming, Mommy!" Sarah exclaimed. It was hard to believe that this was the same child who'd been so miserable all week long.

The bedroom pillows had red and white stripes.

"These are candies," Sarah told David.

David fell over one by mistake. "I've got candy on my hands!" he squealed.

Giggling, he and Sarah took turns pretending to lick the candy off.

"Candy cane!" Sarah shouted ecstatically.

"Candy cane, Mom!" David called to Heather.

Then they offered up a bouquet of giggles and sank, mirthfully, to the floor.

———

There was no sight I found more beautiful than the sight of them holding hands. It had taken a while in coming, because they'd been different, of course, in their fears and desires.

David was boisterous, cuddly, physical, fast, eager for food and attention and trouble, usually in that order. He could scale a couch or a bookcase or a table in a matter of seconds, and then perch, a three-foot-tall promise of chaos, or of irrepressible hilarity. He was the kind of boy whose knees would always sport Band-Aids and whose face would always be slightly sticky.

Sarah was quiet, imaginative, sometimes cautious, sometimes fearful, only truly giddy and chatty when she was alone with Edgar or me. She would sit for long stretches of time with a book or a puzzle or a cup of juice, lazily kicking a foot back and forth and seeming to ponder abstruse mysteries. Her favorite game was I Spy, which we played, as she grew, with increasing complexity. "I spy a red rose," she'd tell me, and I'd comb her room for ten minutes while she smiled to herself deliciously, and finally she'd show me a pea-sized rose in the fabric of her doll's dress. "I spy a pig," she'd tell Edgar, and, when he had finally given up, she'd show it to him in a shadow on the wall. At night, she would curl up into my arms and sigh on my shoulder with ancient love.

David had reached for her, and she'd recoiled. Until, one day, she hadn't.

Now they paused in their skipping and stood by the living room window, holding hands. They spoke, in whispers, of who knew what. From behind, they looked like twin dolls, or like some small figures poised to move on a clock. Their proportions were perfect, their posture exquisite, their hair the same color and tumble of curls.

"Look at them, Heather," I said, and we stared at our children in shared amazement.

———·———

Ten minutes later, all three kids were wilting before a tape of *Fantasia.*

"Let's turn this off now, okay, kids?" Dad asked. "What channel is Guy Lombardo on?"

"Don't start this again, Dad," Heather said.

"You know what I mean," Dad said. "The countdown."

"I'll find it," Edgar told him.

"Ten more years till the year 2000," Dad said as Edgar located the scene of Times Square.

"Thought about your resolution?" I asked him.

"Great," Heather said. "Encourage him."

"I'm too old to make resolutions," he grumbled.

As a young man, he had inherited the practice of an older doctor, and so for many years his patients had all been older than he. He had been able to luxuriate in the sweet smugness of youth. Even in his fifties, when his eighty- and ninety-year-old patients were dropping off the earth with stunning predictability, he had been invincible and immortal and too busy to notice that time was passing for him as well. Now he had finally noticed, and everything he experienced seemed to get filtered through the intractable screen of his short, irresistible future.

"I've got a resolution for you," I told Dad. "Why don't you resolve to stop being like this?"

"When you're seventy-two, we'll talk," he said.

"When she's seventy-two," Heather told him, "I don't think you'll be interested."

Predictably, he didn't laugh. He had settled into semiretirement, giving lectures and making occasional rounds, but he hadn't begun to settle into being in his seventies.

"Always Heather first," Dad said. "What's your resolution this year?" he asked her.

"Let's see," she said. "To work on my marriage."

"Don't be sarcastic."

He turned to me. "Erica? A new baby this year?"

Heather saluted me silently.

"Dad," I said. "Please. We don't know."

"She's got plenty of time," Heather said.

"Well," Dad said. "Maybe next year at this time, there'll be more of us."

"And maybe there'll be fewer," Heather said, which she meant as a threat.

———

Dad stood up slowly and raised his glass.

Behind him, the globe on top of the Times tower glowed like a falling moon.

"Ten! Nine! Eight! Seven! Six! Five!"

Edgar squeezed my hand.

"Four! Three! Two! One! Happy 1990!"

"A toast!" Edgar said, holding up his glass.

"To the future," Dad said.

"To the past," I said.

"To the moment," Heather told us, and she was beaming at the children.

———

In the three years and eight months that had passed since Sarah's birth, I had learned to view the world not only through my usual assortment of classical myths but through the stories in Sarah's books.

Weekly, I fought the temptation to stand before my students and say: "Class, please turn now to page fourteen of *The Cat in the Hat Comes Back!*"

I almost could have pulled it off. In this Seussian masterpiece, the Cat appears on a wintry, Momless day, dives into a bathtub, where he eats a cake, reads a book, hoists an umbrella—and leaves an inky pink cat ring. As the Cat and the kids try to clean up the ring, it merely metamorphoses, from bath ring to dress stain to wall splotch to shoe spatter to rug spot to bedspread smear and finally to backyard catastrophe.

The ring, I thought that night, like so much in life—family carping, say, and also family love—never disappears, only changes.

Winter and Spring, 1990

"Wasn't It Snowing Before?"

I called Edgar. Heather called Dad. I called Richard. Dad called me. I called Edgar. I called Heather. Heather called Dad. Richard called me. After the news was exchanged, all we could say was: "Did you talk to Heather?" "Did you talk to Richard?" "Did you talk to Heather?" "Did you talk to Dad?"

Uncountable phone calls, and nothing to say. David was dead. He'd been hit by a car.

Between calls, I walked into Sarah's room. She was taking her nap, and I watched her breathe. I knew when she woke I would need to tell her, so I wasn't going to wake her. But the sight of her sleeping was frightening to me. I needed to hold her. I thought I was going to hold her too hard. She moved an arm in her sleep. I thought: I am not going to let you out of my sight.

The phone rang again. Now it became the facts of the accident, replayed as if they mattered. Where had it happened? Who had been driving? Had he been hurt? How old was he? It was what we needed to talk about. It was as if knowing the way that it happened were going to allow us to change it.

David had been standing on a street corner, holding his sit-

ter Debbie's hand. The car had gone up on the curb and flipped
over. Debbie and David had both been hit. Debbie was fine but
was still in shock. The driver was fine. And David was dead.
The driver was eighty-seven. He had been late for a visit with
his children. He had stepped on the gas instead of the brake. If
the driver hadn't been late, David would be alive. If he hadn't
had children, David would be alive. If they'd gone to visit him,
David would be alive. The ifs stacked up like palpable objects,
building an unimaginable box.

The phone rang again. There were things to arrange now: a
service, a funeral, a burial. How could a child be put in the
earth?

"Heather wants him buried," Dad told me.

"I know," I said.

"She should cremate him."

"She doesn't want to."

"I know," he said.

"I know," I said.

What we said didn't make much sense.

I called Edgar.

"Heather wants him buried," I told him.

"Well, that's what Heather wants," he said.

Richard called me.

"Heather wants him buried," he said.

"I know," I said.

Heather called me.

"I have to go identify him," she said.

"What about Richard?" I asked.

"On his way back from Boston."

"Why don't you wait?"

"Because I have to see David."

"I'll come with you," I told her.

"I've got to leave now. So I can be back before Jeffrey gets home from school."

"Does he know yet?"

"No. Does Sarah?"

"No."

"Do you have to teach this afternoon?"

"No," I said. "It's Friday."

"Oh."

"Don't go without me," I told her. "Rosie's on her way. And I've got to wait for Sarah to—"

"To what?"

It took a long time before I could speak. "To wake up," I said.

There was a silence. I knew she was crying and that she wanted me to think that she wasn't.

"Just wait," I told her. "I'll be there as soon as I can."

———

"Did you have a nice nap, sweetheart?" I asked when Sarah woke. My voice sounded ridiculous to me.

Sarah yawned, covering her mouth, which seemed unbearably beautiful.

"I need to pee," she said.

"Okay."

I went with her to the bathroom.

I was watching her pull up her panties when she met my eyes with a placid expression.

"I saw David," she said.

"You what?"

"David's going away," she said. "I dreamed him. He's too big," she said.

I found I had sat on the side of the tub.

"Too big for what?" I asked her.

"Too big for here. He told me."

"He told you what?" I said, but I realized that I was crying, and that my voice came out a shout.

It was the first time that she'd looked scared.

"I'm not going to tell you!" she cried out, and ran back to her room.

———

The morgue was in a large white room of Roosevelt Hospital. A tall black policeman showed us the way. It took forever for them to bring David's body out.

Heather kept throwing her shoulders back, taking deep breaths, straightening her spine. She was going to meet this head high. Her strength made it harder for me to be strong. Her strength always had.

"Are you ready, Dr. Rosen?" the officer asked Heather. A nurse was standing beside him.

"I'm ready," Heather said.

He folded the sheet down gently, like a bedcloth, and until the last moment, I realized I was thinking that David wouldn't be underneath it.

The top of his head was swathed in gauze, but there was no sign of blood. His eyes were closed, and his mouth was slightly open; there was a gray-blue cast to his skin, and his lips were smooth and lavender, like the inside of a shell.

I touched Heather's arm, and she moved slightly away from me.

She was staring at her dead son. He had been a month away from his fourth birthday. The nurse and the policeman and I were staring at her. She put a hand on David's foot, and then his waist, and then his chest, and then his neck, as if she had to pull herself up, touch by touch, until finally she could stroke his cheek. Her fingers were shaking, but her spine was still straight. Then her fingers brushed his lips, and she gasped. The nurse moved into position, but Heather took a last look at David and turned away. She inhaled. She exhaled. She looked up at the officer.

"My husband and I haven't made arrangements yet," she said.

"Of course not. Call here when you have, Dr. Rosen," he said.

He gave her the telephone number and a bag filled with David's things.

I was holding Heather's hand now, whether she wanted me to or not. We were digging our nails into each other's palms the way we had when we were kids and got the giggles at the theater and were trying not to laugh.

———

The sunlight on the street was a shock.

"Wasn't it snowing before?" Heather asked me as we looked for a taxi.

"I don't know," I said.

"It must have been," she said.

"I don't remember," I said.

"How can you not remember whether it was snowing or not?" she asked.

"I just don't, Heather," I said.

"It must have been snowing," she said.

A cab pulled up, and I got in with her. I thought she would have to break down at some point, and I wanted to be with her when she did.

"You don't need to come with me," she said after giving the driver the address.

"Dee," I said.

"Okay," she said, and the cab pulled off, moving through the cold, sunny streets of New York, which looked impossibly harmless.

———

"Sarah," I said to my daughter that night. She was sitting with Edgar and me on the couch. In her hand was the stick of a grape ice pop that had turned her lips dark purple.

"What?" she asked, putting down the stick.

"Daddy and I have something to tell you. Something that's sad and bad," I said.

"What?" she asked.

I felt a dreamlike sense of falling.

"David's dead," I told her.

She looked up. Her eyes blinked.

"He was in an accident," I said. "He was hit by a car on the street. Debbie was holding his hand, but he still got hit, and he died. He's dead."

"Where is he?" she asked.

"He's dead," I said.

"Is he in heaven?"

I looked at Edgar, who nodded at me.

"Yes," I told her.

She thought for a moment. "Let's go find him," she said.

At three and a half, Sarah knew her ABC's, and how to count to a hundred, and just about every color of the rainbow, and the cast members of *Sesame Street,* and what her favorite books were, and how to eat around the pit of a peach. But she did not know about heaven. I didn't know she knew the word. No one we knew had died since she'd been born, and she'd never once asked where my mother was.

"We can't go to heaven," I told her.

"David did."

Edgar said: "You can only go to heaven when you die."

She pondered this. Then she shrugged and said, "So?"

I smiled at her. I touched her hair. I said: "Sweetheart, we don't want to die."

"Why not?"

"When you die, it's forever," I said. "You can't come back. And you can't eat ice cream. You can't see the people you know."

"I could see David."

"But you wouldn't get to see Daddy and me."

She let this sink in. Her eyes narrowed.

"Then who can David see?" she asked.

Miserable though the whole thing was, I had to be touched by her logic.

"No one really knows," I said. "But I think he can see my

mommy, because I think she's there also. And there are lots of great people who will play with him and take care of him."

"I spy David," Sarah said.

I looked at Edgar, alarmed, but he was one step ahead of me and took down the photograph from Sarah's bulletin board of the two of them in Halloween costumes. He handed the photograph to her.

"What if he could visit?" she asked us, staring at the picture.

"He can't, darling," I said.

"What if I could visit him?" she asked.

"You can't visit David, sweetheart," said Edgar, "and David can't visit you."

She hopped off the couch and went to the toy shelf and found the basket where we kept the Playmobil dolls. I thought about David's blue man, which he'd always kept in his pocket, along with two yellow marbles and a broken watch of his father's. I wondered dizzily where these things were now but watched while Sarah took her doll, made a slide out of her leg, and steered the figure down it.

I wanted her to cry, to wail, to show the proper emotion, to understand how deep a sadness it was. She didn't cry. She played until bath time and then went easily to sleep.

———•———

"She just doesn't understand yet," Edgar said as we tried to sleep ourselves.

"Do you?" I asked him.

"Not really," he said. He got up from bed.

"What are you doing?" I asked him.

"I've just got to go in and check on her."

We dozed and wept and watched her all night. Finally, at four in the morning, Edgar got up again and brought Sarah, sleeping, into our bed.

"She's fine," I told him.

"I'm not," he said.

We draped our arms over our daughter and finally fell asleep.

My mother had died in summer, when the heat and the humid air had seemed to bathe and absorb and prime our tears. The heat had let things flow. Now it was February: bleak and brittle, and everything seemed frozen, locked in. When we buried David, the earth was ice.

The rabbi handed the shovel to Richard. It was customary, he told him, for the Jewish people to bury their dead. But the ground near the grave was slippery, and it was hard for Richard to get a foothold. He nearly slipped in as he shoveled the earth, and Heather gasped, then put out a hand to steady him and to hold him back. The rabbi took the shovel from Richard and said he had done enough.

I looked at Dad. He looked at me. At Mom's funeral, he hadn't settled for ceremony. He had kept shoveling earth till his hands were raw, and he was crying blindly. So we'd all taken turns—even Heather, pregnant with Jeffrey then— weeping and sweating beneath the awful sun.

No one was crying by David's grave, because Heather wasn't crying. Our breath turned into white smoke, and we shivered and didn't speak.

I sat between Heather and Edgar in the limousine going back to the city. Richard had chosen to sit on the jump seat: He'd tucked a full flask of scotch underneath it, and once the car started moving, he bent almost double to dig it out. He took a long drink, then another, then offered the flask to Heather. She shook her head and looked out the window. I did the same and looked at Heather. Edgar took a sip, then handed the flask back, and Richard polished it off.

"We should have brought Jeffrey," Richard told Heather, screwing the cap back on the flask.

Heather didn't answer him.

"He should have been here," Richard said.

There was another silence, a longer one.

"He's probably going to think that we *sent* David away or something," Richard said.

Heather turned, very slowly, away from the window. "You don't take a six-year-old boy to watch his brother get buried," she said.

Her tone was sharp, but her eyes were impassive. I wondered if she had taken a pill or had just found a way to bank herself down. I marveled at the fact that it was possible to bury one's child and not start screaming and never stop.

She looked back out the window.

Edgar took my hand and squeezed it hard.

Then Richard let out a huge sob, hugging himself in his dark overcoat.

Heather didn't look at him. She started tapping her foot

on the floor. I touched her shoulder. She shifted away. Her nose turned red, and tears spilled down her face. But she wouldn't look at the rest of us. Her foot kept tapping against the floor, trying to sustain a rhythm, as if rhythm were order.

———

Sarah and Jeffrey were waiting with Rosie and Debbie at Heather's apartment.

"They had some lunch—" Debbie started to say.

"You're fired," Heather said to her.

We all looked up.

"Heather—" Richard began, but Heather silenced him with a frozen stare.

Debbie started to cry, but she said nothing, just stared down at the floor. Finally, she gained her composure and looked up at Heather.

"Well, then, I'll stay until you find someone—" she began.

"No. I'd like you to leave right away."

"Can I say good-bye to Jeffrey?"

"Of course," Heather said, and turned to hang up her coat.

The doorman rang up from downstairs. Edgar went to answer it.

"Heather," Richard said softly. "Don't you think Jeffrey's lost enough?"

"That bitch was with my son when he died," Heather whispered to him fiercely.

"She couldn't have helped it. No one could."

The witnesses had all verified this. Debbie herself had been hit by the car, and the car had come out of nowhere.

"I want her gone," Heather said. Then she opened the front door to greet Richard's parents and sister, and Dad.

———————

Edgar shook hands, poured drinks, gave embraces, but he never let Sarah out of his sight. He had gained, in a night and a day, the habit of moving through space with invisible sight lines attached to her.

"Stop watching so hard," I whispered to him.

"I'm not," he said, looking over my shoulder.

"You're doing it now."

"Doing what?"

"Watching her."

"I can't help it," he said. "I can't."

"You're going to scare her," I said. "You're scaring me."

He wasn't listening. I pulled him into Heather's bedroom. Reluctantly, he came with me, still trying to keep an eye on Sarah.

I put my arms around him.

"How can we get up each morning and not be with her?" he said. "How can we leave her with Rosie like this? What if something happened to her?"

I stared at him.

"I know," he said.

"Remember what you told me when she was born, and I asked you the same questions?" I said.

"No."

"You told me that I couldn't live my life this way. That no one could. That I had to live my life, and let her live hers, or I'd drive all of us crazy."

Beyond Heather's window, eight floors below, two black women crossed a street side by side, one pushing a baby carriage, the other pushing a wheelchair.

"We've got to live our lives," I said.

He nodded, then raced back to find Sarah.

—————

I found Rosie in the kitchen, washing the dishes and weeping at the same time. I was amazed by Heather's brutality with Debbie, and I didn't want Rosie to think I wasn't. I put my arms around her. She had started working for us the autumn after Sarah's birth. Middle-aged and Jamaican, she had three grown children, a dead husband, and a wealth of loyalty. She was religious, superstitious, and kind. She'd made friends quickly with Debbie, with whom, by coincidence, she shared the same hometown. They'd seen each other at school pickups and had faithfully made play dates for the kids—and themselves—at least three afternoons a week.

"Poor Sarah," she said now, between her sobs. "And poor Debbie—" she began.

"I know."

"Debbie feels so awful anyway. And now she won't have anybody. And Jeffrey—"

"I know," I said. "And David."

Rosie disengaged herself and wiped her eyes with the back of her hand.

"No. David's with God," she said. "David's all right. It's the mess he left behind."

—————

I called my boss, Bruno, to ask for time off.

"You'll need a stand-in," he said gruffly.

"Just for a day or two," I said, hoping he'd want to offer me more.

"Take two weeks," he said.

"Thank you."

"I'm thinking of you."

"You are?"

"I've been remembering how damned strong you were when your mother died. I don't think it's fair that someone as young as you should have to deal with so much," he said.

"My sister has to deal with more," I said.

"But I'm not her friend. I'm yours," he said, and left me with a guilty flush of vague pride and vague yearning.

———·———

On Monday morning, I dressed Sarah for the nursery school class that she and David had gone to together each weekday morning since September. Edgar and I had decided that he should take her, so I could be free for Heather. She didn't call, though, so I called her.

"What are you doing?" I asked her.

"Getting Jeffrey dressed for school," she said.

"What's Richard doing?"

She exhaled.

"Heather?"

"He's blaming me," she said finally, "for not moving out of the city."

"He's not."

"He thinks if we'd moved, David would still be alive."

"Is that what he's saying?"

"It's what he's thinking. I've got to go. We're going to be late."

"Isn't Richard taking him?"

"We both are. They're doing something in Jeffrey's class, to explain to the kids what happened."

She hung up, and then it struck me that the teachers in Sarah's class might do the same.

I threw on some jeans and a sweatshirt, raced out the door, and ran to her nursery school. What was I expecting? Some kind of circle group, maybe, with one of the perky teachers holding up a dead philodendron and asking, "Can anyone tell us what happened here?" And I don't know what I was thinking I would do if I found such a group in progress. Hoist Sarah up in my arms and say, "This child needs love and friendship! Share your paints with her, and your stacking clowns!"?

I ran up the steps to the classroom and stood at the door, looking through the thick windowpanes. It was business as usual: comforting, colorful—children sitting at low tables, painting at easels, serving make-believe food.

Sarah was building a block tower, no more alone in her play than the other kids were, but, to me, seemingly forsaken. I looked around for the teachers. There were three of them, coaching and smiling, milling from child to child and chaos to chaos in that calmly detached but attached way that I'd always found enviable.

One of them, Paula, saw me. She came to the door.

"Mrs. Ross," she said, stepping outside to join me. "I'm so terribly sorry." She touched my arm. "I told your husband. It's such a shock. Awful. We were all so fond of David."

"I know."

"It must be terrible for you," she said.

"I was just wondering," I told her, "what you told the kids."

"We told them that David had died, and that we would miss him, and that they should ask their parents to explain it to them tonight."

"Oh," I said.

"Three to four is a hard age," she said.

"Sarah—" I started, and looked in at her. The sides of her tower were perilously high.

"We'll be keeping a special eye out for her. Don't worry. Kids are resilient," she said.

"They were close," I said. "They were best friends. They were—"

"I know," she said. She looked down the hall. "Do you want to pick up his things?" she asked. "It might make it easier on your sister."

Stricken, I followed her glance to the cubbies, where David's name, on a hand-lettered tape, was a specter I hadn't planned on.

"Sure," I said, hoping I wouldn't cry.

She said: "I'll be right back with something for you to carry them in."

There were sneakers, socks, fresh underpants, a Mickey Mouse sweatshirt, and two paper plates that were covered with blue glitter and green stars.

Paula appeared beside me.

"I'm sorry," she said. "This was all I could find."

She held up a white plastic trash bag.

"That's okay," I said, scooping the clothes into it and gently placing the plates on top.

I was out on the street moments later, leaning against the grimy building and hugging the bag close to my chest.

When I called Heather in the afternoon, she said she was trying to sleep.

I put the plates in my sock drawer, and I threw David's clothes away.

The next morning, Heather called me.

"What are you doing?" I asked her.

"I have to go through David's things."

"Now?" I asked her.

"Yes. Now."

"Why now?"

"Because."

"Can't it wait?"

"Wait for what?"

"For—later," I said.

She said: "Do you think this will ever get easier?"

"Why not get someone else to do it?"

"Like who?"

"I'll do it," I told her.

"No."

"Why not?"

"Do it with me," she said.

"Okay."

"But now."

———

Someone had closed the door to David's bedroom, but now Heather opened it without ceremony.

What we saw was a child's life—flights and intentions—suspended in time and in primary colors: a half-finished puzzle, a half-built tower, the tin soldiers in their arcane formations, the Mickey Mouse clock with its empty, odd arms. There were games on David's table that he had been in the middle of playing. Red rubber boots that he'd not put away. A stack of bottle tops that he had been saving for snowman's buttons.

"You start with the closet," Heather said.

"Heather."

"There's plenty of clothes there for Sarah," she said. "I'm going to get some bags."

The second she left the room, I threw the puzzle pieces into their box. I scooped up the tin army. I knocked down the tower and put the blocks on the shelf.

"I told you," Heather said from the doorway, "to start in the closet."

So I went to David's closet, and sorted clothes, and pretended that I'd let Sarah wear some, and tried not to watch as my sister went on to dismantle the rest of her son's short life. She sorted; she stacked; she labeled; she boxed. She didn't shed a tear.

———

Dryope and Iole were sisters. They were walking by a stream one day when Dryope picked a beautiful flower to give to her infant son. But the flower, it turned out, was really a nymph. Once plucked, it started bleeding and was determined to seek revenge.

So Iole had to watch while her sister was turned into a tree and forced to lose her son.

In Heather's case, I felt, these two things were happening in the reverse order: The loss of her son had come first, and now the hardness was following.

———

Three weeks to the day after David's death, Heather went back to work.

She had hired a new sitter, Gloria, part-time, because Jeffrey, at six, was in school for eight hours and really only needed to be picked up and fed his dinner.

I could not fathom, could not accept or completely construct, the reality of Heather's opening her arms each day to hold other people's children. I knew that work was work, and that it could be familiar and soothing: Edgar and I were both comforted by the routines of our classes and papers to grade. But Heather's work seemed savagely cruel. On hospital days, she made bedside rounds, traveling through the maternity ward to give cheer, reassurance, and needed warmth. On office days, she faced mothers fretting over viruses, croups, cuts, ear infections, measles, mumps, allergies, bites, milk, vitamins, height. She had to face, with every appointment, the obvious fact that these children would get, or were already, well, and that if, by some strange occurrence, all their mothers' worries and all her sage advice could be collected and stored in one house, or heart, they would never be enough to prevent what had happened to David.

But the only thing Heather complained about was the sympathy of the parents.

"I can't stand the ones who know," she told me one night.

"Why not?" I asked her.

"They have this look. They get this look. I can tell, they're dying to ask me what's wrong with their kid, but they feel guilty just being in the same room with me."

"There's a difference," I said, "between guilt and concern."

"I know," she said. "But sometimes they—"

Her sentence trailed off.

"They what?" I asked her.

"Nothing."

"What?" I said. "Sometimes they what?"

"Sometimes," she said, "they try to hug me."

"Why is that so bad?"

"Because it makes me cry."

"What's so bad about crying?"

"You know I hate crying," she said. "Don't start with me about crying."

"Sorry."

"Anyway, these are my patients' parents. The whole idea is, I take care of *them*."

"Maybe," I said, "it'd be easier for them if you just found a way to admit it was hard."

"It's not hard," she said. "It's my work."

"Come on, Heather. Who do you think you're kidding?" I said.

"I'll tell you what's hard," she said. "What's hard is everyone thinking that they know what I'm always feeling."

I took a wild guess that she meant me.

———•———

I tried to imagine how it would have felt to have been, like Sarah, suddenly untwinned.

I sent Heather a copy of the poem we had loved so much in our childhood:

> *Tweedledum and Tweedledee*
> *Agreed to have a battle;*
> *For Tweedledum said Tweedledee*
> *Had spoiled his nice new rattle.*
>
> *Just then flew down a monstrous crow,*
> *As black as a tar-barrel;*
> *Which frightened both the heroes so,*
> *They quite forgot their quarrel.*

———•———

When I wasn't worrying about Heather, or missing her, or missing David, or working, I was trying to watch Sarah. Unlike Edgar, I wasn't insisting on extra sweaters, or telling her not to climb on things: I wasn't obsessed with her physical safety. I looked for the signs of damage. I looked for loss of appetite, nightmares, mood swings, playground fights, clinginess. All I saw was a sad little girl who said, straight out, that she missed her cousin and wished that he could come back.

Then, one Saturday morning, six weeks after David's death, I found her playing with the two paper plates that I'd put away in my sock drawer.

She looked embarrassed when she saw me.

"I'm sorry I went in your drawer," she said. "Can I have them?"

I nodded.

"Will you put them up?" she asked.

I found the box of thumbtacks and started to put them on her bulletin board.

"He really likes them," she said.

"They're very colorful," I said.

She looked at them sideways, tilting her head.

"He says that it's nice there," she told me.

"What?"

"In heaven," she said.

I looked around her bedroom, oddly surprised by its emptiness. How was it, I wondered, that Edgar had not miraculously heard these words from inside his shower, bounded out with a towel draped around him, and offered the perfect response? I wondered what he would have said. I wondered what my mother would have said. I looked, with rue and longing, at the dresser-top copy of *Dr. Spock*. Then Sarah went back to coloring, and I didn't say a word.

———

"Well, are you worried?" Edgar asked me that night. We were lying in bed at the end of the day. He was appealing to my maternal instincts, which seemed like a low blow.

"I don't know," I said.

"What were her exact words?"

"She said David said it was nice in heaven."

"And that's all she said?"

"That's it," I said.

He punched up the pillows in back of his head. "Well, what do you think?" he asked me.

"I told you, sweetheart," I said. "I don't know."

"Maybe it's normal," he said. "Maybe it's healthy. Maybe it's her way of dealing with it."

"Maybe."

"But what do we do? Do we say, 'Oh, that's nice, sweetie, tell us all about it,' or do we say, 'You can't be talking to David.'"

"No," I said.

"No to which?"

"We don't tell her she can't be talking to him."

"But she can't be."

"That's like telling her Freedo can't brush his teeth."

Freedo was Sarah's teddy bear, veteran of crib and stroller, playground and potty; recipient of countless make-believe nap times, unwanted ablutions, and outgrown clothes.

"What does Spock say?" Edgar asked.

I smiled. From the start with Sarah, I'd been pitilessly teased—by Edgar, by Heather, by Richard, by Dad—for the faith I maintained in that golden book. The words in its index alone had brought me hours of peace, a soothing pediatric poem:

Bottles

Bowlegs

Boys

Cups

Curiosity

Cuts

Nudity

Nursing

Nuts

Tics

Tonsillectomy

Toys

But for once Dr. Spock had failed me. Under "Death, fears of," I learned that they were normal around Sarah's age.

Under "Playmates, imaginary," I learned that a little imagination was fine but that too much was worrisome, and (though he didn't come right out and say so) that it was up to me to tell the difference.

"Spock doesn't say anything," I told Edgar.

"I guess you can't ask Heather," he said.

"Let's just see how it goes," I said.

"You mean play it by ear."

"Go with the flow."

"It's late," he said.

"I know."

"Christ."

"Yeah."

Then we fell asleep.

———

My father had begun making weekly visits. Saturdays to Heather and Richard and Jeffrey, Sundays to Edgar and Sarah and me.

On the last Sunday in March, nearly two months after David's death, Edgar let Dad in the front door while I finished dressing Sarah.

"Grandpa!" she shouted when she heard his voice. She ran toward him, mouth open, socks off, then stopped two yards away from him with a look on her frozen face. The look was all too familiar to me: a fusion of hope and dread.

"Hello, darling," he said to her awkwardly. He bent down to see her. "Do I get a kiss?"

She raced back to where I was standing.

"Say hi to Grandpa," I told her.

She wrapped her arms around one of my legs as if it were a tall mast on a ship in stormy seas.

"Hi, Grandpa," she said to my upper thigh.

"Sarah," I said, "give Grandpa a kiss."

"She doesn't have to perform," he told me. Pointedly. Judgmentally. As if I had somehow forgotten the myriad hoops that I'd once had to jump through for him.

"Twenty minutes," he'd said to me once, when Sarah was just a year or so old. "Twenty minutes is about the limit of time I can spend with them when they're this age."

"Twenty minutes," I'd simply repeated.

"Well, how long can you stay interested when all they're doing is knocking down blocks?"

"Longer than twenty minutes," I'd said.

If I wanted my daughter to give him a kiss, it was simply because I felt it would take such obvious sweetness to conquer his impatience.

Now Dad shook Edgar's hand and patted his arm, gave me

a kiss on the cheek, and reached down to stroke Sarah's shoulder.

"Have you talked to Heather or Richard?" he asked me as he watched me hang up his coat and hat.

Our talks had always begun with Heather, but now he talked about nothing else.

"Didn't you see her yesterday?"

"Yes."

"Didn't you talk to her?"

"Yes. But Richard was there."

"So?"

"So I couldn't talk to her about Richard."

I laughed.

"Why are you laughing?"

"Because, Dad. When has she ever talked to you about Richard?"

"I think they're in trouble," he told me.

"That's what you said on New Year's Eve."

"I know."

"They need each other more now," I said.

"They should. But that's not always how it goes."

"Didn't you come to see Sarah?" I asked him.

"Sorry."

"Let's get you some coffee," I said.

We walked into the kitchen, where Sarah was watching intently while Edgar put Oreos on a plate.

"Well, so, *did* you talk to Heather?" Dad asked me.

I sighed. Then Sarah said: "I talked to David."

Now it was Dad's turn to freeze.

I gave him a warning look, over her head, which I desperately hoped he would understand. "Here's the coffee, Dad," I said. "Want a cookie?"

"No thanks."

He was looking at Sarah as if she were a small, lethal device that was about to explode.

"Want a cookie, sweetheart?" I asked her.

"In heaven," Sarah said, "cookies are shaped like what you think about."

"That sounds like fun," I said, sending a reckless shrug toward Edgar.

Then we all went into Sarah's room for the requisite twenty minutes.

———

My father called later that evening.

"Did you talk to Heather?" he asked me.

"No."

"You didn't tell her?"

"Tell her what, Dad?"

"What Sarah said about David."

"No."

"Good. That's good. I was thinking that it would probably only make her very sad."

You are a mass of intuition, I wanted to tell him.

"Good thinking," I said.

"What are you going to do?" he asked.

"I'm not going to do anything, Dad."

"Don't you think you should get her some help?"

"No, I don't."

"You sound pretty calm about this."

"She also tells me that Freedo's favorite food is macaroni and cheese."

"Who's Freedo?"

I sighed. "Her teddy bear."

He was silent a moment, processing this.

"Dad," I said, "does David make you feel better or worse about being seventy-two?"

"What do you mean?" he asked me warily.

"What I mean is, you've been feeling pretty miserable about getting old."

"You'll understand someday."

"It's not that I don't understand," I told him. "What I mean is, you know you've had seventy-two years, and David didn't even have four. Doesn't that make you feel that you've been at least a little bit lucky?"

"Maybe," he said.

I told him: "Baudelaire wrote, 'The only way to forget time is by making use of it.' "

"What the hell did Baudelaire know?" Dad said. "He probably wrote that in his forties."

———————

I looked up Baudelaire's dates. Dad was right. He had died at forty-six.

———————

"What's going on with you and Richard?" I asked Heather when I called her later that night.

"Nothing's going on. What do you mean?" she asked.

"I don't know. I just wondered how you were doing."

"We're doing fine," she said. "Gotta go."

She hung up.

"Budweiser," I whispered.

———

I knew that David had brought Heather into the orbit of Sarah and me, and that we had all spun around together for three years, charmed by the company and the voyage. Now, we had learned, David had been a comet, and Heather, pulled from the course, was soaring away alone again.

———

"You look tired," Bruno said Monday morning as we walked up the stairs to our offices.

"It was a long weekend," I told him before I could stop myself. "Sarah told us about heaven."

Bruno climbed a few steps in silence. Then he paused at the landing. "When my wife died," he said, "my boys held their own service for her."

I'd known that he had been married, but I hadn't known that his wife had died.

"How old were the boys?" I asked.

"Five and six."

I looked at him, aghast. He smiled at me kindly.

"They laid out a dress of hers, and a handbag. The older boy, Jim, said some prayer he knew."

"What was the prayer?"

"I don't know," he said. "They found it in a comic book."

———

Sarah's fourth birthday was April thirteenth, two weeks from the coming Friday. Under normal circumstances, of course, David would have topped her guest list, and the other children would simply have been invited because they were in her class.

"Are you sure she even wants a party?" Edgar asked me as I wrote out the invitations.

"What four-year-old doesn't want a birthday party?" I asked him.

"A four-year-old whose best friend just died," he said.

"I can't ask her if she wants one, darling. If I ask her, it'll seem as if I'm telling her that she shouldn't."

He nodded.

"What should we do?" he asked.

I shrugged and smiled. "What else?" I said. "Make a wishing well."

On the way home from school the next evening, Edgar and I stopped at a hardware store and picked up a large cardboard box.

When we walked in the door, Sarah ran out to meet us. She shouted, "Mommy," and hugged my knees.

"Is it for my party?" she said when she saw the box.

"Yes."

"What is it?"

"You'll see when I paint it."

She smiled up at me. "Will it be pink?"

"Of course," I told her.

I stroked her hair. She sneezed, and Edgar looked at me, instantly alarmed.

"Bless you," I told her. "Go get a tissue."

Rosie came out to greet us.

"Is everything okay?" I asked her.

"Oh, fine," she said. "Everything is fine." But she shook her head no as she said it.

Edgar led Sarah away to the kitchen, asking her if she thought she had a cold.

"What is it?" I asked Rosie, knowing I knew.

"She said she'd been talking to David," she whispered. "My poor baby. Lord," she said.

I sat down. "What did you say?" I asked her.

"Nothing," she said. "But I'll tell you, it gave me the chills."

Rosie had come from a large family. Two of her sisters and one of her brothers had died before they'd reached thirty. At sixteen, she'd witnessed her father's murder. When Rosie had chills, it gave me pause.

"That child—" she began, and shook her head. "My poor baby," she said again.

"I know."

"She talked about this to you all before?"

I nodded.

"I once heard tell of a child who heard voices that told him to walk off a bridge," she said.

I stared at her.

"Not that she's going to do that," she said.

"Sarah's always had a great imagination," I said.

"If that's all it is," Rosie said.

"What?"

"I've heard tell of spirits who hold on, you know."

"Okay," I said. I stood up. "For now, let's just listen to what she's saying."

———

Before David's death, I'd been looking forward to Sarah's fourth birthday party. The third had been canceled by roseola, the second had been a melee, and the first merely a prolonged photograph. With the fourth, I'd been hoping to start giving Sarah a taste of what my mother had done for us.

My mother had thrown the best parties in town. They'd had themes and decorations, perfect prizes, burgers and french fries for lunch. They'd had games of her own invention: word games, art games, puzzles, races. She had always made Heather and me two cakes—one for each of us to decorate—and she'd baked in handfuls of small metal trinkets wrapped up in pockets of wax paper. Other mothers would have blanched at the prospect of kids choking on crumb-covered dimes and lucky charms, but our mother had had almost exotic faith, and our friends liked us better because of it.

The crowning glory of each party had been the homemade wishing well. It had started as just a grab bag filled with trolls and whistles and rubber balls. But each year, it had grown more elaborate, until, by the time we turned ten, she had constructed a large cylindrical box and painted it with faux stones and ivy, frogs, ladybugs, and flowers.

So when Sarah was finally in bed that night, I took out the paints and the brushes and a box of stickers I'd been saving for months, and with Edgar sitting in the big cozy chair, I spread out a drop cloth and got to work.

———•———

Guiltily, I called Heather to tell her.

"I know there's no way you can come," I said. "I just knew you'd be mad if I didn't tell you."

"Why wouldn't you want to tell me?" she said.

"Come on, Dee. You don't need to see these kids."

"Joe's going to be on vacation that week," she said. "It'll be crazy here. There's just no way."

"I understand," I told her.

"No you don't. I'll really be busy," she said.

"I know."

"I'll bring Sarah a present," she said.

"You don't have to," I said, but she'd hung up.

———•———

There were eight of them now in her nursery school class, and not one of them had a cold or the flu or an aunt visiting from Texas. They all came—tumbling into the living room like a mad, tiny acrobatic troupe. Their mothers or sitters came too, of course: women I'd known only by nods and smiles from the school corridors and cubbies. I had not really tried to know them. I'd had Heather and the safety of our old insulation. I understood that in coming years, I would need to make more of an effort.

We had ninety minutes to fill before we could bring out the pizza and birthday cake.

"Okay, everyone," I said, clapping my hands. "Everyone gather round."

The children all formed a circle around me, and I was briefly heady with power.

"A few rules," I said. "If anyone needs to go to the bathroom, ask your mommy or baby-sitter. You can play here or in the hallway, but don't go into the kitchen. No throwing anything. And no grabbing."

I looked at them. They were quiet. I didn't trust them.

"And if anyone needs to go to the bathroom," I said again, "ask your mommy or baby-sitter."

They seemed bored. They'd heard all this before.

"Now," I said, with my most winning smile, "everyone take a balloon."

I had a bagful of them—uninflated, of course—eight red, eight white, to avoid crises of aesthetics or regret.

Above the ensuing stampede, I shouted, "There are pens on the coffee table."

They actually sat, and they actually drew.

"When you're done," I shouted above the din, "Sarah's daddy will blow them up for you."

They were done in what seemed like ten seconds but might have been a full two or three minutes.

By the time Edgar had inflated the last of the balloons, the kids were all over the living room, and his face was a remarkable gray.

"You okay?" I asked him as Lily, Noah, and Johnny ran past me into the forbidden kitchen.

"The singing," he said.

"Yes?"

He'd planned to take out his guitar.

"I can't," he gasped. "Not yet. Plan B."

I heard the pop of a balloon. I sent Rosie into the kitchen to field the three kids, and I set off in search of a balloonless child. It turned out to be Sarah.

"Sweetie," I said, "what happened to your balloon?"

"I popped it," she said.

"Why?" I asked her.

"I wanted to."

"Why?"

"I didn't like it," she said.

"Do you want to make another?"

"No."

I was lonely for her, and terrified, but just then a high-pitched scream came from the corner of the room, where Cathy was now being pinned by Judy, Jim, and Alexa, who fell against her rhythmically, shouting, "Squeeze the lemon! The lemon is the pits!"

At the coffee table, Will, Johnny, Noah, and Lily were now addressing the party bags I'd laid out after the balloons, decorating them with an assortment of stickers, glitter, glue, washable markers, and, in one case, spit.

Sarah clung alternately to my leg and Rosie's, with the occasional brief foray to Edgar's. She looked, now and then, toward the front hallway door, as if she were waiting for David to walk in. I half-expected to see it too, and I hated the fact that I had to and couldn't explain the word *never* to my child.

I squeezed her hand.

"It's okay to miss him," I told her.

"I know," she said to me evenly.

We were through with everything but the food in an hour and seven minutes.

I searched my memory and came up empty.

"Duck Duck Goose," Edgar muttered to me.

"Are we that desperate?"

"Duck Duck Goose," he yelled, clapping his hands.

When Heather and I were children, we had devised a way to rig Duck Duck Goose. We had always been afraid that we wouldn't be Goose, so if things were going badly, we would give each other a look and then we'd know to Goose each other. The other kids always fell for our act, the feigned suspense as we circled the ducks—Duck . . . Duck . . . Duck . . . whose head would be tapped?—and then the seeming surprise of GOOSE! and the wild fake chase around the ring. I'd always known when she wanted to lose and when she wanted to win.

Now the children formed a reluctant circle at Edgar's feet.

"Let's start," he said.

"Who should start?" Sarah asked him.

"I want to start!" four voices chorused.

"Let's let the birthday girl start," Edgar said.

"He says it's a silly game," Sarah said.

I tried to pretend I hadn't heard.

"Who does?" Noah asked.

"Kids—" Edgar and I began in unison.

"David," Sarah told them blithely.

"David's dead!" Judy shouted with brutal bluntness.

"I talked to him," Sarah said calmly.

"No!" Judy shouted again. "You didn't!"

The other kids looked bewildered.

Judy's mother, Nancy Weiss, appeared at the door.

"What is it, sweetheart?" she asked Judy.

Judy stood up, breaking the Duck circle, and pointed a finger at Sarah.

"*She* said she talked to David," she said. "But David's dead and he can't talk. You told me."

Nancy circled Judy in her arms. I did the same with Sarah, though she was perfectly calm and poised.

"That's right, sweetheart," Nancy told Judy. "David can't talk anymore. He's dead."

"He talks to me," Sarah said unbendingly. I loved her for holding her ground.

The other mothers and sitters appeared, looking on with both sympathy and alarm.

"If he's dead, can he eat?" Will asked.

"If he's dead, can he play Duck Duck Goose?"

"If he's dead, can he drink soda?"

"If he's dead, does he have to brush his teeth?"

"Okay, everybody," I said, standing up. "How 'bout some birthday cake?"

"Why didn't you tell me?" Heather asked me on the phone at eight o'clock the next morning.

"Tell you what?"

"About the party."

"I did. I told you I was giving Sarah a party."

"Not that. What she said."

I froze, guiltily.

"Who told you?"

"Judy's mother. Nancy Weiss."

"What did she say?"

"She told me that Judy said Sarah said she was talking to David."

"She *called* you?"

"No. She brought Judy in. Too much birthday cake."

"Serves her right."

"Erica," Heather said.

"Sorry."

"How long has this been going on?"

"I don't know."

"But she's said stuff like this before?"

"A few times."

"Why didn't you tell me?" Heather asked.

"Why do you think?"

She was silent a moment.

"Do you want me to get you a name?" she asked.

"A name?"

"Of a therapist. A child psychologist."

"She's always had a great imagination," I said.

"I want to talk to Sarah," she said.

———

She came later that afternoon, leaving Jeffrey with Richard, and Dad on his way there. She brought Sarah a gift that was wrapped in Mickey Mouse paper.

"Can I open it?" Sarah asked.

"Kiss me first," Heather said, smiling.

Sarah kissed her, and let Heather hug her. It moved me. I

couldn't remember if they'd even seen each other since David's death.

I thought it must have been excruciating for Heather to hug a child David's size, but she held on tight, and Sarah did too. I realized that I had been missing not only David but Heather with Sarah too. A few seconds passed. I was going to speak when I realized that Heather was crying. It was shocking, and an enormous relief, and I knew enough to say nothing.

"Sarah," Heather said to the back of her neck. "Tell me. Your mommy says you talked to David."

Sarah nodded.

"How does he talk to you?" Heather asked gently. She had stopped crying now, and she was calm. Her tenderness toward Sarah seemed as enormous as her sorrow.

"He comes in through the window," she said.

"Which window?"

"The one in my bedroom," she said. "And he talks to me in my head."

"Does he come a lot?"

"When he's lonely," she said.

"Is he lonely a lot?"

"Pretty much," she said. "He misses you and his daddy and Jeffrey."

"Does he miss you, too?"

"No. Because we talk."

"Will you tell him I miss him?"

"He knows," she said.

Heather looked down at Sarah's shoes.

"I miss getting him dressed in the morning," she said. "I

miss holding him the way I'm holding you now. I miss seeing you two play together."

It was the first time in years, if not decades, that I'd heard her admit she recalled anything with sadness and with sentiment.

It crushed me to think it had taken the death of her son to give her a past she missed.

"He knows all that," Sarah said to her.

Heather tossed her shoulders back. "Do you want your birthday present now?" she asked.

"Yes."

"Well, open it, then," Heather said brightly. Sarah slid down from her lap. Heather kissed Sarah's head, patted her back, and straightened her shirt and skirt, as if they were about to embark on a long journey together.

New Year's Eve, 1963

"Erica's Just Taking the Drink Order"

It's six o'clock on New Year's Eve, the day before 1964. Heather and I are ten years old. We sit at our desks in our twilit rooms and silently spar with each other.

As always, there are five tests this week. But because it's a holiday Tuesday, we have been told to do them, alone, at home. They are language, reasoning, spatial relations, counting, and memory.

Dr. Newsome told us last week that he sensed we were trying to rush through our tests. The other twins in the study looked at us harshly, feigning surprise and dismay. But the Amitai twins are known cheaters: They've been swapping answers in the bathroom all year. And the Davidson twins pass notes sometimes. And the Durning twins keep a secret score pad that supposedly tracks the whole group's progress.

"Remember," the doctor told us last week. "It doesn't matter who's faster, or who gets more of the answers right."

Heather and I started laughing.

———

I match the word pairs. I ponder the meanings. Cat is to dog as mouse is to what? I try to connect nine points with three lines. I do long division. I do fractions. I fill in the squares on the answer sheets. I list all the objects that I can remember the doctor placing on the table last week. I know that there was a bell, a pill vial, a dictionary, a pack of cards. I know that there was a notepad, a pencil, a photograph, and a miniature car. But that is only eight things, and in the weeks past, there have always been ten. I beg my memory to respond. Something small and green, I'm thinking, and also something larger.

Next door, I know, Heather is trying to beat me. I am trying to beat her too.

Something green and small. A frog? No. A sugar bowl. Green? Some child's plaything? Or maybe there were only eight, and the doctor is trying to trip us up.

"Done!" Heather yells as she passes my room. I throw down my pencil and run to my door.

"I'm done too!" I tell her.

"I was done first!"

We race, side by side, to the kitchen, where Mom is dressed in a beautiful caftan and looks up at us with an unknowing smile.

"Girls," she says. "Not so fast. There's plenty of time before midnight."

She's totally missed the point, which is that both of us want to be waitress tonight.

"What's for dinner?" we ask her in unison.

"Chicken, broccoli, and red rice," Mom says. She checks the rice as she says it.

Heather grabs a notepad from the kitchen counter. I grab the mug of pens. Stalemate.

"Choose," she says.

"Odds or evens?"

"Odds."

"Once, twice, three, shoo."

"Best two out of three," I say.

"No way. You didn't call it."

She takes the pens from me and sits at the counter to write out the menu, making the words in her tall, perfect letters, and adding a border of scrolls and flowers.

"Lovely," Mom tells her when she's done.

Meanwhile, I've taken Mom's extra apron down from its hook on the side of the stove. So Heather, not to be outdone, finds a white paper napkin and drapes it over her arm.

"I'm doing the drink orders," I say.

She tears the menu page off the notepad and hands it to me reluctantly.

"What have we got, Mom?"

She dictates, and I write down orange juice, milk, ginger ale, champagne, water, club soda, apple juice.

I draw a border of flowers also and show it to Mom.

"Lovely," she says. "Okay, girls. Bring me the orders."

We race into the living room, where Dad is reading the newspaper.

"We've come to take your order," I say.

"What's on the menu tonight, waitresses?"

"I'm the waitress," Heather says. "Erica's just taking the drink order."

"Well, what have we got?" he asks me.

I read to him from the menu. He pretends, briefly, to ponder his choices.

"Champagne," he finally says.

"One champagne coming up," I tell him, and run back into the kitchen before Heather can take Dad's dinner order.

———

Heather is in the red group of fifth grade. I am in the blue group. We have finally persuaded our mother to stop dressing us alike. Heather is on the volleyball team. I am in the glee club. Heather likes Libby Singer. I like Felice Lavec. But we share the same teachers, the same locker, and the same crush on Mrs. Stevenson, who teaches American history.

In study hall, when the whole fifth grade sits each day in alphabetical order, Heather and I are desk buddies, sitting side by side at the lift-top desk. Still, when Mrs. Elzinger calls the roll, my name is always first.

In the evenings, we have the same homework assignments. Heather won't help me, and I won't help her, but we compare answers when we're done, and sometimes we change things later. On Tuesdays after school, we go together to our father's hospital, where for nearly a year now he has had us enrolled in the study of twins that one of his colleagues is doing.

We know the premise of the study. The premise is that the closer a relationship is between twins, the better their memory, word skills, math skills, and overall ability are going to be. There are identical twins in our group too. All the fraternals, like Heather and me, are trying to prove that we can be brighter. This means proving that we can be closer. Heather and I ache to be different. We ache to outdo each other. It's confusing to have to stay together to have any chance of real greatness.

"Did you finish your tests?" Dad asks us as he comes into the kitchen.

"Erica didn't," Heather says.

"Yes I did."

"Max Newsome told me you're racing each other," Dad says.

"We're not!" we both say.

Sometimes the only thing that unites us is the need to prove we're united.

Heather gets to carry the champagne glasses in.

I get to set the table.

Heather gets to dance first with Dad.

I get to sit next to Mom on the couch.

Heather gets asked for her New Year's resolution first.

I get asked to turn on the TV and find what channel Guy Lombardo is on.

Long after everyone's gone to sleep, I tiptoe into Heather's room and take her tests from the shoe box in her closet where I know she hides her most valuable things.

I thumb through the pages, looking for the memory test.

"Name as many objects as you can remember that I put out on the table last week," the question reads.

I see her answer:

Pill bottle
Notepad
Pencil
Cactus

She will always remember less than I do, and slightly different things.

Spring, 1990

"If She Doesn't Know It's a Fantasy,
Then You've Got a Problem"

It was May, and heaven was shaping up nicely.

Sarah said David liked it there. You could be any age that you wanted to be—not just the age you had been when you died.

"So you could be a baby in heaven if you wanted to, Mommy," she said one day, "and I could be a grown-up."

There were rooms, as far as I could understand, that had mirrors and sparkles and flowers, and you could sit on tall ice-cream-parlor chairs around tall ice-cream-parlor tables.

There were swimming pools that had no deep ends. Into these pools you could toss green Legos, which turned into plants that were known as Deents.

You could wear your favorite pajamas each night, and they would never be in the wash, because they would never get dirty.

There were playgrounds laid out on vast, clean green fields. There were daisies and daffodils that you could pick; when you picked them, they didn't die, she said.

There were other fields that were like huge trampolines, where you could keep bouncing as long as you liked.

I listened to all this with sadness and awe. But I told myself she would outgrow this world, just as she had outgrown her baby toys, her "no" phase and her "why" phase, and her passion for make-believe birthdays. This was a girl who said rainbows should have swings beneath them, who drew pictures of fish eating seaweed salad, who said soap on her arms was like evening gloves, who said butterflies were made of butter.

Who was I to decide for my daughter what fantasies were the good ones?

———

On the first Sunday in May, Heather phoned to say that she'd been on call the day before and had missed Dad's still-weekly visit to her.

"Can I come over?" she asked me.

"Sure," I said. "Is something up?"

"Since when can I not just come over and see you?"

Since the worst thing that can happen to a human being has happened to you, I wanted to say, and you've become either too prickly or too cold or too miserable to touch.

"Of course you can come," I told her.

She showed up an hour later, alone. Jeffrey and Richard had gone to a ball game. Dad hadn't even appeared yet, so Edgar went out to take a run, and the three of us settled in Sarah's room.

We sat at her tiny white table, which she adorned with plastic place settings for four and construction-paper place mats.

"Want some tea, Mommy?" she asked.

"Thanks."

The cups were an old set that Mom had saved. Heather had broken the pot years before. Sarah poured out the pretend tea from one half of a smiling Russian doll.

"One lump or two?" she asked sweetly.

"One, please."

The sugar cubes were old buttons.

"Aunt Heather?" she asked.

"Two lumps," she said.

"I'll make you some cake, too," said Sarah, and we watched her hop off her chair and busy herself at the play stove.

Heather watched Sarah pensively.

"I've got lots of plates and pretend food and stuff," she said. "Jeffrey hasn't used it for years."

"He doesn't want you to do that," Sarah told her.

"What?"

"David doesn't want you to give them to me."

"Oh, Sarah," she said. "I'm sure he wouldn't mind."

"No. He does mind," she said simply. "The cake is ready now," she added. She brought it over—four bright, colored blocks—and served it to us ceremoniously.

"Who's the fourth one for?" Heather asked her.

"Maybe David," Sarah said.

Just then, Edgar came back in from his run.

"Maybe the fourth piece can be for Daddy," I told her.

Sarah said: "No! It's David's!"

Heather shook her head in wonder.

"Does he still come in through the window?" she asked.

"Uh-huh," Sarah said. "At night he does."

"So he still talks to you in your head?"

"Uh-huh."

Edgar appeared in the doorway just in time to hear Heather's question. He looked from Heather to Sarah to me. I shrugged.

"What's David doing there?" Heather asked Sarah.

"Playing," Sarah said.

"Does he still feel lonely?"

"Uh-huh. But he told me about the seasons," she said. She picked up an errant crayon and started to draw on her make-believe place mat.

"What seasons?" Heather asked her.

Edgar asked: "Anyone want some apple juice?"

"Um, David says heaven's just like summer or spring or winter or fall," Sarah told Heather.

"Why is that?" Heather asked her.

Sarah looked up, as if trying to remember a song she had learned in school. She held up her lovely hands to count. She said: "Music, Arts and Crafts, Snack, and Gym. And after Gym, then you go back."

"To where?" I asked.

"To here, Mommy, of course," she said.

"And that's what happens after heaven?" Heather asked.

"Uh-huh," Sarah said. "It's just like after nursery school you go to kindergarten."

———

"We've got to get Sarah some help," Edgar said that night after Heather had gone.

"She'll outgrow it," I told him.

"When?" he said. "It's been like two months."

"Two months is nothing."

"Two months is a long time for a kid."

"Well, so is four years," I said. "Did you think Sarah was just going to pick up her toys and forget David ever existed?"

"Do it for me," Edgar said. "Let's just call someone."

"I think you're overreacting," I said.

———

Dr. Rachel Koenig had an office on West Eighty-seventh Street. Edgar had gotten her name from Joe Worth and sworn him to keeping the secret from Heather.

Edgar called the doctor on Monday. The first hour she had was more than two weeks away. I wondered at the success of her practice, and found its implications of widespread youthful neurosis mildly comforting.

In the meantime, Heather began to call. She called most evenings after work. She'd start out pretending to talk to me: How were my classes? How was my husband? Had I seen the sneakers on sale at Jay's? When I'd ask her how she was doing, she'd tell me something harmless about her work: how the new receptionist was reading Kant on her lunch break; how the kids were all getting ear infections from swimming. Then there would be a pause and she would say, "Is there a Cookie around who wants to say hello to me?"

"Sarah," I'd say, "it's Aunt Heather," and I would feel a flush of joy and relief when I saw the joyous look on Sarah's face.

She would bound to the phone immediately and pace back and forth, talking, just as I did.

"In the park," she'd say, and there'd be a silence. "On the slide," she'd say. "No, backwards," she'd say. Sometimes she would laugh, or giggle. Sometimes she would sing Heather a song.

"I don't know," Edgar and I heard Sarah say one night to Heather. "Maybe if you listen very hard."

"Listen very hard to what?" Edgar hissed at me.

"Shh," I said.

"I don't know how," Sarah said again. "He just talks to me. I don't know how."

———

"Let's get away for the summer," Edgar said that night after we'd tucked Sarah in.

"What do you mean?" I said.

"You know. Get away. From the city. From—"

"What?"

He shrugged.

"From Heather?"

"She's encouraging Sarah."

"I don't know," I said to him, knowing. What I knew was that, despite everything, I loved it when my sister called at night.

———

On Thursday, May twenty-fourth, at the peak of final exams, Edgar and I both got stand-in proctors and hailed a cab together to go back downtown, toward help.

Somehow, Edgar and I had both reached our thirties without ever having had therapy. Anomalous in this way—mistrustful, too—we fought in the cab on the way down about the prospect of Sarah's needing help at all.

"If we're this nervous," I said, "how do you think Sarah's going to feel?"

"I'm not nervous," he told me. "I'm just concerned."

"Oh right," I said.

"Don't snap at me."

"I know when you're nervous. Your lips are dry."

"I thought you agreed that she needed this," he said.

"I don't know what she needs right now. And I don't think you do, either."

"All I know is, she thinks heaven sounds like fun, and I sort of think that's scary."

———————

I had read enough about psychotherapy not to expect the clichés. I was disappointed. From the moment Dr. Koenig greeted us in the tiny waiting room to the moment she ushered us back out (suggesting she'd like to meet Sarah herself), I felt scrutinized, pigeonholed, and indexed like the case history I was sure our little family unit would become.

But she was relaxed in her system, constricting though it seemed to me.

"I'm a lapsed Freudian," she explained with a smile as she sat in a leather armchair, tucking her feet up cozily.

"What does that mean?" Edgar asked her, pulling a small doll from the recesses of his chair.

"It means," she said, reaching forward to take the doll from him, "that when child psychotherapy began, the minimum expectation was six hours a week. The feeling was that you couldn't get anything done in less time. You had to have real contact with the child."

I looked over at Edgar, but he didn't look back at me.

"Anyway," Dr. Koenig said, "I don't believe that six hours

is essential. But I do accept the Freudian premise that there are certain stages of development that are fairly fixed in childhood—Oedipal, latency, anal, oral, and so forth. And the work I do here with children is predicated on that assumption."

"What about death?" I asked.

"Excuse me?" Dr. Koenig asked.

"What about death? What about a tragedy? Her cousin was killed in February. We feel that her problems are because of that."

She smiled kindly, but within that kindness I detected what I thought was a sliver of amusement.

"I'm so sorry about the boy," she said warmly. She looked at Edgar. "You told me a little bit on the phone. Why don't you tell me more now?"

So he told her about Sarah's birthday party, the talks she was having with David, and her ever-more-complex descriptions of heaven.

"And how old is Sarah?" the doctor asked.

"Her birthday was April thirteenth. She's four."

"Well, four," Dr. Koenig said, "is the age for death and birth questions anyway."

"That's what I've been thinking," I said.

Edgar looked at me.

"You have?" he asked.

The doctor's eyes bounced from Edgar's to mine and hungrily back again.

"Well, at three to four," Dr. Koenig continued, "that's the age when a child first starts to understand that her parents existed before she did. A four-year-old gets the idea, I came from you. And with that understanding come all the questions about how babies are made."

"She hasn't asked us that yet," I said.

"But she's asked you about heaven."

"No. She's *told* us about heaven," I said.

"Well, in the end the question will be how real she thinks it is. A child of three or four often has an imaginary friend, usually likes to play make-believe. And often she seems to blur the line between reality and fantasy. If she doesn't know it's a fantasy, then you've got a problem."

"How can you tell?"

Dr. Koenig smiled.

"That's why they pay me the big bucks," she said.

———————

Edgar and I walked to the street corner in silence. Then he hugged me, hard and sweetly.

I started to cry.

"I know," he said, stroking my back.

"Damn it," I said.

"I know," he said.

"Poor David," I said. "Poor Heather."

"Poor Sarah," he said.

He flagged a cab. We got in. I blew my nose.

"What do you think?" he asked me.

"I think she's a four-year-old girl who just lost her best friend, and this is her way of dealing with it."

"It's freaking everyone out," he said.

"I know," I said. "But that's too bad."

"You think she knows she's making it up?"

"Yes. Don't you?"

"I'm not sure," he said.

We passed a school that was just letting out. Children spilled down the steps in pairs, trios, and quartets. I ached for my child.

"I wish she had a brother or sister," he said.

"I know."

"I wish you were pregnant," he said.

"I know. I wish we hadn't waited."

We knew we would have to wait longer now, but we hadn't talked about it.

"She's got to make some new friends," he said.

"Let's find a play group for her."

"I'm not sure it's that simple," he said.

"Nothing's simple," I said.

"Let's just look," Edgar said to me that night. "Let's just look for a house. There's still time."

I was grateful he wasn't insisting on the doctor.

"Where would we look?" I asked him.

"I don't know," he said. "Jersey. Connecticut. Westchester. Just some house with a backyard. What's the point of being teachers unless we can have real summer vacations?"

Time off was one of the few perks of teaching, and it was true that in summers past we had always regretted not taking better advantage of it. Edgar had spent his childhood summers at camp. I'd spent most of mine in the Berkshires, in a small wooden house that my parents had bought and rebuilt as the years went by.

We'd gone up there gamely some weekends in autumn and winter after my mother's death, including the weekend of New Year's Eve. Twice, we'd arrived, settled in, had some lunch, and then Dad had announced that he felt sick. He had actually had to lie down both times. He had blamed it, both times, on the food we had had, never noticing that the rest of us were fine, never admitting that there might be some other reason. But he wound up renting the mountain house out. He had been too attached to sell it, and too sad to live in it without her.

I would have loved to take Sarah there, but the rent was much higher than we could afford, and I didn't want to ask Dad. Instead, I had heard of a place from Bruno, who lived year-round in Hastings-on-Hudson. Neighbors of his were taking a leave. They would let us have their place, cheap, for three months.

On the weekend after the doctor visit, we rented a car and drove out to see it. Sarah sat in the backseat, alone, with her lovely face tilted against the window, and a breeze combing back her short, curly dark hair.

"What's it like?" she asked us.

"That's what we're going to find out," I said.

"Are there horses?"

"Horses?" I laughed. "I don't think so."

"Do you like horses?" Edgar asked.

"Yes."

"What does a horse say?"

"Neigh!" she shouted.

It was nice to know there were some questions that still elicited the same answers.

———

The house was on a small hill. Through the trees, we could just see the Hudson River.

The owner's wife, Martha, showed us around. There were three ample bedrooms, a study, a playroom, a great kitchen with a large pine table.

In the backyard, an old swing set hung, long neglected. Sarah immediately ran to it.

"Our children spent all their time out here when they were young," Martha said as she led me toward the garage. She was opening the door when I heard Edgar scream, "No!"

Fear spun me around.

"Sarah!" I shouted, running before I had even seen where she was.

She was simply standing beside the swing set, looking at Edgar as if he'd lost his mind.

"What is it?" I asked him.

"The chain on the swing. It's broken," he said.

"Yes?"

"Sarah started to climb on."

I gave him a level look.

"Are you okay, Sarah?" I said.

"Yes, Mommy."

"Okay. Well, the swings are broken. Don't climb on them, okay?"

"Okay."

She went off to count the flagstones in the patio.

Martha looked at us oddly.

"We love the house," I told her.

"So do we," she said, still distracted.

Edgar said: "We'll be in touch with you." Then he called to Sarah, and we piled into the car. Edgar double-checked her seat belt.

Martha watched as we left the driveway.

I put on a tape and whispered to Edgar, "You've got to get a grip."

———

Heather had left two messages on the machine while we were gone.

I called her before I had taken my coat off.

"What are you doing?" she said, sounding breathless.

"We just got in from checking the house out."

"Listen," she said. "I don't think you should take it."

"It's great," I said. "A big backyard. Lots of rooms. It's wonderful. Why not?"

She took a breath.

"Heather?"

"Because," she said. "I think I'm going to take the summer off, and I think we should all go to the mountain house."

———

She came over in the evening with Jeffrey. Sarah and he stood eyeing each other. Their only link had been David.

"Jeffrey," Heather said. "Why not go play with Sarah?"

They wandered, reluctantly, into her room, sensing, as children occasionally can, the need for real sacrifice.

"Want a drink?" Edgar asked Heather.

"Yes."

That was surprising.

"What would Richard do if you took the summer off?" I asked as Edgar went to the kitchen for ice.

"I don't know," Heather said. "Come too. Probably. I don't know."

Richard worked mad Wall Street lawyer hours.

"What's going on?" I asked Heather.

"He's making me crazy. He still wants to move. And I think we all need to get away and think about it for a while. If he comes with us, that's fine. If he doesn't—"

"Come where?" Edgar asked as he walked back in.

"To the house."

"In the Berkshires?"

"Yes."

"What does Dad say?" I asked Heather.

"He says he might want to come too," she said.

———•———

Edgar was wary, at best.

"Everybody?" he said.

"Yes," I answered, beaming.

He sighed.

"Edgar," I said. "It's my *family*."

"I know."

"It means a lot to me."

"I know."

"If you really don't want to—" I started.

"No."

"What?"

"You want it more than I don't want it."

"Do you really dislike them so much?" I asked.

"That's a rotten question," he said.

"Edgar. Her son just died. She needs me."

"She'll have your dad."

"He needs me too."

———

"Did you talk to Heather?" Dad asked on the phone when I called him, midweek, between grading exams.

So I told him I had, and that I loved the idea.

"What if Richard doesn't come?" Dad asked.

"He'll come," I said. "He needs it too."

"Well, I'd better call up the agent," Dad said.

"I think this is going to be great," I told him.

———

There is a Japanese folktale about a boy named Urashima who married a mermaid and lived with her in a castle below the sea. After some years, he became homesick for his parents and so longed to see them again that he decided he had to find them. His wife gave him a casket to travel in and told him that as long as he didn't open it, it would protect him on his journey.

When he came home, Urashima found that centuries had passed since he'd been gone. Distraught, he opened the casket and was transformed into an old man, then a corpse.

My interpretation of this story was that the awareness of the time that had passed since he'd been a child had killed him.

New Year's Eve, 1983

"What's Wrong with the Walls?"

Dad has started dating. Her name is Margaret, and I've met her three times. She has great teeth, a good figure, and a loud, slightly anguished laugh. Her dresses crackle with static cling, and her eyes teem with ready sympathy. But Dad hasn't brought her to Lenox for New Year's, so Heather and I have a topic while we gather wood at the mountain house on the last day of 1983.

It has been only half a year since Mom's death. Dad has been furious, dazed, bereft, navigating a wild course between his determination and his dread. He says he must think of the future. The past hugs him in his dreams. Most mornings, he calls me to tell me his nightmares. They are haunting, hypnotic, transparent, but every day, as I offer my sympathy, he cuts me off, saying, "Well, what's the point?" and then asks if I've spoken to Heather.

Heather is still nursing Jeffrey. Her breasts are large and her moods unsteady. Resolutely, she leads me back behind the house to the woods where, with our mother, we once gathered flowers in spring, berries in summer, and leaves in early autumn. Now it is winter, and Heather and I look for firewood.

The floor of the forest is covered with snow; the sun falls through the branches, landing in stripes and shadows at our feet. Where we walk, the sun turns our footprints pale blue.

"So what does Dad say about Margaret?" Heather asks. Her face is flushed with the cold. She scours the ground for fallen branches as if she is looking for bits of gold.

"That this is something he feels he should do."

"Like he doesn't want to," Heather says. She tucks the wood into Mom's canvas bag.

"He doesn't. It's not like he's having fun."

Heather's eyebrow is arched like a spring. "Why shouldn't he have fun?" she asks.

She finds a small fallen tree, and she braces her boot against a branch, straining to snap it off.

"He should," I say. "It's just that he isn't."

"She seems perfectly nice," she says, straightening up, the limb torn free in her hand. "And if she wants to put up with him—"

We walk on and gather more wood in silence, two brown-haired women at twilight, seeing our breath and his future before us.

"That's all," I say, our arms full now. "Why don't we let Dad and Richard do some?"

"We've just started," Heather says grimly, scanning the path that lies before us and starting to search anew.

Since Mom's death, Heather's fury has ripened. She seems to think Dad is a traitor for lacking the medical wisdom to save Mom.

"It's just a phase she's going through," I tell him whenever he asks me about it.

"We're all going through a phase," he says.

Her anger bends and straightens her spine, her arms; it drives her into her work, wherever the work is, whatever the work is. Heather has just had her first child and is just starting her own practice. Her life is built around the furious need to prove something to Dad that he's never taken the time to doubt. But her success is wasted on him. He has never questioned her competence.

When we go back to the house, we fill the wood bin to the top and fill the kindling box. Heather lights a ferocious fire, then looks around for a witness, but Dad is nowhere in sight.

———

Mom's death has scattered the three of us like the seeds of a weird perennial. Each of us is growing into a different version of her, a separate strain.

Heather now perpetuates her stamina and strength. She nurtures her patients and husband and child with a restless but always extravagant heart. She works hours beyond all reason, ever alert and ever ready, and never completely available to anyone. Like our mother, she is at her best and most loyal in times of crisis. Her drive, so much like defiance, still baffles me. But she walks the same clipped footsteps that Mom did.

Dad has become the head of the household in novel and seemingly perilous ways. We are thirty now, but he suddenly feels responsible for the jobs we've chosen, the men we've chosen, the places we live in, the women we are. For the first time, he's bought us our birthday gifts. He clips things from papers. He calls to check in. And he is discovering for the first time what kind of feelings we've saved up for him.

So I, for better or worse, have become my father's surrogate confidante, consulted on matters pertaining to Heather: What is she doing, how is her practice, how is her marriage, how is her kid. It makes me jealous to talk about her, but I hear Dad's loneliness for her and Mom, and that turns me into a brutal scold. I call Heather to remind her to call him. She says I should save the lectures for my students, and she hangs up on me. But then she calls him, and then he calls me, proudly reporting that she has called, and reviewing with me the intricacies of the life he so needs to know, the life she holds above him, giving him someone to miss who is still alive.

———·———

The twilight has turned to evening. The mountains have turned from shapes into shadows. Richard has changed a diaper and looks up to see if awards will be given out. His whole demeanor annoys me: the smug, supercilious looks, the fact that he's older, and richer, than Heather, the fact that he seems to equate good looks and good business sense with a kind of moral rectitude.

Then again, I am lonely, and Heather is not.

———·———

The house is odd in winter. We are used to being here in summer, when all the doors are left open and the nights don't begin until nine o'clock. We are used to the city on New Year's Eve, but we know that we couldn't have faced it there.

———·———

Before dinner, Heather nurses Jeffrey, who is three months old and a warm, pink mystery.

"I think we should think about redoing this place," she says, looking up at the unpainted walls.

"Heather!" I say, as if she's just suggested that we take a torch and burn the place down.

"I don't mean completely redo it," she says. "But let's face it, it's looking a little neglected."

"We could have our decorator come up and look," Richard says.

"We don't need a decorator," I say. "Our mother never needed a decorator."

We all look around the room, which, faded and dark, does nothing to support my point.

"At least paint the walls," Heather says.

"What's wrong with the walls?" I ask.

"What color would you paint them?" Dad says.

I stare at him, disbelieving.

"White," Heather says.

"That could be nice," Dad tells her.

She smiles and lays Jeffrey down on a small blue quilt. He stares up at her blankly.

"When did you cover these couches last?" Heather asks.

"I don't remember," Dad says, which is his standard answer about the past.

I marvel at his failure to embrace, let alone recall, the past. It is lovely, in a way, because it reveals such faith in the future. Even in mourning, he still seems more interested in what might happen to him than in anything that has. My father is sixty-six years old. By definition, he owns more of the past than he does of the future. But if his life were an hourglass, then the bottom half might as well be broken.

———

Mom kept a store of candles in the living room cupboard. They come in twos, attached by a single wick. Before dinner, I light a pair of them, thinking the whole time of Heather and me. The shared wick burns with a huge flare, and then the candles separate.

Heather stands Jeffrey up on her lap, bouncing him on his chubby legs.

We all stare at the baby, who drools at us grandly and sags to his knees.

"Don't do that to him," Dad tells Heather.

"It's good for his muscles," she says firmly.

———

At dinner, she points out the need for new china, the need for new glasses, the need for new chairs.

Dad nods, taking it all in. If he is troubled at all by his daughter's wish to dismantle his wife's house, he doesn't let on.

Perhaps, I think, his openness to consider changing the house is like his resolve about Margaret: something he feels he should do as a way of forcing himself forward. I am awed by his courage, and hurt by it. I do not know how to let go. I don't even know whether I should want to let go.

"I may just rent the place out," he tells us.

"That's a good idea, Dad," I say.

"Either way, though, it could use work," he says, and

Richard again starts talking about what wonders a decorator can do.

After dinner, Heather and Richard stroll out to the porch, come back in to get their jackets, and say they are going to take a walk.

"Now?" Dad asks.

"Yes."

"It's nearly midnight."

"Watch the baby," Heather says.

So Dad and I refill our glasses.

Dad turns on the radio—and doesn't waltz. The radio plays an old song:

> *Maybe it's much too early in the game,*
> *Ah, but I thought I'd ask you just the same,*
> *What are you doing New Year's, New Year's Eve?*

The patchwork quilt on the wall has faded. The old black telephone sits on the desk, a promise, a gleam, of connection, but to whom, I do not know. I hear:

> *Wonder whose arms will hold you good and tight,*
> *When it's exactly twelve o'clock that night.*
> *Welcoming in the New Year, New Year's Eve.*

I think I'm going to call Bruno. I'm going to say hi. I'm going to say Happy New Year. He'll say something charming and lively, something that no one else in the whole world would say.

I look at Dad, who is drifting in thoughts. I look at Jeffrey, who lies on the rug near me like a cast-off puppet. The music goes on:

> *Maybe I'm crazy to suppose*
> *I'd ever be the one you chose*
> *Out of the thousand invitations you'll receive.*
> *Ah, but in case I stand one little chance,*
> *Here comes the jackpot question in advance,*
> *What are you doing New Year's, New Year's Eve?*

Since college, I haven't once been in love. And somewhere in London, a guy named Paul whom I dated for nearly a year and a half is already sleeping, not dreaming of me.

———

Later, I lie in bed, half-asleep, hearing the sounds of Jeffrey fussing, and Richard and Heather squabbling about who should get up and see to him.

I fall asleep remembering summers past, when moths flew at the windows at night, and our parents kept watch below.

Summer, 1990

"I Found Out About Arts and Crafts"

Sarah had known how to count to ten when she was only fourteen months old, but she'd just recited the numbers then, as if she was saying a nursery rhyme. At school, they taught her to count for real by coloring in little circles or squares so she'd know which things she had counted.

Mourning my mother had been like that. I had had to do it one step at a time: walking past Bloomingdale's, watching *Born Free,* hearing Sinatra, using her sewing box, smelling her perfume, looking at photographs, eating tangelos, seeing white tulips, buying Dad shirts. The ache had been fresh in each setting: a new discovery, a new disclosure of loss. And then would come the relief of knowing I had one less setting to conquer, one less circle to color in. Then Bloomingdale's would become just a store, *Born Free* just a sappy movie.

We left for the mountains in early June. I had not seen the house in seven years. In that time, I had learned how to live without a mother. I had fallen in love with a man she'd never meet. I had given birth to a child she'd never hold. But apart from the winter just after her death, I had not been back to her second home, the place she had loved and had made us love. I had not yet colored the mountain house in. Time heals all wounds, I'm sure it's true, but not until after the wounds have been felt.

———•———

Edgar and Sarah and I would be the first ones there. Heather and Jeffrey would come in two weeks, and Dad, who had lectures that he couldn't cancel, a few days after that. Richard had decided that he would come too, but he said he had lots of loose ends to tie up, and he wasn't sure when he would make it. I was becoming more doubtful that he would come. It was not just because he and Heather were fighting. It was because so much of Richard's full and fond sense of himself seemed to come from insisting how busy he was. He always spoke about trying to make time, as if time were an unfixed commodity.

The mountain house was five minutes by car from Lenox, a small, perfect town filled with thin, tidy streets and thin, tidy people—few of whom we'd ever gotten to know. Our house was set on five acres, with views on all sides of the Berkshires. In summers, we'd rarely left it, making the briefest forays into town, and only when we needed food or news. The isolation had been rare for us all, but especially for our mother, whose charity work and shopping had always kept her out in the city, buzzing and flying from cause to cause. The house had been her refuge, and I imagined, driving north with Edgar and Sarah, that it would become ours too.

———•———

The caretaker had left the key in the old hiding place, a geranium planter, which now held neither flowers nor soil. I made a mental note to fill the planters and make the flowers grow.

"This is where Mommy spent her summers," Edgar told Sarah, and just as I had on the day of her birth, I thought for a moment that *Mommy* meant my mother.

It was breathtaking to come home to her house. The apartment in New York had changed many times since the year of her death. But nothing had changed here, despite the fact that Heather had once urged Dad to redo it. All that was new were the people who now stood on either side of me, taking it in. As we walked into the living room, I saw the couch fabrics my mother had chosen, the rug she'd had woven, the old prints of hot-air balloons from France, and the dozens of old tin boxes that filled the shelves to the right of the doorway. I felt the whole house was a time capsule, its contents sad and oddly outdated but nonetheless put here to be retrieved.

"It needs airing out," Edgar told me as I stood in the living room, trying to smile.

Sarah said: "I spy crying."

Edgar, not having noticed, turned around to see my face.

Sarah asked: "Why are you sad, Mommy?"

"I'm thinking about my mother," I told her.

"Is this where she lives?" Sarah asked.

I pondered this.

"Erica," Edgar prompted me.

"I told you, sweetheart," I said, kneeling down to take off her sweater and smooth her hair, "my mother's dead. She can't live here. But this was where we spent our summers with her when we were children."

Sarah nodded, looking up the stairs.

"Did you sleep up there?" she asked.

I nodded.

"With Aunt Heather?"

"Yes," I said. "Want to see?"

"Yes!"

We left our sweaters in a heap and went upstairs—so that I could be sad there, too.

———

Edgar took Sarah to town for the groceries, and I put all the sheets I could fit in the washing machine, and all the plates and glasses I could fit in the dishwasher. Then I opened windows, disposed of several large dead flies, and walked out the sliding glass doors to the porch. I took a long breath, looking past the toolshed to the woods. I remembered gathering blackberries with my mother, then imagined gathering blackberries with my daughter.

I didn't think there was a heaven, or a God, but in my mind I talked to my mother sometimes as if there were thrones and wings above me, and as if she were an angel with a lingering responsibility.

I was thirty-six years old, and still longed for her arms: the first, the elemental, embrace, the only embrace that had never had memories, echoes, or ghosts inside it.

———

I went inside and upstairs, to the large, lovely bedroom that Heather and I had always shared. I sat on the old, cozy love seat, then lay there, my legs draped over one of its arms. As a child, I'd been able to lie between them. I closed my eyes. In my mind, the room seemed to flicker, going from color to color and year to year. In this room, Heather and I had had a yellow linoleum floor and bunk beds, then pale blue walls and calico curtains. We had had beds in an el and beds in a line and beds we'd put almost side by side. We'd had a long, low white dresser, followed by a tall pine armoire. Then our walls had been painted white, and our toys and books had spilled over the sunny wood floors like things from an ocean left high on a shore.

The room went through all of these changes as I lay, remembering, with my eyes closed. So the thought I had as I drifted off to sleep was that if I opened my eyes at just the right moment, I could catch the room spinning somewhere in the past, and my mother would walk through the door and say, "All right, girls, it's time to sleep."

The house was a two-story colonial in the shape of a shallow U. Upstairs, a guest bedroom made the left arm of the U, and Heather's and my room made the right. In between was a large playroom, and beneath it, downstairs, the living room. The master bedroom was beneath the guest room. Under Heather's and mine were the kitchen and dining room. The house had been almost too large for two grown-ups and two children; for two children and five grown-ups, I thought, it was finally going to be crowded.

Heather and I had made out the room assignments in New York. Dad would sleep in his old room downstairs. Heather and Richard would have the guest room. Edgar and I would have Heather's and mine. Sarah and Jeffrey would sleep in the playroom, with grown-ups on either side.

When Edgar and Sarah woke me from my nap, I said it was time to bring the bags upstairs and get to work setting up the house.

Edgar whispered: "Are you okay?" as we walked down the stairs, and I said I was fine. But I still felt submerged in the past.

————

One of the things I loved about Edgar was how he fathomed my family—and usually managed to tolerate it. It was a quality of grace that stood in direct contrast to Richard's impatience. Richard had always dismissed our family's love as idol worship, our home as cult, our good works as guilt, our closeness as fear of the outside world. He blamed all of this on our parents, and so mourning Mom was suspect to him. Meanwhile, he made money and looked good, and made sure Heather made money and looked good. Like Dad, Richard had always seemed to be waiting for his children to become presentable. I wondered now if losing David was making him realize what he had missed. And I wondered if he'd understand now how relentlessly one could keep missing a person one loved.

————

We had brought one whole bag filled with Sarah's toys, and another of books and art supplies. I made the command decision that she should be allowed to keep these things in the living room downstairs. Along with this came the realization that I didn't want or expect Dad, with his arm's-length list of pet peeves, to be the head of this household.

Side by side, Sarah and I knelt to clear the long shelf by the front door to make room for her toys. We pulled the books off the shelf one by one. They were old books, slightly mildewed, some familiar to me from long-ago summers, some the castoffs of bygone renters. I found my mother's bird-watching book, and the skeleton of an ancient leaf fell out, crushed and colorless.

We put in the box of blocks, a new set of Colorforms Sarah had gotten for her birthday, her Playmobil dolls in their basket, and the sets of dollhouse furniture that Heather had given her for her birthday.

"Maybe we'll build you a dollhouse this summer," I said.

Her eyes widened with pleasure.

"Really?" she said.

"Why not?"

"Could it have three bedrooms?"

"Why three?"

"One for Aunt Heather and Uncle Richard, one for you, me, and Daddy, and one for David."

I had hoped, of course, that in addition to peace and memories and old pressed leaves, we would find some reality in this house.

"What about Jeffrey?" I asked, hoping to steer her toward a friendship that, admittedly, I couldn't fathom.

"No," Sarah said, shaking her head.

"No?"

"No."

"Why not?"

"Because David says Jeffrey was mean to him and never let him play with his Batman."

"Sarah," I said, looking at her levelly. "I distinctly remember watching Jeffrey let David play with his Batman."

"Not the one in the Batmobile, with the Robin and guns that pop up."

That was true. I could not remember ever having seen Jeffrey let David play with the Batman in the Batmobile with the Robin and guns that pop up.

"David says he never let him," she said.

"You mean David once *told* you that."

"Yes," Sarah acknowledged. "He *told* me."

"Right."

"Last night," she said.

———•———

It took us a while to find our own rhythm, to stitch our own patterns out of the day. We discovered the places we most liked to sit in, the times of our meals, and our sleep and play.

I drove to the local garden store and bought huge bags of soil and bright red geraniums. Sarah helped me fill the planters, using her small, sweet hands—and, at one point, Freedo's paw—to help me pat down the soil. Edgar found our old rowboat in the shed and pulled it down to the lakefront with my help, sending whole families of aphids and spiders scurrying for safety.

It was strange not to have Rosie's help with Sarah. I found myself missing the comfort of Rosie's vast certainty, however misguided it sometimes seemed. I missed her cooking our meals for us. But I thought I would miss her being with Sarah more. I had not been a full-time mother since the first months after Sarah's birth, and it was a thrill to discover that almost everything I'd found oppressive about it had changed. It was less a job now than a state of being. Sarah still demanded attention, still had to have three meals and a bath every day. But she liked crayoning, make-believe parties with Freedo, dress-up in my clothes, and, sometimes, in Edgar's. Some afternoons, she would sit for an hour in back of the house, sorting the gravel by colors and then pretending that they were gems. She was displaying the kind of independence that I, as a twin, had never once known but that I, as a mother, adored. And though Sarah asked more questions than a classroom full of students, she understood *now* and *later,* and had a healthy respect for their differences.

It was still too cold to swim in the lake, so we started each day with a long walk into the woods, where we gathered flowers or ferns, or turned over rocks to watch ants do their work. At lunchtime, we came in, washed up, and ate thick sandwiches on fresh brown bread from town. After that, we lay around reading. It was hard not to feel I was doing a hopeless impersonation of my mother. In the early evenings, when I cooked our dinners, Sarah would stand on a step stool beside me, helping, the way I had once helped Mom. I was showing her how to do things that had absolutely no meaning to me, except that they were things my mother had shown me how to do. "A good cook always cleans up after herself," I heard my mother say. I said it to Sarah. I felt the wash of time.

Edgar, meanwhile, seemed slowly to be getting over his own fears for her. He let her run out the back door, let her climb into the tree house that our mother and father had built years before.

At night, when Sarah was sleeping, he led me down the stairs to the master bedroom, where he made love to me with an old fervor.

———•———

"Are you ready yet?" he asked me one night, a week after we'd arrived.

I didn't have to ask what he meant, but I couldn't believe he meant it.

"No," I said. "It's still too soon."

"You mean because of Heather," he said.

"Of course because of Heather," I said.

"If we start now, it'll be born in March. That'll be just past a year since David died."

"So?" I said.

"Sweetheart, it would be different if Heather *could* have another baby," he said.

"There is an operation," I said.

"To reverse it?"

"Yes."

"Does it work?"

"I think sometimes."

"Would she ever want to try that?"

"I don't know," I said. "I haven't had the guts to ask her."

We lay side by side, feeling awkward.

The summer wind blew through the trees outside. I sighed, apologetically, into the sweet spot at his neck.

———•———

I was more lonely than I could admit to him or wished to admit to myself. The house felt too large, too damp, and too haunted. The beautiful views at sunset made me ache, made their audience seem paltry. When I spoke, my voice seemed to echo, as if I were hearing myself in a deep canyon.

Edgar would bound into a room and shout, "I love this family!"

"You mean me and Mommy?" Sarah would giggle.

And I alone kept feeling that there were empty places everywhere.

At night, while Edgar slept, I looked at him skeptically, wondering when he had changed.

I felt unsteady with Sarah, unsure that I still understood her mind.

I wondered why Edgar was so certain that we were ready for another child.

———

I called Heather most evenings after Sarah was asleep.

"How's it going?" I'd ask her, which really meant: How soon are you going to get here?

———

A few nights before she arrived, Edgar said: "It's been so great, being here with just you and Sarah."

I said: "I know, darling." But I was still waiting, inwardly, for my family to arrive.

The real summer, with its rituals of tree-house picnics, skinny-dips, reading by firelight, blackberry picking and blackberry pies, had, for me, not yet begun.

"I miss you," I told Heather on the phone the next night.

There was an awkward, all-too-familiar silence, a silence I should have expected but had been duped into not foreseeing.

"Dee?" I asked her anyway.

"What?"

"I said I miss you," I said.

"That's nice," she said, the old, cold Heather—let's pretend there's nothing between us; let's pretend I don't need you at all; let's pretend that all along I've just been with you because you needed me; let's pretend that the past you love is only a figment of your lonely, freighted, hapless imagination.

"You've only been gone two weeks," Heather said.

"You miss me too," I said.

"What?"

"You miss me too. That's what you should have said," I told her.

"I miss you too, Erica," she said in a breezy singsong, as if I were totally out of my mind.

She came with Jeffrey the next afternoon. It was already June twenty-second.

They were fighting when they stepped out of the car.

"I don't want to hear it!" Heather was shouting.

Jeffrey was looking down sullenly.

"Hi!" I said from the front steps, waving.

Sarah circled my thigh with her arm and leaned out toward Heather with new interest.

"Look at me," Heather told Jeffrey.

He shrugged and turned away. He would be seven in September, and his long legs and skinny body were no longer those of a little boy.

"Look at me!" Heather shouted at him, oblivious to both Sarah and me.

Jeffrey came to within a foot of us, then turned, glacially, back toward his mother.

"Jeffrey," she said again. "Look at me."

"I am," he said.

"At my *face,* not my *feet.*"

Slowly, he raised his eyes to her.

"I want you to tell me you're sorry," she said.

With his right sneaker toe, he sketched an arc in the gravel driveway.

"Sorry," Heather repeated. *"Now."*

Sarah looked from Heather to Jeffrey, bewildered.

"You told me I shouldn't lie," Jeffrey said.

"Well?"

"If I say I'm sorry, then I'll be lying."

Heather slammed the car door he'd left open, trying to hide the wisp of a smile that his logic had inspired.

"Into the house," she said, marching back to the trunk. "I'll figure out what to do with you later."

Jeffrey turned once again and stomped past us into the house. I could hear Edgar saying hello to him, but I couldn't make out a reply.

"Hi, Dee," I said when she'd opened the trunk.

She looked up, seething. She seemed to grunt. No kissing. No hugging. No greeting. Only the old Heather's face, which said: Don't kiss. Don't hug. Don't greet.

"Need a hand with the bags?" I asked her.

"Yes."

"Come on, Sarah," I said. "Let's help Aunt Heather."

Heather straightened up and sighed. "Hi, Cookie," she said to Sarah. "I'm sorry. I didn't mean to scare you."

Sarah brightened, then ran to hug Heather.

I walked to the car and grabbed a bag. I was guiltily delighted that my child could express my feelings with all of the vigor and none of the risk.

———

"So what did he do?" I asked Heather, who had her hand on Sarah's shoulder now.

"What?"

"Jeffrey. What did he do?"

She shook her head, beleaguered, amazed, and took out another suitcase.

"What?" I said.

She exhaled. "Well, he played with the tape deck," she said.

"Yes?"

"After I'd told him not to," she added.

"Did he break it or something?"

"No," she said.

She grabbed the last bag and slammed the trunk closed.

"Long trip?" I asked.

"It was endless," she said. She held out her purse to Sarah. "Can you carry this, Cookie?" she asked, and Sarah nodded happily, then swung the bag over her shoulder.

"Well, you're here now," I said, gesturing into the house and wondering when it would hit her that she was walking back into our childhood home.

"At last," was all she said as we dragged the bags up to the doorway.

———

Jeffrey waited until the next morning, and then he marched up to Sarah and punched her, hard, on her left shoulder.

"Ouch!" she shouted.

"Ouch!" he mocked.

"Jeffrey!" Heather said.

"Sarah!" I said.

We rushed over to confront them.

"Why did you do that?" Heather asked Jeffrey.

"Because I felt like it," Jeffrey said.

"That's not a good-enough reason," Heather said.

"Well, it's the truth," he said grandly.

I reflected that from a mournful, lonely little boy, Jeffrey was quickly transforming himself into a muscular philosopher.

Heather grabbed him by the elbow and led him to one of the two couches.

"Sit there," she said.

"For how long?"

"Time out."

"Till when?"

"Till I say so," she told him.

Then, astonishing me—and the children as well—she knelt down next to Sarah, put her arms around her, and gave her a kiss.

Sarah grinned with glee.

"I'm sorry for what Jeffrey did," Heather said, still holding Sarah protectively. "He *won't* do it again."

———

The immediate issue became the beds. In the playroom, where we had put Jeffrey and Sarah, two couches faced each other, on either side of the fireplace. The first night, Jeffrey hadn't pressed his luck; he had gone to sleep, fairly promptly, on the couch opposite Sarah's. Now, over breakfast on the second day, he kicked his enormous Nikes in rhythm against his chair legs and announced that he didn't want to go to sleep every night looking at a girl.

"I should be in my own room," he said.

"You're sharing a room with Sarah," Heather said.

"Why can't I have my own room?" he asked.

"Because Grandpa is coming, and there aren't enough rooms to go around."

"Why can't I sleep in the attic?" he asked.

"Because it's dirty up there," she said.

"Why can't I clean it?" he asked.

Heather sighed.

"Why can't I?"

"Maybe later in the summer."

"It isn't safe," Jeffrey said.

"What isn't safe, Jeffrey?" Edgar asked him.

"To sleep so close to the fire," he said.

"Mommy?" Sarah asked me.

"Jeffrey," Heather said witheringly. "It's June."

"It was cold last night," he said. "I heard Aunt Erica say she wanted a fire."

More than that, I had wanted the firelight, to have all of us curl up and read our books by.

"We're not building any fires," Heather said.

"I still don't want to have to go to sleep looking at her," Jeffrey said.

"That's not nice," Heather said.

"I know," Jeffrey said.

The grown-ups exchanged a three-way glance.

"Tell you what," Edgar said. "After breakfast, you come upstairs with me, Jeffrey, and we'll move the couch."

"To the attic?" he asked, his face brightening.

"To the other side of the room," Edgar said.

Jeffrey kicked his chair legs again.

"What do you say, Jeffrey?" Heather asked.

"Okay," he said.

"That's not what I meant."

"Thank you, Uncle Edgar," he said.

By mid-afternoon, Edgar had come to the conclusion that it was time to launch the dollhouse. I had hoped that we could save it for a few weeks and wait for a time of rain or at least of profound moping. But it was clear even to me that some project was needed, and badly. Heather had called ahead from New York to sign Jeffrey up for a local day camp, but it wasn't starting until July, which was more than a week away.

Jeffrey had always loved building things: block towers, Lego trains, Tinkertoy scaffolds. So the prospect of hitting the hardware store with Uncle Edgar lit up his otherwise-murky face. He even laid down the electronic game that he had been clutching since breakfast.

"Come on, kids," Edgar said. "Sarah, you too."

"Can it have three bedrooms?" she asked again.

"Yes," Edgar and I chorused, hoping to head off any reasoning that she might be inclined to offer.

Remarkable how Jeffrey changed back into an eager little boy. He virtually ran to the car and, unasked, let Sarah sit in the front seat.

Heather and I watched as the car drove off. I felt the way I always did when I watched Sarah go away from me. I felt an intense tug of sadness, mixed with a giddy sense of space.

———

Half an hour later, Heather suggested we go for a walk.

"Where?" I asked.

"I don't know," she said. "Let's just go for a walk."

"To the lake?" I asked.

"Sure," she said. "Why not?"

Because, I wanted to say, the last time you wanted to go for a walk with me, you had two sons, and one of them was in diapers.

"Okay," was what I said.

"Let's see how cold the water is," she said.

We took our sweatshirts from the same closet where our sweatshirts had once been Sarah's size. Then we stepped out together into the deep, cool mountain sunlight.

We walked past the woods in silence.

"Jeffrey seemed to perk up about the dollhouse," I said, making my first attempt at the conversation I thought she wanted to have.

"Uh-huh," she said.

I looked at her sideways. She seemed to be watching her feet as they walked.

"Do you think that he's changed since David?" I asked.

She said: "No. He's almost seven."

"How's he doing, really?"

"Okay, I guess. I know he's got to be really sad, but it's hard for me to sympathize when it comes out as brattiness."

The grass was long on the path to the lake, unmanicured and untrampled.

"Think there are snakes?" I asked.

"Probably."

———

"It'll be great to have all of us here," I said.

"Yeah."

"Does it bother you to hear Sarah talking so much about David?"

"No."

"Have you told Jeffrey what Sarah's been saying about David?"

"Some."

So I turned to her as we sat by the lake, and I said, "I thought you wanted to talk."

"I do," she said.

"About what?"

"About anything," she said grandly. "What's on your mind?"

"You are."

She skipped a stone across the lake. "The operation," she said slowly, with telepathic logic.

"So have you thought about it?" I asked her.

She pulled up the hood of her sweatshirt, then tugged it back off and shook her hair out.

"Sure," she said.

"And?"

"I don't know," she said. "A lot of times, it doesn't work, and you can't reverse it after all."

"What does Richard say?"

"He's still angry," she said.

"That you did it in the first place?"

"No. He wanted me to do it. He's angry about David."

"Oh."

"I know it's supposed to be a stage of grief or something," she said, "but he was angry the minute it happened, and he's still angry. And he's not angry at fate, or God, or the old man who killed him. He's angry at me."

"Why?"

"I told you," she said, her eyes narrowing, punishing.

"I remember," I said. "Because you didn't want to move to the suburbs. I know. I just can't believe it."

"It's true. And he's right. He really is right. David *would* still be alive if we had moved to Cedarhurst."

"That's where he wanted to move?"

She put up the hood of the sweatshirt again. "You know what I mean," she said.

"Do you really think about that?"

She shrugged.

"Sometimes," she admitted. "Or I think, What if I'd been with him instead of Debbie? Or what if she'd walked a little faster? Or a little slower? Or what if he'd been in his stroller?"

"You can't live that way, Heather," I said.

"Who's living?"

"You are," I said firmly. "Jeffrey is."

"Jeffrey," she said. Tears came to her eyes.

"Tell me, Dee," I told her.

Finally, she nodded. "Sometimes," she said, tears falling past her cheeks to the grass before her, "I just can't stand being with him. It's like I don't want to love him any more than I do."

"You're afraid that you'll lose him, too," I said.

She didn't answer. Finally, she said, "Are you pregnant, Dum?"

I was startled. "No," I said.

"You're not?"

"Would it bother you?"

"So you are," she said.

"I'm not."

"How many weeks?"

"I'm not pregnant."

"You want to be."

"I honestly don't know," I told her.

"It's okay," she said.

She stood up and walked to the waterline.

"So why are you walking away?" I asked.

"I'm not walking away. I'm seeing if I can see any boats."

"Any what?"

"Any boats."

"Oh. Boats," I said.

"Let's get back," she said. "We've got to start dinner."

We walked back past the woods toward home.

"The blackberries are amazing," I told her.

"What?"

"The blackberries."

"Oh."

"We should pick some."

"And make a pie?" she asked.

I nodded.

"I hated those pies," Heather said.

———

Edgar winked at me as he opened the car trunk, by which I understood him to mean that the trip to the store had been a success. And Jeffrey continued to grin eagerly as he helped his cousin and uncle unpack.

We decided that it would drive Dad crazy if we built the thing in the living room. We decided to do it there anyway.

"Maybe he's gotten more tolerant. We haven't lived with him in a long time," I said as Edgar and I moved the old pine coffee table to a side wall where it could serve as a workbench, and Heather stood ready to cover it with a faded sheet.

"I don't think people get better about that sort of thing. Especially not in their seventies," she said.

Just then the phone rang. We laughed. It was Dad.

"We were just talking about you," I said.

"How's Heather?" Dad asked.

"She's fine, Dad," I said. I sighed. I wondered, for the thousandth time, if he'd ever asked Heather how I was. "I'm fine too," I told him. "Edgar's fine. Sarah's fine. Jeffrey's fine."

"So what have you all been doing?"

"Not much. Edgar just took Sarah and Jeffrey to the hardware store. We're going to build a dollhouse."

"That's nice."

I looked over at Heather. She and Sarah were kneeling beside the low shelves, making room for all the new building supplies. Heather seemed not to be acting. She seemed sincerely charmed by Sarah. I was proud, and I was thankful.

"When are you coming?" I asked Dad.

"Tomorrow."

"What time?"

"Around two o'clock. Do you think Heather wants to talk to me?"

"I don't see why she wouldn't," I said.

"Will you ask her?"

"Sure you want me to?" I asked, teasing. But he wasn't teased.

I motioned her over and gave her the phone. She said her patented, brisk hello. All these years, I thought, if I'd been mean to Dad, he would probably have been fascinated by me.

I walked back over to Sarah, who was sitting beside the coffee table, intently drawing a picture.

I gave her a hug that she leaned away from.

"What are you doing?" I asked her.

"Drawing it," she said.

"The dollhouse?"

She nodded.

"What's the dollhouse going to look like?" I asked her.

She shrugged. "We haven't decided yet," she said.

I didn't feel like asking who she'd meant by "we." My hunch was that she'd meant David, and if it turned out that she'd meant Jeffrey, then it would be a pleasant surprise.

———

When Dad stepped from the car the next afternoon, he seemed simultaneously inspired and deflated. He surveyed the house suspiciously, as if comparing it to an expectation and somehow finding it lacking. His glance conveyed owner-ship, pride, loneliness. I felt, as I often did when we hadn't seen each other in a while, completely confused by how old he looked.

"Hi, hi!" he said, the familiar greeting.

We walked out to kiss him, a twin on each cheek.

Jeffrey came leaping out of the house, jumping down from the top step to land at his grandfather's feet. Sarah had come out also, but she was looking at Heather, not Dad.

"Hi, hi!" Dad said to Jeffrey as they walked up to the house.

"It may feel a little weird at first to be in the house," I told Dad.

"All right," he snapped, as if I'd been badgering him for hours, and I thought: Fine. Maybe those who don't believe in ghosts cannot be haunted by them.

———

After coffee, Dad said he was going to lie down.

"I think it was something I ate," he said, and I started to re-mind him of the weekends when we'd come here after Mom's death, when he'd always felt sick to his stomach. But then I stopped, hugely sensing the futility of the gesture.

At night, though—at bedtime—the house was now full, and I fell asleep with an old peace.

———•———

Sarah opened our door the next morning. She was wearing a T-shirt and pink underpants.

"Come on up," I told her. I had one of those moments of wanting to hug her so hard that I frightened myself.

"Did you have a good sleep?" I asked her.

"I found out about Arts and Crafts," she said.

"Really?" I asked her groggily as she settled between Edgar and me.

"Well, they give you sixty-four paints, like the sixty-four box of crayons, except it's paints."

Edgar sat up with grim recognition.

"Why don't you tell us a story that's not about heaven?" he asked her.

She slumped. She said, "No."

"How about I Spy?"

"No."

Edgar looked over at me, dismayed.

"Tell us about Arts and Crafts," I said.

Sarah smiled, delighted. "Okay. Well. The great thing is the paints, and there's a paintbrush for each color too, and the handle of the paintbrush is the same color as the paint, so you always know where it goes, and the blue doesn't get into the yellow, and the red doesn't get into the orange, and the white always stays white. Just white."

She let out a tiny sigh of satisfaction and possible longing.

"Does David paint with the paints?" I asked her.

"Not yet. He's still in Music."

"What does he do there?"

"He sings 'Leafy, Leafy, Here and There,' " she said.

"What's that?"

"A song."

"I know it's a song. How does it go?"

"I don't know," she said.

"How long does it take before you get to Arts and Crafts?" Edgar asked her.

"He doesn't know yet," she said. "But he's going to find out."

"Who's going to tell him about it?" I asked.

"Other dead people," she said.

"Are they scary?" I asked.

She looked at me with intense condescension.

"No, Mom," she said witheringly. "They're just like us, except they're dead."

"That's a big difference, sweetheart," I said.

She shrugged. It seemed, suddenly, like a Heather shrug.

"Can I have eggs for breakfast?" she asked.

"Sure."

"Can I beat them?"

"Sure. Just let me get dressed."

"I'm going downstairs," she said. "Is Grandpa up yet?"

"I don't know," I said, smiling. I loved the fact that even after dismissing me for my failure to understand heaven, she still believed I had magical ways of knowing things I couldn't possibly know.

"I'm going to go down and see," she said.

"Get dressed!" I called out after the door closed.

"Why didn't you tell her it couldn't be true?" Edgar asked me before I could say anything.

"Why didn't you?"

"I just followed your lead."

"I don't want her thinking she can't tell us things."

"Can't we just tell her 'Stop'?" he asked.

"I don't know. Would it work if I said it to you?"

———

Downstairs, the need for eggs had been forgotten. Sarah and Jeffrey were locked in combat.

"Three bedrooms!" she was shouting.

"Two bedrooms!" he said.

"Three bedrooms and a dining room!" she said.

I felt they were enacting the entire drama of New York real estate.

Dad's bedroom door swung open.

"What's the problem here?" he asked before Edgar or Heather or I could ask it ourselves.

He looked as annoyed by their boisterousness as he'd always been by ours.

"It's got to have three bedrooms," Sarah said.

"Two!" Jeffrey shouted.

"I don't think we'll have enough wood for three," Dad said.

"It's got to have three," Sarah said firmly. "One for Aunt Heather and Uncle Richard. One for Jeffrey. And one for David."

"David's dead," Jeffrey said to Sarah.

"He wants a bedroom," Sarah said.

"Sarah—"

"David's dead!" Jeffrey shouted.

———•———

After breakfast, the woe continued. The problem was that Dad, having warmed to the project, had determined that Edgar hadn't bought enough wood to make three bedrooms, and the wood that he'd bought was the wrong kind. He had told the kids that he would take them to town, but now he had disappeared.

"Grandpa promised," Jeffrey said despondently an hour later, when Dad had still not returned.

"I know, Jeffrey," I said. "But Grandpa said he wanted to help."

"But he isn't," he said, his voice approaching a whine. He loped over to the shelves and pulled his electronic game from a high berth. Then he settled sullenly on the couch.

Sarah looked close to tears.

"That's it, I'm finding him," Heather said.

———•———

Five minutes later, she was back.

"Dad's losing it," she whispered to me. "You know where he is? He's down by the lake."

"What's he doing?"

"Reading."

"He really forgot?"

"He said, 'What wood?' " she told me. She seemed less concerned than angry.

"So is he taking them?"

"Who knows?" she said.

"Why don't you do it?" I asked Heather.

"What?"

"Get the wood. Help them build it," I said. I figured her old need to outdo Dad might carry the day, and carry her back.

She brushed her hair away from her face.

"You've always been good with your hands," I said.

"Don't butter me up."

"Please, Mom!"

"Please, Aunt Heather!"

She thought about it. "It's a lot of work."

"Please!"

"Please!"

"Okay," Heather finally said, and reached for her keys and jacket.

Sarah sprang up like a freed prisoner and walked out so closely behind Heather that she was inside Heather's shadow.

New Year's Eve, 1964

"One of You Is Lying"

I am eleven years old the night I first learn that love is not enough to keep someone in a room with you.

Mom and Heather and I are in the kitchen. It's ten o'clock on New Year's Eve, but Dad isn't home from work yet. Mom is washing the champagne glasses, letting Heather and me take turns climbing up to the highest, most dusty shelf so we can hand them to her one by one.

We hear the sigh of the elevator, then the sweep of the metal gate.

"It's him!" Mom says, reaching for a dish towel. She dries her hands and spins around, expectation and stillness in her face. But the front door doesn't open.

"It isn't him," Heather says, her face in profile with Mom's, her voice flat and cheerless.

"He'll probably call any minute," Mom says, tossing her hair over her shoulder and turning back to the sink and the glasses. She stares out the kitchen window a moment and lets the water wash over her hands. For two of the last three years, Dad has had to leave in the middle of New Year's Eve to attend to a patient's emergency.

Heather pokes me in the ribs with her elbow. Hard.

"Quit it," I say.

"Girls."

She does it again.

"Quit it," I say.

"Girls," Mom says.

Heather reaches into the dish drain for one of the glasses.

"What are you doing?" Mom asks.

"I'm going to dry it," Heather says.

"No. It'll dry itself."

"But this way's faster."

"Heather. Leave it," Mom says and then takes a breath. "Why don't you girls go get dressed?" she asks.

In our rooms, we race each other to see who can get dressed first. Heather wins, of course. She comes charging into my room just as I'm reaching my door on the way to hers.

"I think they're going to fight," she says.

"They never fight," I say, echoing one of Mom's favorite—and mostly true—boasts. Others are: "Your mom and dad love each other" and, amid the burgeoning realm of the sixties divorce: "That's never going to happen to your dad and me."

"Of course they fight sometimes," Heather says.

"Prove it."

"You've got gunk in your hair."

I turn to look in the mirror, and Heather puts something down my back.

"Very mature," I say.

I reach around, trying to grab at it, but it falls straight down to the floor. It's only a rubber band.

"Scared you," Heather says.

In the living room, Mom is adjusting the knickknacks and stops to peer into her bowl of old marbles. These marbles were a gift from her father, augmented by years of collecting, and for us they are a forbidden temptation. Something catches her eye. She takes a step closer, and Heather takes a step back. Then Mom reaches into the bowl and fishes a marble out with two exact fingers. She holds it up to the light, then snaps it back into the fist of her hand.

"Who's been playing with these?" she asks. "Erica?"

"No, Mom," I say, which happens to be true.

"Heather?" she asks.

"No, Mom," she says.

I stare at Heather, who's looking at Mom with the sweet innocence of blatant guilt.

"Well, how did *this* marble get mixed in with mine?" Mom asks.

She opens her fist and reveals the proof: a dime-store marble—a cheap clear eye with an ordinary iris of red.

Heather shrugs. I'm still looking at her. We had each been given a small pouch of marbles in our Christmas stockings. I know that this marble is hers, not only because I know I haven't been playing with Mom's but because Heather had traded me her four blue marbles for my four red ones.

"Girls," Mom says.

I am wishing the phone would ring, or that Dad would just walk in the door and say "Hi, hi!"

"Girls?" Mom asks, louder.

"I didn't do it!" I say.

"I didn't either!" says Heather.

"Well, one of you did," Mom says.

The phone finally rings. Dad's mantel clock rings too. Eleven chimes. Mom goes to answer the phone.

"Heather," I say.

"What?"

"That's your marble."

"Let's go listen to what she's saying."

———

We creep into the dining room, which connects to the pantry, which connects to the kitchen, where Mom is talking on the phone, oblivious to our whereabouts.

"Does it have to be you?" she is saying when we take up our posts by the door.

We try not to breathe through her many silences.

"At the office?" she asks, sounding angry. "Why not at the hospital? . . . Do you have to admit her too? . . . Well, I guess I should be grateful for small favors. . . . Yes, George, I understand. No. It's just that it's New Year's Eve. . . . Do you think you'll make it by midnight? . . . I hope so too. . . . Yes, I love you too."

We know that his absence will mean that we'll be punished for the marbles, so we race back to our rooms.

———

I hear the clip of her shoes on the wooden floor in the hallway.

My room is first, and she enters it first.

"When's Daddy coming home?" I ask, before she can say a word.

"Soon."

"Where is he?" I ask.

"Where do you think? At his office," she says. "Now, tell me why you were playing with my marbles. You know they're precious to me. You know my father gave me some of those."

"I wasn't," I say.

"You'd better not be lying."

She goes down the hall to Heather's room. I wait and imagine that I am Dad's nurse. I am wearing a white dress and I'm by his side at the office, helping him get finished sooner.

Mom returns with Heather in tow. Heather is holding her bag of marbles.

"Erica, get your bag," Mom says.

I go to my shelf and find it.

"Sit down," she tells us.

We do.

"I've told you a hundred times that I don't want you playing with those marbles," Mom says. "They're old and they're special to me. But I don't care about that as much as I care about you lying. And one of you is lying," she says.

"It's not me," I say.

"Heather, open your bag."

Heather does so. The marbles spill out on the carpet between her legs.

"See, Mom? I *have* all these red ones," she says.

"Erica?"

I open my bag too. A dozen marbles come tumbling out: blue and yellow and green. No red.

Heather looks at me, evil triumphant.

Mom looks from Heather's pile of marbles to mine.

"Heather," Mom says finally. "You lied."

"But—"

"You've got eleven. Erica's got twelve. Go to your room. Right now," she says.

Mom kisses the top of my head and goes back down the hall to get angry at Heather because Dad is still not home.

———·———

In the front hall, I slip on my coat and open the door and ring for the elevator and go down to the street.

———·———

Dad's office is on West End Avenue and Eighty-third Street. Our apartment is near Riverside Drive on Seventy-ninth Street. The difference is one dark street and four well-lighted ones. Just last weekend, Mom allowed Heather and me to walk there alone and meet Dad.

Now I am going on my own. I'm going to be Dad's nurse and help him finish and bring him home.

The doorman is on the phone with a tenant, and I walk quickly past him.

It is cold and silent on the street. The other families are all inside. I think: Their fathers are already home beside them, not having to do Dad's important work. He's probably saving a life, I think, and I'm going to help him do it. He will see me walk into his office, and he will hug me and say, "Hi, hi! I'm so glad you came! Let's go home now to Mom."

My fingers are cold. I've forgotten my mittens.

I pass a discarded Christmas tree whose tinsel, like an old man's hair, is blown by the wind.

On the corner of West End Avenue, under the streetlamp, by the garbage can, a fat man is walking a fat dog. It looks like a cartoon, because the dog kind of looks like the man. I don't look at him when he looks at me, though. Mom has taught me two things about walking. She's said: "Always walk in the middle of the sidewalk, because people come out from alleys, and cars come up on curbs." And she's said: "Never look straight into the eyes of a strange man if he's looking at you."

But I have to stop next to them at the corner, waiting for the light to turn. The dog makes a sudden leap toward me, and the man jerks him back on a metal chain. The dog makes a deep, mean sound, and I watch as his paws scrape at the sidewalk.

I turn to my left and decide to walk a block in that direction. I know I should just wait and cross the street, but I'm scared of the dog and the man, and the light won't turn green, so I walk where I shouldn't.

I hear the dog bark, once, behind me, and then the sound of his paws on the pavement. My heart starts to beat fast, and I look around for someone. But the doormen are all inside their buildings, warm, hidden, and protected.

On the next corner, the light turns green, and I cross the avenue quickly, watching the car lights blur as my eyes tear up.

"Hey!" I hear the man shout, and I start running as fast as I can.

———

I stop running a block later, on another avenue, with stores. Our grocery store is around here somewhere, and I walk one more long block, looking for it.

I find another grocery store, and it is closed. I stop walking. The tears are warm on my freezing face. I look around and see no one, still.

Another block farther, there is a phone booth. I run to it, look through my pockets, discover two nickels, and dial Dad's office.

"Dr. Marks's service," a woman's voice says.

"Hi." My one word comes out, hot and choked.

"Hello?" the receptionist says.

"Hi," I say again. "This is Dr. Marks's daughter."

"Yes?"

"Erica," I say.

"*Yes?*"

"Is he there?" I say.

"This is his *service*," she says.

"Well, can you reach him?"

"He's home."

"No he's not."

"He signed out," she says.

"I don't have another dime," I say. "I'm on a street corner." I start to sob.

"Honey," she says. "Where are you?"

"Outside."

I try to make my voice calm down.

"Can you call him?" I say.

"Of course. You just sit tight. Tell me what corner you're on."

"I don't know."

"Just calm down, honey, and look at the street sign."

I look.

"Broadway," I say.

"And what cross street?"

I look again.

"Eighty-second Street," I say.

"Well, stay there."

"Okay," I say.

"Promise you'll stay there."

"I will," I say.

"Do you want to hold on?"

"No. Just call him," I say, and I hang up, mortified, to wait to be rescued from rescuing him.

———

When he comes, the breath clouds pour from his mouth like smoke.

"How could you?" he yells at me.

"Daddy!"

"How could you? How *could* you?"

He hits me across the face. It stings.

"Daddy!" I whisper.

"Never again!"

He grabs my arm by the elbow and yanks me away from the booth. He looks straight ahead.

"I wanted to—"

"Quiet," he says.

"I wanted to—"

"Quiet!" he shouts. "Or you'll be sorry!"

He leads me home in seething silence. I keep my head down as we walk past the doorman inside.

In the elevator, he finally looks at me.

"I just wanted you to come home," I say.

I know now he'll hold me and hug me and say that he loves me as much as I love him.

"What were you *thinking?*" he asks, though I've just told him.

"Mommy was mad, and we wanted you there," I say.

"You scared the life out of us!" he shouts.

"I'm sorry," I say, and start crying again.

———

In the apartment, I run past Mom to my bedroom, and I soar onto my pillow and cry. I'm waiting for Mom to come in and tell me she understands, that it's all okay. But she doesn't come. I cry louder. I cry so she'll come. And finally, the door opens. Mom and Dad stand above me, rigid and silent.

I see the look on their faces.

"You don't love me anymore," I say.

Dad's face twists with furious sarcasm. "Right," he says.

Mom reaches to smooth the hair from my face but gives me a look that says I should know better.

They turn, together, and walk out the door. Then Dad flicks off the light with the side of his hand, as if he's cutting something in two.

Summer, 1990

"I've Got Something in Mind for You"

Sarah, Jeffrey, and Heather spent most of that last week in June huddled in the living room. The new wood that Heather had bought remained untouched in a heap by the couch. But stacks of new and discarded plans piled up on the coffee table. I was amazed by Sarah's patience as she concocted and helped to embellish these plans. And I watched, with equal amazement, while Heather drew and redrew them ceaselessly and let Jeffrey color them in.

"What's taking so long?" I asked them on Tuesday.

Three pairs of combative eyes looked up.

"What do you mean, 'so long'?" Heather said.

"I don't know. I thought you'd start building," I said.

"We're *drawing* the *plans,* Aunt Erica," Jeffrey told me.

"Yeah, Mom," Sarah added. "We're *drawing* the *plans.*"

"Well, I guess you're drawing the plans," I said.

Along with Dad, I offered my help, but it was repeatedly shrugged off. That didn't bother me a whole lot. I walked in the woods with Edgar and gathered blackberries and made a pie. Despite her previous protests, Heather actually ate two slices. I swam in the lake with Edgar and Dad.

And I watched the threesome that Heather, Jeffrey, and Sarah seemed to be forming. It was no substitute for the foursome of Heather, Sarah, David, and me. But I sensed that it kept Heather's mind off her marriage and softened slightly the absence of David, an absence that was itself threefold: Heather's son, Jeffrey's brother, Sarah's best friend.

I loved Edgar all over again. Whether it was the fullness of the house or simply the sense that Sarah was happier, I didn't know. But as we paddled out into the lake each morning to swim, I'd see the sun gleam in his hair and I'd swim up behind him and kiss his neck.

With the dollhouse, all arguments about room number and room occupants had faded. I hadn't heard the words *David* or *heaven* for days. I tried not to gloat with Edgar over the wisdom of my commonsense approach. He was happy too, and he watched her less. Even Heather seemed to be walking with a slightly lighter step.

On Monday, July second, Jeffrey started camp.

The bus came to the front door, and Heather and Sarah walked out together to say good-bye. From inside the house, I watched Jeffrey step on board the unfamiliar bus with the unfamiliar driver and the unfamiliar children. I was floored by his courage. I heard the cheerful good-byes from Heather. But as the bus drove off, I saw what looked like terror on her face.

She sat on the front steps with Sarah and put her arms around her. I went outside.

"What time will he be back?" I asked Heather.

"Not till three," she answered.

She looked completely lost. She was silent. I couldn't think of anything to tell her.

"Come on, Aunt Heather," Sarah said.

"What?"

"Come on! The dollhouse! Let's go!"

"Sarah, why don't you let me—" I started.

"No, it has to be Aunt Heather!"

"Aunt Heather might not be in the mood," I said.

"That's okay," Heather said to me.

"You don't have to," I told her.

"That's okay," Heather said. "Come on, Cookie. Let's go."

"She's such a comfort to Heather," I said to Edgar that night as we got ready for bed.

"I don't want to talk about Heather," he said. He was grinning. I looked in the mirror, and was surprised to find myself smiling too.

"I've got something in mind for you," Edgar said from the bed, which I knew could mean only one thing. So I reached mechanically into the dresser for the pouch where I kept my diaphragm, and then I stopped myself and glanced in the mirror again. I looked old.

From my purse I took out my calendar, with its pattern of little red-circled days spread out like the answer card on a standardized test, and I counted the days of the months to myself. These were the twenty-eight-day months, of course, which had started when I was thirteen, forcing time into maddening cycles. It had often struck me that these built-in proofs of time's cyclical nature had made me feel less peace than fatigue and futility. And that Edgar, on his one long male linear ride, had a better sense of renewal than I. I counted and counted again.

I looked up at Edgar. "The timing is perfect."

"Really?" he said.

"On the nose," I told him.

"Come here," he said.

I dropped into his arms.

"Are you sure?" he said. "Are you ready?" he said.

I kissed him.

When we conceived Sarah, it had been a warm July night in the city, and Edgar had said, "What are we waiting for?" and I'd had no answer to give him. It had been sweet, and it had been sexy, like a new and slightly silly game. I'd made love pretending that I was making a baby, with no reason to believe that that was what I was really doing.

This night was different. We knew so much. We knew Sarah, and we'd known David. This night felt like a sacrament. I wept as we made love.

I had my hands around the hard, thick muscles in Edgar's arms, and he held both sides of my face as if, with our arms, we were already enclosing the tiny, the new, the miraculous.

I woke in the middle of that night, feeling the mystery of my own body, something I realized that Edgar could never feel. It was like having a secret, and it made everything different, richer, more startling. The odds were so overwhelming to me: the odds of the time being right, and the thought that we could be one cell—and who knows what slightest motion— away from a boy or a girl, a delight or a nuisance, a rail or a dumpling, a teacher or a tax attorney.

I stared at the ceiling, remembering the whole implausible process of carrying and giving birth to a child, and wondering if it had started, and what it was that had started if something had. Then I felt young.

———

There had been a door broken open after Mom's death, a door through which a succession of Dad's women had walked, lunged, shimmied, stumbled, and roamed. None of them had gone the distance, of course, and after a while, he had stopped trying.

"This aging business," he'd said to me once, shortly after he'd broken off some affair.

"You mean your patients?" I'd asked him.

"No. I mean me."

"You're not old," I'd told him. Of course he was old. He'd been old since the moment he'd buried his wife.

"There are so many things that I wanted to do. I wanted to teach. I wanted to write—"

Regret had never been part of his repertoire. Neither had self-pity. I'd been shocked and angry to find that he'd lived nearly seven decades and was no closer than I was to an understanding of death. I'd wanted to believe that death was more than a destination you couldn't know until you had reached it. I'd wanted to believe that you could see it as you drew closer, the way we saw the mountains rise up on the road to the Berk-shire house.

"Well, maybe when you retire in five or ten years, you can start teaching then," I'd said. I'd hoped that if I pretended he'd live forever, he would live longer.

Dad's face had stretched away from me, his eyes startled by loneliness.

"Ten years!" he'd said, clearly amazed by the depth of my stupidity. "In ten years, if I'm still around, I'll be seventy-six."

He'd looked at me, across the generations, as if we'd been citizens of separate countries. But I hadn't been young since Mom's death either. From the first time I'd learned of her illness, I'd felt I was standing on one side of a vanishing wall, the wall that had shielded and sheltered me, and against which I'd always leaned, and in whose cool, broad shadow I had always been able to play and plan. Mom's sickness took the wall down brick by brick, and on the other side of it had been the mystery of her absence and the certainty of my death, and the knowledge that all stories, no matter how sweet or sad, would end in the same way. I could not remember being young, at least not in the way that Dad meant it. I couldn't remember living clockless, unaware of time's one-way arrow.

———

But I might be almost pregnant. I woke in the morning with that sweet double doubt.

"Think we did it?" Edgar asked me, smiling.

"No," I said.

"Yes you do," Edgar said, his warm, large arms closing around me as he said it.

I looked into his eyes. I had noticed long before that whenever I looked into Edgar's eyes, they were ready to look back into mine. His eyes could build a room, a shelter, a small private place—no matter what spaces surrounded us.

But of course I couldn't know how another pregnancy might change that room, or Sarah, or Heather, or me.

New Year's Eve, 1966

"I Think They're Kissing"

Our apartment is only six floors up, and it faces West Seventy-ninth Street. Even late at night, when most of the other street noises have faded, I can lie in bed and hear from my window the routine sighs of the crosstown buses lumbering down the avenues. But these sounds never wake me. Instead, they lull me to sleep each night as if they are breezes in country trees.

What wakes me tonight is my mother's voice.

"Listen to me!" I hear her shout. "The girls are thirteen years old, for God's sake!"

My father says something that I can't hear, then: "You've known how I've felt about all this for years."

A bathroom connects our bedrooms. I get to my feet and inch open my door. Their door is open an inch or so too.

"I'm thirty-eight years old," she is saying. "It's not just as simple as one, two, three."

"They know a lot more now than they did thirteen years ago," Dad says.

"I'd think," Mom says, "you'd be worried about me. I'd think that you'd worry about my health."

167

"Jack Simmons is the best man."

"Great, George. Find me the best man. That makes it simple. That solves everything."

"Lower your voice," my father says.

"They're sound asleep," my mother tells him.

I run next door, to Heather's room.

"Heather!" I whisper, shaking her. "Heather! Wake up!"

"What is it?" she asks me.

"Fight!"

She sits up, blinking blindly, puts on her glasses, and tosses her covers back. We dash back to my room. We lean over, side by side, listening at the door. I can feel her breath and the heat of her body, still warm from her sleep.

"Where would we even put it?" we hear Mom ask.

"Heather's room," Dad says. "We'll put the girls in together."

Heather straightens up, as if in sudden pain.

"I was thinking of going back to work," Mom says.

"You've been saying that for ten years."

"I've been thinking about it for ten years."

There is a long silence, and I take a step back from the door, just in case.

"What about the girls?" Mom finally asks him.

"The girls will love it," Dad says.

Heather sits down next to me.

"They'll be a big help to you," Dad says.

"Who are you kidding?" Mom says. "I can barely get them to make their own beds."

I sit down beside Heather. I look at us in the mirror that hangs on the door. Her eyes are enormous and filled with tears.

"They're going to have a baby," I say.

"You always go wild over babies, Gloria," Dad is telling Mom.

"They can't," Heather whispers.

"They're going to," I whisper.

"They can't," Heather says. "She's too old."

"She's not."

"You loved it when they were little," Dad says.

"I know, George," Mom says.

"You're going to love it again," he tells her.

We can't hear her answer.

"She's going to do it," Heather says. "I can't believe it. She's going to do it."

"I think they're kissing," I say.

"He's always wanted a boy," Heather says.

"That's not it," I say, but I'm not convinced.

"Not now, George. It's so late," Mom says.

"Better late than never," he says.

There is another silence.

"You know," Mom says to him finally, "it might be another girl."

"Hush now," he says. "Come here," he says.

This silence lasts a longer time, and we know to close the door.

Summer, 1990

"I Want to Stay Here with Aunt Heather"

We went to the Fourth of July parade and stood in the sun, an unmerry band, watching sweatily as the floats went by bearing men in militia costumes who were red-faced with heat and pride. The drums drummed and the air felt thick.

"I'm melting," I said to Edgar.

"Well, when we get home," Sarah said to me, "I'll make you alive again."

We looked down at her.

"How?" Edgar asked.

"I'll just make Mommy alive again. I'll give her a red ice-cream cone."

Edgar laughed, and it was the first time in weeks that I'd seen him delighting in Sarah's dreams.

Each night, albeit surreptitiously, I checked off a day in my calendar, willing the time to pass so that I could know that another life had begun.

Construction on the dollhouse had finally started, and now the living room smelled perpetually of sawdust and carpenter's glue. Nails, brads, and shavings collected briefly under the coffee table, only to be tracked to the more exotic locations of kitchen floor, backyard, and bedcovers. Sarah and Heather knelt head-to-head, as if they were shooting marbles. Late afternoons and weekends, when Jeffrey was home from day camp, they would sometimes grant him minor concessions: a sleeping loft in his bedroom, a secret compartment in his closet. But it was less and less his project, more and more Sarah and Heather's obsession. Faithfully, I left them alone and reveled, from a distance, in the way they appeared to be helping each other.

Dad seemed not to notice either the mess or the enjoyment. He was unusually distracted.

"Thought I'd go to the post office," he said on Sunday morning, and he had to be reminded that the post office wasn't open on Sundays.

"How about if I take everyone for ice cream at Bill's?" he asked the next night. Bill's was an ice-cream parlor that had closed a decade before.

In the mornings, he was up before the rest of us, and he drove into town to buy the *New York Times.* His habit was to read the front section first, then the business news, whiz by the sports and reviews, and finally reward his efforts by a long session with the obits. At first, studying him, I told myself that he was probably just reading them the way I read wedding and birth announcements—we were both just looking for people we knew. But soon I came to realize that that had little or nothing to do with it. Dad had a purpose all his own. Each morning, he would carefully jot down the ages of the people who'd died that day, and then he'd tote the numbers up, divide by the number of dead people, and write the average down. A great day, I gathered after watching this ritual for a week or so, was any day that produced an average age of seventy-five or older.

Even apart from this obvious eccentricity, it seemed that he had changed, quite suddenly, into an old man. His chest had hollowed, and his shoulders had sloped, and when I saw him in his swim trunks, without his shirt on, I found myself amazed by how much less of him there was. Watching him fumble for names and dates and hearing him tell stories he'd told before made me alternately impatient and concerned. But there seemed to be nothing that I could do. I certainly couldn't ask him how he felt. Like me, Dad loved the idea of having the family together. But once we had all assembled, he seemed to have little or nothing to say, except to ask me occasionally how I thought Heather was doing.

———————

"No, Richard," I heard her bark into the phone the next Wednesday night, after the children were asleep.

She was standing in the kitchen, basically hiding behind the refrigerator.

"No," she hissed. "I don't give a damn if you come or you don't."

There was silence as she started listening, and as we listened for her next reply. Edgar, Dad, and I exchanged curious glances.

"What's he doing down there, anyway?" Dad whispered to us.

"He's finding deductions and loopholes," I told him, "and making money. Lots of money."

"Well, you can spend as much time as you want looking," Heather continued. "That still doesn't mean I'm going to live there."

"Where?" Dad asked.

"Quiet, Dad," I said.

"Live where?" Dad said.

"Because for one thing," Heather was saying, "Jeffrey would have to leave all his friends. And for another, I'd have to give up my practice." A pause, then: "I don't want to commute. I spend little enough time at home as it is." Another pause, then the punch line: "And I don't want to leave my family," she said.

I watched Dad's and Edgar's eyebrows shoot up. But I wanted to cry for Heather. I felt how lonely she had to feel.

"Fine," she was saying with crisp certainty. "You know where we're going to be."

———

"I don't know if I even want him to come," she told me the next morning.

"He really wants you to move?"

"He's looking at houses."

"Really?"

"Really," she said.

"So just tell him you don't want to move."

"I did. You heard me last night."

"You need time together."

"I think we need time apart," she said.

———

A week later, on the morning of July eighteenth, my breasts hurt when the shower water hit them, and I knew that I was pregnant. For the seventeenth time in seventeen days, I took out my calendar and counted and recounted. I might, at most, be two days late. It was not much to go on, but I still knew. I stood in the bedroom clutching my towel around me, clutching my calendar, glutted with thoughts. I thought with great joy about how to tell Edgar and, then, with guilt and sorrow, Heather. I realized I hoped it would be a girl.

I let the towel fall, and I looked in the mirror: a body that after four years had finally achieved some semblance of its former self; a face whose worry and laugh lines no longer depended on worry or laughter.

I looked out the window and down to the lake, where Edgar was hooking up fishing gear.

I threw on some shorts and a T-shirt and opened the bedroom door. Sarah had just woken up.

She stretched and yawned, and I sat down beside her and hugged her.

"Good morning, sweetheart," I said.

"Mommy?" she said.

"What? Did you sleep well?"

She nodded.

"Mommy?"

"What?"

"David says she's going to be borned."

"Born. Who?"

"David. He says I'm going to have a little sister."

For four years, with each tiny stage of development that Sarah had mastered, Rosie had told me, with wild certainty: "This child has been down here before."

When she'd seen the birthmark on Sarah's neck, she'd told me that birthmarks were the scars of fatal accidents from previous lives. She had said: "This child has been down here before."

When Sarah had learned the alphabet at sixteen months, Rosie had said: "This child has been down here before."

When, at only two, Sarah had recited an entire poem one day, Rosie had said: "This child has been down here before." And then she had looked at me with a slow, wise nod and said: "This is your mother right here, come back to be in your life and take care of you."

"Oh, Rosie," I'd said.

"This child is an old lady," she'd said.

Now, by some eerie coincidence, this child seemed to have divined the future by talking to a dead boy.

In Greek myth, Persephone was said to sit at a great loom, weaving new bodies for old souls. Pluto, who stood for both fertility and rebirth, lived below the ground, enshrouded in darkness and mystery, receiving the souls of the dead.

In Egyptian myth, Osiris was said to have come from India to Egypt in the body of a bull, and to judge the dead as they passed before him from life to other life.

But I allowed myself to think about other myths as I walked out the back door to find Edgar. I thought about the myth of Lucy Ricardo and the myth of Laura Petrie. I thought about the myth of Samantha Stephens and the myth of Mary ("George Lassos Stork!") Bailey, and all the other big- and small-screen wives who had had to hint, knit, faint, and weep in order to tell their oblivious husbands that the stork—and they'd had to use that word—was finally on the way.

What had these husbands been thinking? Where had these husbands been? These were not ancient myths; they were the myths of the fifties and sixties. Hadn't anyone heard of birth control then? Did women in those days just decide it was time to have children and Frisbee their diaphragms into the wastebaskets? And once they'd gotten pregnant, how had they managed to wait through trips to the doctor, rabbit tests, and, in the case of Lucy Ricardo, long Cuban numbers at nightclubs before they'd finally sprung the news?

With Sarah, I'd known I was pregnant before my first missed period was due. Edgar had known it too. Somehow, we had managed to miss the glory of "Yes, it's true, dear," and the giddiness of "You should be sitting down," and the calm certainty of "Don't be silly, dear, I'm fine."

———

Edgar had taken the rowboat out in search of the fictional fish that were said to swim in our lake. In the few weeks that we'd been at the house, I had not seen him catch anything quite as long as his foot, but he loved the tackle, the bait, the routine. He loved the quiet waiting, and he loved to swap tales with the handyman, Jim, about the ones that had gotten away. Jim bewitched him with stories of great fish brought to justice, and Edgar was determined to find a place in Jim's anthology.

I saw Edgar off in the distance now, wearing an old Yankees hat and a denim shirt. The father of my two children, I thought. I could imagine with perfect clarity the merry, proud look that would come to his face when he heard me tell him the news. It would be just like Sarah's birth, I thought. Through months of an awkward pregnancy, I had bucked myself up by imagining how Edgar would look when he first saw the face of his child. That look had not disappointed me, and I knew that this one wouldn't either—unless I ruined it by telling him what Sarah had said about David.

I shouted once, loudly, but he didn't seem to hear me, so I walked back into the house and called Sarah, who came down the steps to me slowly.

"Want to come to town with me?" I asked.

"I want to work on the dollhouse," she said.

"It's a beautiful day. You should be outside."

"She'll just be in the car with you," Heather said from the kitchen. "And then in the shops."

"You should all be outside," Dad shouted to us from the deck, where he lay, still working on one of the speeches that the hospital had asked him to give in the fall.

"I want to stay here with Aunt Heather," Sarah said.

"Suit yourself," I said, feeling somewhat unsteady.

I took the keys and got into the car, and then I recalled the best part of pregnancy, which is the feeling that one is never quite as alone as one appears to be.

—•—

At the Main Street market, I planned and bought dinner: baby potatoes, baby carrots, baby onions, and veal, AKA baby cow. It didn't involve any woolens, but I imagined that if I could wait until dinner, it might have a nifty effect on Edgar.

At the Lenox drugstore, I bought a pregnancy test, grinning stupidly at the salesclerk. I hated the weight gain of pregnancy, the boozelessness, the caffeinelessness, the months-long parade of petty symptoms, each one completely untreatable. But I loved its armor, its agelessness: how alike it made me with every woman who'd ever borne a child. And oh, how I loved being two in one.

———•———

I did the test as soon as I got home. I watched with nervous joy as a blue line appeared in the test window, broken slightly, like an exclamation point.

———•———

"I'm making dinner tonight," I told Heather when I went back downstairs to put the groceries away. She and Sarah knelt by the big table, drawing what I took at a glance to be possible wallpaper patterns.

"Fine," Heather said without looking up.

Sarah reached for an orange crayon, her face furious with concentration.

I started to unpack the groceries, peering past the kitchen counters to see if she planned to look up at all.

Then I returned to their table and stood for a while, gazing down at their work.

"Where's Dad?" I asked Heather.

"He went for a walk."

They were drawing some striped wallpaper now, crayoning on the same piece of paper, their lines about to meet.

"That's really pretty," I said.

Sarah looked up brightly.

"Orange and green," I said admiringly.

"It's not orange. It's yellow," she said.

I watched till their crayons met.

"Sarah," I said.

"What?"

"Look at me."

"What?"

Her brown bright eyes were utterly pure.

"We're going to Ticka," she told me. "David says."

"To tickle?"

"To Ticka," she said.

"Who's Ticka?"

"A place."

"What place?" I asked.

"Ticka."

I looked at Heather, who merely shrugged.

"How do you get to Ticka?" I asked Sarah suspiciously.

"You die," she told me. "David says."

"I want you to go outside," I said. "It's a beautiful day. It's summer. You know?"

"Later," she said.

"No. Now," I said.

"Mommy!"

"Now."

"Mommy!"

"Run upstairs. Before I get angry. And put your bathing suit on."

She actually looked toward Heather, who had enough sense not to say a word.

I waited until I heard the last of Sarah's footsteps on the stairs.

"What is going on here?" I asked her.

"What do you mean?"

"You know what I mean. What's all this stuff about Ticka. And David."

"She's building this house for him," Heather said.

"Still?"

"Yes."

"Why?"

"It's kind of hard to explain."

I stared at her, hard. "Try," I said.

"Okay. Sarah says David says that in heaven you have to take Arts and Crafts."

"I know that," I said.

"Okay. Well, in Arts and Crafts you get to do lots of cool stuff yourself."

"And paint with all those paints."

"Right. But then in order to move on to Snack, you have to get somebody on earth to make something, because it's like they're making something you've shown them how to do, or something like that, or like they're making something that you'll use when you come back in some way, and so you have to get people to make things, and every time anyone makes something, it frees up someone to leave Arts and Crafts, and then they get to go on. And as far as I can tell,

we're making David a house and he's going to live in it when
he comes back, which will please Richard enormously."

I stared at her, speechless.

"I may not have it exactly right," she said.

I continued to stare.

"What?" she finally said.

"Do you think you might have told me that this was going
on?"

She shrugged. "I thought you knew," she said.

"The first day, she said she wanted the dollhouse to have a
room for David. That's all."

"So?"

"So I guess I was hoping that that was all."

"Well, it wasn't," Heather said.

"And you've just been going along with it?"

"Erica," she said. "It's make-believe."

I looked at her again. "Dee. Please. As a doctor. As a mother.
You wouldn't be worried about this?"

She laughed lightly. "Of course not."

"Does she *say* that it's make-believe?"

"Not exactly."

"Well, don't you think it should stop?" I said.

"Why?"

"You know why."

"No I don't," she said.

I knew that this could not be the case. But I wanted to believe
that she was right about my daughter. I also knew Heather had
just lost her son and that her marriage was stretched tight by
grief. I knew that I would be telling her, later that night, that
nine months from now, there would be a new child.

I picked up a crayon to put it away.

"Leave them," she said.

"I'm just cleaning up."

"Leave it," she said. "We've got lots more to do."

Our eyes met, four mirrors. Then Sarah came back.

"You look great," I said.

"This suit's too small," she told me. She tugged at the back of it, then at the top.

"We'll get you a new one," I said. "Come on out. Let's go and see if Daddy's caught something yet."

"He never catches anything," she said.

"Don't be fresh."

"Well, he doesn't."

"Maybe this time, then, you'll bring him some luck."

I followed her out the front door, leaving Heather, Ticka, and the dollhouse behind us.

———

We sat in the field by the shore of the pond, and we counted the different kinds of flowers.

For years, my mother had kept a book—a loose-leaf binder arranged by month—in which she'd pressed each flower sample she'd found and pasted in photographs by their sides. I had not seen the book in years, but I could still remember the names of some flowers so long ago searched for and long ago found: pitcher plants, yarrow, Saint-John's-wort, jewelweed, knapweed, fleabane, baneberry, rue. But I struggled to match their names to the flowers that Sarah leapt through the field to find.

My father ambled over to us.

"I was just telling Sarah about the wildflowers," I said.

He nodded indistinctly.

"Remember how Mom catalogued them?" I asked.

He squinted, as if the sun was in his eyes.

"Dad?" I asked.

"Did she?" he asked.

"Dad. She kept that book? The loose-leaf binder? With all the samples pressed in it?"

"I guess I've forgotten that," he said.

"I guess you have."

"Well, there goes the memory," he said with a grin.

"What memory?" I asked him.

He smiled.

"Whatever happened to that book?" I asked him.

"What book?"

"Mom's book. With the wildflowers."

"I don't know," he said. "Maybe it's up in the attic."

"Can we look for it?" Sarah asked.

"Maybe sometime," I said.

"When?"

"Sometime," I said. "Let's swim."

Her eyes narrowed suspiciously, the eyes of a city girl.

"In *here*?" she asked.

"Come on."

"It's gunky."

"It won't hurt you," I said. "It's only gunk."

My father, of course, should have ratted on me, should have told Sarah how much I'd hated the water when I was her age, and for just the same reason. But of course he would not remember that. It was no more discernible to him than the lake's lightless bottom was to us.

———

We paddled out just far enough to feel the lake getting cleaner and colder. After two years of toddler "swim magic" lessons with Rosie, Sarah was quite a good swimmer. But Edgar was long out of swimming range, just a hat and a boat in the twinkling distance.

We treaded water side by side.

"See Daddy?" I asked.

"He's so little," she said.

"He went out a long way."

"Can I tell him?" she asked.

"Tell him what?" I said.

"Tell him about the baby that's going to be borned."

"Born," I said reflexively.

Had she heard our talks from next door late at night? Could she read my thoughts, or my menu plans?

"Can I tell him what David said?" she asked me.

"Sweetheart. David's dead," I said. I was firm but smiling. "You know that, don't you?"

She turned in the water, away from me, and started trying to swim away, her long, skinny arms like the spokes of a wheel.

"Sarah!" I shouted.

She didn't stop.

"Sarah!"

She flailed madly, that gorgeous, ineffective kid's crawl, with her head flipping wildly from side to side, and a splash and a spray with each stroke. In a few yards, she was exhausted, and I grabbed her foot from behind.

"Mommy!" she shouted, grinning, as if we were playing a game.

"Gotcha!" I said, in the same spirit. But I knew we were in the water and that she was scared and too far from shore.

I held her like a baby and treaded water.

"Want a ride?" I asked her.

"How?"

"Put your arms around my neck," I told her.

"Okay," she said, and I swam us back in.

On the shore, we caught our breath, side by side.

"You're a good swimmer," I said.

She beamed at me.

"But don't ever do that again," I said.

She looked down at her feet, which were muddy and wet.

"It's dangerous," I told her, "to swim that fast, and to swim that far away from me."

———

Edgar finally came in at four, his face and forearms burned pink and freckled. He carried a small bucket filled with small fish.

"Sarah!" he shouted. "Come see what I caught!"

She ran over to inspect the haul.

"Can we have them for dinner?" she asked.

"Sure!" he said, beaming back at her.

"Not tonight," I said.

"Why not?" she asked.

"Why not?" he asked.

"Because. I've got something special planned."

Heather came in to pour herself a glass of water.

"Veal," Heather said.

"Veal?" Edgar asked.

"What's a veal?" Sarah said.

"I love veal," my father called from the living room.

"Why veal?" Edgar asked.

"You'll see," I said.

"Why can't we have veal tomorrow?"

"Because."

"Daddy caught all the fish," Sarah said.

"It won't take me long to clean them," he said. "We can fry them in lemon and butter."

"Sounds great, Edgar," Heather told him.

"Please, Mommy?" Sarah asked.

Both of them looked at me, eager and hopeful. I forced my shoulders to shrug.

———

Edgar took the fish down to the lake to clean, and the child down to the lake to watch. I was aching for a moment alone with him, especially since my plans for the baby dinner had gone awry. But I put the veal in the freezer and set about cleaning the kitchen.

I kept thinking about what Heather had told me. I knew probably five thousand myths, but I had never heard a myth about heaven that was anything like Sarah's.

"It's make-believe," Heather had said to me, with that lofty condescension that I'd loved and hated in equal measure and never known how to answer.

Myths, I thought, were make-believe too, created to give their makers a sense of order where none was apparent.

So I willed myself to believe that Sarah was fine and that Heather was right.

———

An hour later, Edgar was taking a much-needed shower, and Sarah was taking a much-needed bath, and Jeffrey came running in from camp with a stopwatch bumping against his chest and his two hands cupped together.

"What is it?" Heather asked him as we stood side by side, chopping things for the salad.

"I need a jar," he said.

"What is it?" Heather asked again.

"A cockroach."

"Well, get it out of here," she said.

He walked forward as if he were carrying the rarest specimen known in nature.

I found an old mayonnaise jar under the sink.

"Will this do?" I asked him.

I unscrewed the lid, and he dropped his cargo in.

Heather and I bent down to look.

"It's not a cockroach," she said, as if she were making a medical diagnosis. "It's an earwig."

"What's an earwig?" he asked.

"This," she said with a shudder.

It was hopping around inside the jar, its wings popping out with each desperate jump.

"It has wings," Jeffrey said, his wide, bright eyes nearly touching the jar's glass sides.

"That's so it can fly away," Heather said. "Why don't you let it fly away?"

"It's got a claw," Jeffrey said, picking up the jar and unintentionally thrusting the creature back down to the bottom.

"I'd let it go," Heather said.

"I'm going to name it Billy," Jeffrey said.

"Billy," we chorused.

"What does it eat?" Jeffrey asked. "Do you think it eats lettuce?"

"It's not a rabbit," Heather said.

"It has to eat something," Jeffrey said, wounded.

"Maybe grass," I said.

Heather glared at me.

"Grass!" Jeffrey said. He screwed on the lid, picked up the jar, and ran out the front door.

Heather exhaled. "I'm going to kill Richard," she said. She threw down a dish towel and followed her son out into the yard.

I suddenly couldn't bear the thought that she wouldn't be able to share my glee.

———————

The steam from Edgar's shower was still in the air, and he was lying on the bed, a towel wrapped around him, a look of sunburned contentment on his face.

"Hi," he said.

"Hi."

I settled beside him. I kissed his shoulder, which smelled like the sun.

"I'm pregnant," I said, my eyes jumping to meet his. I wondered, at the same instant, how he could be so consistently

Edgar: His face showed joy without any panic, terror, regret, second thoughts, even mild alarm.

"I knew we'd done it," he said. "Are you sure?"

"I did a test."

"When?"

"This morning."

"And you waited this long to tell me?"

"Barely."

He hugged me, then kissed me deeply.

"How do you feel?" he asked.

"Excited. Scared."

"Why scared?"

"I don't know. It's going to change everything."

"Everything's going to change anyway," he said, the kind of comment that made me adore him.

———

Throughout dinner, Billy sat in his mayonnaise jar, which was perched nastily on the kitchen counter. This seating plan had been the best-available compromise between having the jar on the dining table, which was what Jeffrey wanted, and having the jar and its contents smashed on a rock, which was what Heather wanted.

"He's not eating the grass," Jeffrey said.

"He's gross," Sarah said.

"You tell him, Cookie," Heather said.

"He's not gross," Jeffrey told her. But he looked very worried, and Billy looked very dazed.

"You might," Edgar said to him softly, "try putting some air-holes in Billy's jar."

Jeffrey leapt up from the table, as if on springs.

"Mom," he said.

"What?"

"I need airholes."

"We're eating dinner."

"But Billy can't breathe. Uncle Edgar?"

"What?"

"Make me airholes?"

"After dinner."

"I'll do it, Jeffrey," Dad said to him.

Heather and I looked at Dad in mild amazement.

"I don't like seeing things suffer," he said.

So the oldest and youngest men in the house got to work with an ice pick and hammer.

Through the pounding, I looked at Edgar. Under the table, he took my hand.

"When's Uncle Richard coming?" Sarah asked abruptly.

"I don't know, Sarah," Heather told her.

"Soon?"

"Either soon or never," she said gaily.

"He'll come," Sarah said.

"I hope so," Heather said.

"I hope so too, Heather," I said directly.

"Can I go help?" Sarah asked, through our stares.

"Are you done?" Edgar asked her.

"Yes."

"Then you can."

She scraped the chair back and went to the living room, where Dad and Jeffrey had moved with the jar.

Edgar, Heather, and I sat alone.

"Your turn to wash, Erica," Heather said.

"I've got news," I said, looking down at the table, then up, back into Heather's frozen smile.

"You're pregnant," she said.

"Yes."

"I knew it," she said. "Why'd you lie to me?"

"I didn't. I just found out today."

"You told me you weren't pregnant."

"I wasn't pregnant then. I am now. I'm sorry."

"Sorry for what?" she snapped.

She started clearing the dishes. Edgar stared at her stupidly. So did I.

I got to my feet and then started to clear.

"How pregnant are you?" Heather asked accusingly.

"Two seconds pregnant," I said. "And be quiet. I don't want the kids to know yet."

"I suppose you'll want me to find you a doctor."

"Yes."

"Well, I don't know if I know anyone here."

———·———

Two weeks later, I wound up going to the local hospital. Dad had finally called a former colleague who had a house nearby, and she had said that I should see the folks in town. So Edgar and I left Sarah with Heather and Dad and drove to Stockbridge, the next town over.

The obstetrician was named Dr. Merry, an encouraging name for a doctor if ever I had heard one. He was terrifically handsome, and smug about it, or perhaps about things in general. Nurses and a receptionist seemed to hover about him with gleaming, unmarried eyes. I imagined that Dad had once had the same effect.

"Well, it's in there," Dr. Merry told me festively as he finished the briefest exam and snapped off his rubber gloves.

Edgar looked sober but happy.

"Any complaints?" Dr. Merry asked me.

"No."

"Date of your last period?"

I told him.

He took a plastic disk from his pocket and found my supposed due date: March twenty-fifth, squarely between David's birthday and Sarah's.

"You could make it to April Fools' Day," Dr. Merry said.

"We've been through that before," Edgar told him. "Our daughter was born in April."

"Well, then, you're old hands," Dr. Merry said.

"Right," Edgar said.

"Get dressed," Dr. Merry said.

"Okay," I said.

"I don't need to see you for a month," he said, "unless something comes up. Except your lunch."

The door closed merrily behind him.

"What a delight," Edgar muttered.

"Well, at least I'm official now," I said.

———————

It was lonely, but quite familiar, to be pregnant with only Edgar seeming to care or be happy about it. With Sarah, I had felt that my pregnancy was a minor but specific miracle. I had walked around for nine months feeling slightly smug and hugely maternal. But Heather had already had Jeffrey, and she had gotten pregnant again a month before me. When I'd called my father to tell him the news, he had said, "That's great, sweetheart." He had not said: How are you feeling? When are you due? How does Edgar feel? Are you thinking of names? I'm so happy. When can I see you? Mom had hard pregnancies. Mom had easy ones. A lone and simple "That's great, sweetheart." I didn't expect more now.

I didn't get more.

What I got was a series of impatient looks.

"What is it, Dad?" I finally asked him one night. It was early in August, but chilly, and we had all been reading around a fire.

He beckoned me into his bedroom. He shut the door.

"How's all this going to make Heather feel?" he said.

"All what?" I asked.

"Your having a baby. Especially with Richard not around."

"We'd waited long enough," I said.

"Has she talked to you about it?"

"Not really."

"She won't talk to me."

"Well, that's nothing new."

"Why do you think she won't talk to me?"

"I don't know, Dad," I said. "Why don't you ask her?"

"I don't think she wants me to. Anyway, it's done now," he said.

"What?"

"You're pregnant."

"Yes, Dad."

He stared out the window, right past my eyes.

"Dad," I said. "Couldn't you at least pretend to be happy for Edgar and me?"

"I am happy for you, darling. It's Heather I'm thinking about."

There was a group of large boulders out in back, a remnant of who knows what glacial age, and I'd often gone there to think big thoughts as a teenager wanting to make a point.

Now I snuck out the back door, not wanting anyone to see where I'd gone, let alone to know I was crying.

I sat with my back up against a rock and wondered with fear and anger if I should ever have gotten pregnant. When would it have been fair, or right, or fitting, for me to have a child? Was I supposed to have waited for Heather to deal with the grief she seemed bent on escaping, to work out the marriage she insisted on neglecting, to have the surgery she didn't want to contemplate so she could bear another child herself before I went ahead with my life? Yes, I thought to myself. I was supposed to have waited for all these things.

I made myself think about David, remembering his bouncing gait and the way he'd looked when he was learning to walk. I thought about his eager hugs, his chubby feet, his cubby at school. And the way he had brought us together.

The sky was the darkest purple. For years, Dad and Heather had teased me about how I'd worshipped and quoted the past we'd all shared. It was true I had carried the past around with me—as if the past were a child itself. I'd nurtured it, loved it, protected it, even imagined love coming back from it. I'd memorized its every feature and marveled at its changing nature, and I'd watched it growing larger as time went by, until finally I'd had a real child to watch who was helping me put the past in its place.

I hugged my knees to my chest. I felt alone with my body, which meant that I felt alone with the future.

———

There was blood the next morning—three small spots of pale pink on my white underpants.

"Sonogram," Dr. Merry ordered at the hospital two hours later.

Edgar gripped my hand.

I saw the beating heart of a green computer blip: thrilling, reassuring, and completely divorced from my body. I would have been no more surprised to see the outline of a tree. Something was there inside me, growing, beating, moving, taking life. That was all I needed to know.

"There's been a small separation from the uterine wall," the technician said.

"Bed rest for two weeks," Dr. Merry announced with his now-familiar, impenetrable cheer.

"Total bed rest?" I asked.

"Yes."

"Total?"

"You can get up to use the bathroom. You can move around a little. But don't climb any stairs after you get home. Don't lift anything. Or anyone."

"That's it?"

"That's it," he said. "Schedule another sonogram for two weeks from Monday. Call me if there's more bleeding."

———

"Two weeks," I said to Edgar as we drove glumly home through incongruous sunshine.

"You can catch up on your reading," he said. "But what am I going to do with Sarah?"

I looked into the distance, where the heat shimmered on the open road. Talk about David had ceased again, and Heather had promised to tell me if she heard it start again.

"Heather can help you with Sarah," I said.

"That's true, I guess," Edgar said to me.

I put my hand on my stomach.

"Is it going to be okay?" I asked him.

"I think so," he said, but darkly.

"Make it okay," I said.

"All right."

"I'm scared," I told him. "I don't want to lose her."

"Her?"

"It. Him or her. I don't know. Maybe I'm not supposed to do this yet," I said.

He laughed. "According to whom?" he said.

———

Edgar made the bed with fresh sheets, and Sarah and he gathered wildflowers out back and brought them upstairs to the bedroom.

We told the kids that I'd hurt my back.

"How?" Sarah asked me as I plumped up the pillows.

"I don't know, sweetheart," I told her, wanting to keep things as simple as possible.

"What do you need?" Edgar asked me sweetly.

"I don't know," I said.

"Magazines," he said.

"Yes."

"Books."

"Yes."

"The TV."

"I guess so," I said.

They brought these things to me, one by one, then each gave me kisses and promises. "See you later." "We're right downstairs." "I'll play outside." "I'll take care of things."

So I read. I read the myths of siblings. I read about Enumclaw and Kapoonis—thunder and lightning in Indian lore—and about Isis and Osiris, who ruled the heavens of Egypt. I read about Bahubali and Bharaba, in Jainism two brothers who battled for dominion over the land. The vanquished one, Bahubali, did penance for his defeat in a forest, standing still for a year while snakes and vines crept up his legs. By way of acknowledgment, Bharaba built him a huge and magnificent statue. He could afford to. He had won.

I read the myths of twins: Esau and Jacob; Apollo and Artemis; Romulus and Remus; Castor and Pollux. Always the twins were opposites, rivals; yet the completion and end of each other. Always the twins were two in one, and, alone, were one in two.

And I thought about how birth and death sometimes stood too close together to bear.

New Year's Eve, 1967

"Dad Always Wanted a Boy"

Two months early, our mother goes into labor on New Year's Eve. Heather and I are fourteen years old. It's the first New Year's Eve of our lives that we aren't expected to spend with our parents. It's the first New Year's Eve without promises of waltzes and resolutions. We watch Dad lead Mom off, in crablike silence, and feel no sympathy for her pain. Her pain, we figure, is all her fault.

We wear Indian-print dresses and wire-framed glasses, and our hair falls past our shoulders. I put my feet up on the leather couch, and Heather kneels like Cinderella next to the fireplace.

In the corner of the room, the Christmas tree is balding and fragile. Heather lights a joint and inhales. Dad's clock, the one on the mantel shelf, tsks in endless disapproval.

Heather exhales and hands me the joint. We learned to smoke last summer at camp, but our opportunities have been few. We're still nursing the modest stash that we smuggled home in our steamer trunks.

It's just past 11:15. It feels as if we've been up all night. I sit on the living room couch and watch Dad's clock for a full five minutes, trying to catch the minute hand in the act of moving. Its passage, however, is seamless. It moves from five minutes to ten without seeming to move at all.

Heather leaves the room and comes back a moment later with a pair of poultry shears. She snips off a high branch of the tree.

"What are you doing?" I ask politely.

It is half an hour till midnight, and we are stoned in our parents' home, and Heather feeds the branch into the fire. It sputters and flares and smells wonderful. We start laughing, and then we tear at the tree. The bristles and branches scrape our hands, but we don't notice until later. We nearly smother the fire with the branches and have to add kindling and rolled-up newspapers to keep the flames from going out.

A few minutes before midnight, we turn on the TV. We see a husband embracing his wife. We see a woman wielding a glass of champagne. Then the camera pulls back, and we see thousands of people wearing ridiculous hats and looking up toward the Times Square ball. Whenever the camera points at them, they stir like bits of confetti.

"Well, what do you know," says Guy Lombardo from the bandstand at the Waldorf-Astoria ballroom. "It looks like it's time to begin the countdown."

"And for this," Heather says, "I gave up Becky and Darcy's party."

"You wouldn't have gone anyway," I say. It is true. We are always expected to be with our parents at midnight on New Year's Eve. But ever since Mom became pregnant, Heather's pretended that she doesn't care what they want, or what they have ever wanted.

"Ten! Nine! Eight!" the crowd on the TV screen shouts in raucous unison.

I think of the boy I met at camp. I decide if he calls, I will tell him I love him.

"Seven! Six! Five!" the crowd shouts.

I wonder if I will ever kiss a boy at midnight in somebody else's home.

"Four! Three! Two! One! Happy New Year!"

White numbers float on the TV screen: 1968. The orchestra starts playing "Auld Lang Syne." From the street below our windows, we can hear some screams and shouts.

"What does 'Auld Lang Syne' mean?" I ask Heather.

"They're going to make us share your room, you know," Heather says, ignoring my question.

"*Auld* probably means *old*," I say.

"And they're going to make us take care of it," she says.

"But *lang*," I say. "Maybe *long*?" I ask.

"And change its diapers," she says. "Babies spit up, too."

"I wonder how she's doing," I say, giving up my line of questioning.

"She's fine," Heather says. "She's done it before, you know. And we were early too."

"She hasn't done it for fourteen years," I say.

I stare at her. She stares at the fire.

"Munchies," Heather says.

"Sometimes you're brilliant."

I go to the kitchen and open the refrigerator and look at the smoked salmon and the caviar and get the box of petits fours instead.

We sit in front of the fire, feeding the Christmas tree to the flames and eating the petits fours. Then we eat the chocolate candy canes from the tree. Then we eat the gingerbread cookies. Then we eat the popcorn.

Heather stares off at the distance.

"You know that movie *It's a Wonderful Life?*" she asks me hazily.

I nod at her.

"What kind of parents name a kid Zuzu?" she says.

———

They have saved a crib. They say they don't remember if it was Heather's crib or mine, but it has been stored in the building's basement, along with a small white wooden dresser, a changing table, and a host of cardboard boxes filled with bedding, toys, grungy hand puppets, and perhaps a dozen pairs of matching terry-cloth stretchies.

I am stunned to learn that they've saved all this. But Heather tells me she isn't surprised.

"Dad always wanted another," she says, with her new, and savage, certainty. "Dad always wanted a boy."

At two in the morning, Dad calls, sounding tired and distant.

"Is it okay?" I ask him.

"We don't know for sure yet," he says. "It'll be a while still. Why don't you both get some sleep?"

I have never held a baby before. I dream that night that the baby is put into my arms, and that it fusses and squirms and wriggles free and falls, and that somewhere between my arms and the floor it turns into a china doll. Its head breaks on the floor.

———

They both get to hold him before he dies. They give him a name, though he will not live. They call him Adam. His lungs are so weak that he cannot use them to make a cry. His eyes open once. Dad closes them.

———

Dad calls us after it's all over, and Heather and I never get to see him.

For weeks, for months, the house is in mourning. Whenever our mother laughs, she cries. Dad is more absent than ever, working weekend shifts and holidays.

"It's all his fault," Heather whispers to me one Sunday morning while we wash the breakfast dishes together. Her fury at Dad, born the New Year's before, has now learned how to speak.

"She wanted a baby too," I say.

"Not as much as he did. He made her."

"Shh. They'll hear you."

We listen for them. There is silence.

"It's like Dad doesn't even remember that we ever made him happy before," Heather says, and this is largely true. It's the first time that either of us understands how useless the things of his past are to Dad.

I decide I will hold the past for him, for us, just in case anyone needs to remember how warm and snug and lovely it used to be. At the same time, Heather seems to decide that if Dad can get by without it, then she can too. Years will pass before she'll be able to express a fond memory.

Summer, 1990

"I'll Just Do This So You Won't Be Cold and You'll Always Be Getting Kisses"

After three days of bed rest, the morning sickness started: morning sickness that lasted all day, a dull, ill, rampant queasiness with the power not only to make me weep but to change the taste of water and air. I had felt it for only a few days with Sarah, and prided myself on that fact, as if it reflected a healthy psyche and showed how happy I was to be pregnant.

Now I sipped steadily from glasses of iced herbal tea, brought to me by Edgar with smiles of sympathy and mercy. Heather gave me a bar of French soap, which I kept in the drawer of my night table, and when the smells of food from the kitchen below seeped upstairs, I held the soap to my nose as if it were an oxygen mask and tried to relax and breathe deeply. Cheerios were the one food that didn't repel me. Edgar would fill a bowl for me every morning—dry, no milk—and I would swallow them, one by one, like pills. I lost five pounds in a week.

Occasionally, I would hear a shout from down below: a squabble between Jeffrey and Sarah, a protestation of some sort from Dad. But mostly I heard the steady murmur of Sarah's and Heather's voices, and the pounding of nails, and the frequent surprises of reassuring laughter.

———

On my fourth afternoon, with the house silent, I snuck up to the attic, step by slow and forbidden step. I found old box springs and mattresses, an assortment of mismatched chairs, a broken mirror, some old lamps, and a cache of unlabeled boxes holding solid, if moth-eaten, memories. There were school papers of Heather's and mine in a progression of handwriting styles; there were trophies and badges; loose photographs; a deflated volleyball; several swim floats; and, at last, my mother's flower book, which I opened with equal parts of sadness and love.

Her photographs showed the bright gold of black-eyed Susans and Saint-John's-wort, the rich, pert pink of spotted knapweed, the rusty red of pitcher plants. Beside them were their pressed ghosts: pale, burnt colors, grays and beiges, thinner than paper petals, flecks of broken leaves. I wondered how long it had taken them to lose their colors. In what month of what year had the colors just vanished, up there in the attic, leaving only the photographs as proof of what had been? I was thrilled by Mom's understanding that this would happen, and I recalled how we'd teased her about taking the photographs when she had the real flowers. And then I saw one flower that I had forgotten, a flower called live-forever. The photograph showed it pink and purple, with star-shaped flowers in bushy clusters. The note Mom had written beneath its name said: "Can regenerate indefinitely!"

———

That evening, I called to Sarah, who came up to my bed almost shyly.

"I found something special," I told her.

Her eyes opened wide.

"What is it?" she said.

"Look."

From the bedcovers, I pulled out Mom's flower book. Sarah glanced at it, downcast.

"This is what Grandpa and I were telling you about," I said.

She nodded and looked at one page politely.

"Can I go to town with Aunt Heather for ice cream?" she asked me.

At night, I dreamed that my bed was a boat, sailing me on through a lake of billowing sheets and into a darkening sky. I woke with a hand on my belly, as if I could sense, even in my sleep, how much protection the future demanded.

I had read long ago about the pair of identical twins who had been separated for forty years but who, when they finally met, discovered that they had each been married twice, first to women named Linda, then to women named Betty, had had sons to whom they'd given the same name, and, in childhood, two dogs that they'd each named Toy. And the pair of identical twin girls, also separated since birth, who, upon meeting, had shown up wearing the same outfit and learned that they'd each had a miscarriage, followed by two boys and a girl. Heather and I had had every childhood illness together, had gotten toothaches, mysteriously, at the same time, and canker sores in the same places, and ear infections in the same ears. In college once, separated by two hundred miles, we had both come down with mono, with the same fever on the same day. It seemed to me that if she had lost a child, then I might have to also.

I wanted the baby now desperately, and so I felt fragile and responsible. I ached for a baby, and Sarah seemed huge.

I ate my Cheerios, sipped my tea, and allowed myself to imagine two. Two sets of clothes, toys, linens; a second small pillow, a second box of apple juice to pack for the park. There would be two baths in the evening; two sources of mischief or woe in the night; two reasons for being awakened at dawn. More important, there would be two sets of feelings, failings, talents, monsters, fantasies, and dreams. Would the second one be a boy or a girl, aggressive or reticent, mean or kind? Could the second one ever stun and enthrall me the way that Sarah did? Could I imagine the sweetness of two sets of eyes, two napes of the neck, two sets of shoulder blades that looked like angel's wings?

I had always been one of two—born in a pair, after fighting nine months for food and space with a girl who would always argue with me. But I didn't want Sarah to grow up without the chaotic mixture of friendship and loathing that having a sibling entailed. The mere fact that Heather was helping with Sarah now seemed a perfect example.

———

But occasionally, hearing them laugh, I would think that having them close to each other was no guarantee that either of them was going to want to be close to me.

———

Jeffrey's earwig, Billy, breathed his last on Thursday, August ninth, and Jeffrey glued him to a piece of cardboard, coated him with shellac, and hung him over the couch where he slept.

"It's gross!" Sarah shouted in horror when she saw this little trophy that night.

She was right. It was entirely gross, but nothing compared to the cache of horrors he'd stashed in the bottom drawer of his dresser.

In this drawer, the contents of which I'd made a forbidden excursion to examine, were two broken snakeskins, a piece of a nest, at least a dozen diseased-looking feathers, and a Band-Aid box filled with tiny bones that I took to be parts of mice.

So while Sarah had Heather march upstairs to inspect and denounce the dead earwig, I saw the look of furtive power in Jeffrey's eyes, and I knew he was thinking about the other things in his drawer and the dazzling effect they might some-day have. I was, after all, not the only one who was feeling a bit excluded.

—•—

That night, Sarah woke up shouting.

I threw back the covers.

"Stay there," Edgar said. "You're not supposed to be walking around."

He rushed into the playroom. Through the doorway, I could see that Heather, amazingly, was already there.

I got up. I walked in and held Sarah.

"What is it, sweetie?" I asked her.

She was crying but still seemed to be asleep.

"Sarah," I said.

Her head flopped on my chest. Her hair seemed moist and sweaty.

"Sarah," I said again. "Sweetheart. Sarah."

But she was really fast asleep, and whatever had startled her seemed to be past.

I laid her back on her pillow.

"Probably Jeffrey's damned earwig," Heather said.

I looked over to see if Jeffrey was awake.

"I'm going to get rid of that stupid thing," Heather said.

"That wouldn't be fair to Jeffrey," I said. "And we don't even know if that was Sarah's dream."

"Shouldn't you be in bed?" Heather said.

———————

"You're going to have to make sure that Sarah starts doing some other things," I said to Edgar the next morning.

He nodded.

"I mean it, Edgar," I said. "I don't want her spending these whole two weeks with—"

"With Heather," he said.

"With no sunshine," I said.

"Do I have to remind you," he said, "that you're the one who wanted your family together?"

"Oh, I hope not," I said. "Do you?"

"I thought you thought it was good for Heather," he told me.

"I do."

"Sarah's not talking about David," he said.

"I hate Heather calling her Cookie," I said.

"You're getting jealous," he told me.

"You've got to spend more time with Sarah," I told him.

"She'll lose patience. She's Heather," he said.

———

In the mornings, Sarah still climbed into bed with us, her hair a tumble of fine arcs and rings picking up the sunlight that came through the windows, her skin smelling sweetly of yesterday's sunshine and yesterday's mountain leaves.

She always gave me the dollhouse report, telling me about the halting progress with all the nervous passion of a brand-new property owner. Heather was her landlord and her architect, but her wayward contractor also. Heather had already split several pieces of wood by using nails that were too thick. She had bruised several fingers, had cut one with a saw, and, it seemed from what Sarah told me, had decided to start over from scratch at least three times.

"You'd think," Sarah had said one morning, cracking me up, "that she'd know how to put up a wall."

Nothing else seemed to interest her remotely. Even Freedo, who had still been clutched in Sarah's lap on the trip up from the city, now sat on the living room shelf, looking, for the first time, shabby and worn.

The dollhouse furniture that we'd brought up from New York and that had, after all, inspired the project in the first place was, like Freedo and Sarah's other former playthings, simply neglected in favor of the various building tasks.

"You ready to put in the furniture yet?" I had asked her innocently one day.

"What furniture?" Sarah had said.

"*Your* furniture. That we brought here."

"No, no," she'd said with a sober stare. "Aunt Heather's got to finish building first."

———

In the afternoons, I went crazy with longings: the longing to be with Sarah, to take Heather's place, to go downstairs and outside.

I would hear the door close when Jeffrey left for camp and Dad left for his noontime walk and Edgar left for his fishing. The sound of each door closing was painful and only sealed in more painful sounds: the giggles and laughter from Heather and Sarah, now far more annoying than comforting; the squeals of mock outrage; the new jokes and nicknames.

I thought about how separate Heather and I had been before Sarah and David were born. I thought about how scared I had been that his death would untwin us all over again. I told myself I should be happy that my sister was not only showing an interest in my daughter but was palpably being helped through and past her sorrow because of it. I told myself this, and then I would find myself calling down the stairs to ask for a glass of water, or a too-early lunch, or an update on their progress. I was as envious of their closeness as I had ever been of anything. But I tried to remind myself that they were both in mourning and that each of them gave the other as much solace as they could find.

———

Then one morning, a week into my confinement, I looked through a crack in my door to the playroom and saw Heather braiding Sarah's hair.

"What a great idea," I heard her telling Sarah. "We can use pushpins for the doorknobs."

Sarah whispered something to Heather.

"It was David's idea," was what I heard.

"It's great," Heather whispered to her, and she kissed the top of Sarah's head.

Sarah leaned closer and said something else and then looked around furtively, unaware that I could see her. It seemed that she was whispering so that I wouldn't hear.

Heather whispered back. "Let's go downstairs," she said, "and you can tell me about it there."

I wanted to call out and stop them, but I realized that they would only find another place, even farther away from me, where they could talk about him.

———•———

"She's getting a crush on Heather," Edgar announced to me that night.

I was nauseous, and I was seething, an unfortunate combination. So I just stared at him a moment, trying to find a way around the fight I knew we were going to have.

"Erica?" Edgar said. "Did you hear me?"

"How could you even notice?" I said.

"What?"

"How could you even notice what Sarah was feeling or doing? You spent the whole damned day fishing."

He looked completely startled.

"What do you expect Sarah to do when you're not even around?" I said. "Of course she's going to get close to Heather if no other grown-up is there."

"I was gone for a couple of hours," he said softly.

"You were gone all afternoon," I said.

"You don't want me to go fishing?"

I picked up my bar of soap and inhaled.

"She was spending just as much time with Heather before you had the bleeding," he said, which was entirely true and therefore the last thing I wanted to hear.

"She's more interested in Sarah than she is in Jeffrey," I said.

"Or you," he added.

I felt discovered. "Or me," I finally conceded.

"Don't take it out on me," he said.

"They're talking about David again."

"Since when?"

"I'm not sure. I just heard them today," I said.

He sat on the edge of the bed.

"What are they saying?"

I shrugged. "David stuff."

"Heaven?"

"I guess. I don't really know."

"Should we take her home?" he asked.

"How can we? I'm pregnant and I'm in bed, remember?"

"Don't get snippy. Of course I remember. I mean after you're up."

"I don't know. Don't shrinks take August off?" I asked.

"We could get her away from Heather," he said.

"Let's see. In the meantime, try getting her out."

I felt powerless and awful.

—————

Richard called Heather the next night to tell her that he was going to come up for the weekend. I'd never been so delighted by the prospect of seeing him.

"That's great," I told her when she told me.

"Yeah."

"Isn't it?" I asked.

"Sure it is."

"You guys need some time together," I said.

"Don't tell me what I need," she said.

She looked around the room suspiciously, as if expecting to discover that I'd secretly been crocheting a baby blanket or building a bassinet.

I said: "You promised that you would tell me if Sarah started to talk about David again."

She started to feign surprise.

"I *heard* you," I said.

"It's no big deal," she said.

"What makes you so sure?"

She shrugged. "How do you feel?"

I sighed. A show of affection. It was more seductive to me than a show of remorse and, from her, it was just as rare.

"I feel pretty awful," I said. I wondered if anything bad that I felt would or should ever merit sympathy from her.

"I'm sure it'll be okay," she said.

I nodded.

"I wonder if David's right," she said.

"David?"

"Yes. David."

"Right about what?" I said.

"That you're going to have another girl."

It didn't surprise me that Sarah had told her, but it floored me that Heather seemed serious.

" 'Just make-believe,' you told me, Heather. Remember?" I said.

She shrugged. I stared.

"What?" she asked me.

"I didn't know—"

"What?"

"I guess I didn't know you believed in that stuff."

"In what stuff?"

"In life after death," I said. "That's what we're talking about, you know."

She shrugged again.

"Do you?" I asked.

"Do you?" she asked.

"No."

"Really?"

"In Arts and Crafts? In Snack?"

"Maybe that's just a translation," she said. "Or maybe that's how it is for kids."

I felt almost embarrassed by her need. "When Sarah was born," I told her, "I thought for a while that maybe she was Mom."

"You did?"

"Yeah. I don't know. I guess I hoped it was true. I don't know."

"Well, no one *knows,*" she said.

"Dad knows there's no such thing," I said.

And Heather had always seemed just as intensely, even fearfully, rational. I didn't think I believed in an afterlife, but I was as suspicious of Dad's virulent realism as he and Heather had always been of mystery. Why be that certain, that utterly sure? Why insist so absolutely on an absolute lack of magic?

Dad had always dismissed, with one haughty exhalation of breath, the kooks, the loonies, the seers, the sayers, the people who'd almost died and had seen bright lights, and the people who said there was a God. To him, all faith was slightly pathetic, an invention of little minds for big problems.

The night that Mom died, I'd asked Heather where she thought Mom was.

"What do you mean?" she'd snapped. "She's in the bedroom."

"No," I'd said. "I mean *really* is. The real Mom. Where do you think she is?"

From the moment of her death, I'd had the exquisite sense of being watched.

Heather had said: "Erica. Mom's body is in the bedroom. The rest of her is in your mind. Mom is nowhere now. She's dead."

I'd stared at Heather. "You're scared," I'd said.

"Scared of what?"

"Scared of Mom. You're scared of being haunted," I'd said. Then she had run out of the room.

"Remember what you did when Mom died?" I asked now.

"Remembering is your department," she said.

———

For five days, Jeffrey had been speaking of nothing else but his father's arrival. But late on Friday afternoon, when Richard's horn finally honked up from the driveway, Jeffrey came running up the stairs and launched himself onto his playroom couch.

"Hey," I called to him from my bedroom roost.

"What?"

"Come here," I said. "I can't go there."

He entered the bedroom shyly.

"Your dad's downstairs," I said. "Don't you think he wants to see you?"

"I wanted to see him, and he didn't come," Jeffrey said with exemplary logic.

"How does that thing work?" I asked him, pointing to the stopwatch that was always dangling from his neck.

"You click this button when you start, then you click this one when you finish."

"What do you want to time?" I asked him.

———

It took five minutes and twenty-two seconds before Richard started to climb the stairs.

It took seven seconds for him to arrive at the door, and—though Jeffrey didn't time it—nearly a minute of edgy chit-chat with me before he remembered to hug his son.

He had lost both hair and weight, and the effects seemed to cancel each other out. He looked like a fifty-one-year-old man who was trying to hold on to something.

But for the first time I could remember, I was truly happy to see him. How would Heather be able to build the dollhouse when she had to rebuild her marriage?

———

Later that night, Edgar and I lay listening for I wasn't sure what: the sound of a slap or a violent explosion, the sound of sex or laughter, the sound of a marriage mending or breaking. We didn't hear a thing.

———

Monday morning, August twentieth, I took a shower, dressed in real clothes, descended the stairs from my exile—and was dismayed to find that my freedom had done nothing to restore either my energy or my appetite. Clutching my bar of soap as if it were a lucky charm, I surveyed the breakfast table. It was cluttered with family members, each of whom was eating something different, and differently repellent. I sagged. I sat down in the nearest chair, which happened to be by the dollhouse.

This was the first time that I had seen it in two weeks, and I found it not only benign but wondrous. Though still unfinished—and unfurnished (heaven forbid there would ever be *dolls* in the dollhouse, let alone doll chairs or doll tables)—most of the rooms were already rich with textures and vivid with seeming warmth. There was carpeting in the bedrooms, where sculpted strips of white masking tape made picture moldings and floorboards that set off the painted walls. There was wallpaper in the living room that resembled the floral print in Heather and Richard's own. A pushpin made the doorknob on the closet door, which was neatly balanced on hinges made of cardboard and safety pins.

I marveled at the power of grief, how it could be strong enough to pull from Heather so much ingenuity, so much patience, so much precision.

"This is amazing," I said, though no one heard me above the clatter of plates. I stood up and went to join the family.

"It's amazing," I said to Heather. "The dollhouse."

Heather and Sarah beamed.

"How did you two *do* all that?" I asked.

Heather looked at Sarah as if they had a million secrets and couldn't spare a single one.

"It took time," Heather said to me, smiling.

———•———

"Where are you going?" Sarah asked us five minutes later as Edgar and I stood at the front door.

"To the doctor's. I told you, honey," I said.

"Why?"

"To check on my back."

"What's wrong with your back?" Dad asked me.

Above Sarah's head, I gave him a meaningful, impatient glare. He walked us out to the front steps, out of sight and hearing of Sarah.

"What's wrong with your back?" he asked again.

"Dad. Nothing," I said. "That's just what I've been telling Sarah. You know. I'm going to the hospital."

"Why?"

"Why? You know. To have a sonogram."

"Why?"

"To make sure the baby's okay."

"Whose baby?"

"Dad," I said.

"You're pregnant," he said.

"Dad," I repeated, breathless now. "Don't you remember?"

———•———

"One crisis at a time," Edgar said when we closed the doors of the car.

"Oh my God," I said.

"Let's not jump to conclusions."

"Oh my God," I said.

"He's getting old," Edgar said. "Sometimes he forgets things. You know that. It doesn't mean that he's sick."

"What if he is?" I asked Edgar.

"Could we just get through the next hour?" he said.

The roads were shaded by ancient elms, and we drove through dappled light. I talked to my mother inside my head. I said to her: Don't let him be losing his memory. I said: Don't let Dad be sick. And then I said: Don't let me lose this baby.

"What are you thinking about?" Edgar asked me.

"Fate," I said.

"The baby's or your father's?"

"Both," I said. "And the connection."

"There's no connection," he said.

"How can you be sure?"

"Because if there was any fairness to it, then why is David dead?" he asked.

"Maybe I have to lose this baby because Heather lost David."

"That's not an equal trade either," he said.

"Well, maybe I have to lose this baby and Dad has to lose his memory because Heather lost David."

"You think someone is keeping score?"

Of course I believed, deep down, that he was right. When things are going well, it is always possible to construct a just universe. When things go a little bit badly, you can always find signs and warnings. But when a small child dies on a heartless February morning, the notions of logic and equity start to seem like a rich person's luxuries: things that only the lucky can have.

Still, as we drove on, I found myself making a startling trade inside my mind. I traded the unborn baby for my father's memory—in effect, the future for the past. I could start our own future again, I thought. But the past, represented by Dad, seemed far too finite to give away.

My father was the gatekeeper to a somewhat-exotic kingdom, the kingdom of my past and of my sense that I was safe. He had never been a very willing gatekeeper, and since Mom's death, it had never been a very large gate. But there he had stood none-theless, the most direct access I had to my childhood. The fact that he himself never seemed to want to open that gate—never wanted to step inside—had occasionally been frustrating and often sad, but hadn't changed the essential geography.

Make it be all right, I said to my mother in my mind.

Then I realized that I was talking to a woman who had been dead for seven years. Where, exactly, did I think she was? What, exactly, did I think she could do? And who was I to be telling Sarah that she couldn't be talking to David?

Dr. Merry was uncharacteristically somber, surveying the sono-gram screen in silence as the technician tapped meaningless words on the keyboard.

"You're nine weeks pregnant?" the technician asked me.

"I should be," I said. "I hope so," I said.

The cold jelly went on my stomach, and then the micro-phone. A web of green lines appeared on the screen. I strained up from the table to see them.

"Is there a heartbeat?" I finally asked.

Up until the last second, I could imagine it going either way.

"Yes," he said. "It looks fine. No problem."

So different things would happen to me than had happened to my twin.

Galloping back through my mind came the child: running, red-faced, clad in a snowsuit (somehow I skipped past the whole first year). She was tumbling into my open arms; she was kissing my cheek with small, cold, chapped lips. She was back, in my head, and a little girl. She was mine. She was going to be fine. My daughter. We would have eighteen winters together before I would have to let her go.

"Everything's fine," Dr. Merry said.

"Only fine?" Edgar asked.

"Sweetheart," I said. "She's *fine*."

———

"So?" Heather said when we walked in the door. She and Sarah had wallpaper samples spread out in two rows along the floor.

"It's fine," I said.

Sarah didn't look up.

Heather tried to smile but produced a grimace instead. I tried not to look too sorry for her.

"Where's Dad?" I asked her.

"Out back," she said.

I asked Sarah to get me a tissue, and I told Heather what Dad had said that morning.

She shrugged. "He's getting old," she said.

"I know that."

"He's been forgetting things all summer," she said.

"I know. But this seemed a little extreme."

"Who knows?"

"Where's Richard?" I asked.

"With Jeffrey."

"At camp?"

"No, I kept him home. They went for a walk or something."

Sarah came back with the tissue.

"Have you been in here all morning?" I asked her.

They shrugged in perfect unison.

"I can play with you now, sweetheart," I said to Sarah.

She didn't make a move.

"Come on, Sarah," I said. "Get your bathing suit on."

As she went up to dress, I walked, alone, down to the lake. Dad was just coming out of the water, wrapping himself in a faded beach towel.

"Hi," I said.

"Hi, hi. Water's great."

"So," I said tentatively. "We got good news."

"Good news about what?"

"The baby."

"That's great, sweetheart."

I peered at his features intently, trying to fathom his level of comprehension.

"What is it?" he asked me.

"Nothing," I said, and hoped that was the case.

I wanted to reclaim Sarah, reclaim my life, my appetite, my future, my family. But over the next few days, Dad forgot three times where he'd put his shoes and twice what he'd wanted for dinner. He forgot that Heather and Sarah had already painted one of the dollhouse bedrooms.

At the same time, he had no trouble remembering that August twenty-third had been his and Mom's anniversary; that the bed in the attic had been bought for their first apartment, and that its box spring was stained with red wine that he had spilled on a Thanksgiving Day.

So I concluded that he was systematically being forced back into a past that he had never, in good health, taken the time to appreciate.

———

"It might not be Alzheimer's," Heather told me while we were husking corn for dinner on Friday night. Edgar was giving Sarah her bath, and Jeffrey and Richard were outside. It had now been a week since Richard's arrival, and I was still waiting for Heather to show more interest in him than in Sarah. "It might have been a minor stroke," Heather told me. "That sometimes affects the brain the same way."

"Oh, is that all," I said.

"Well, it is fairly common."

"Shouldn't he see a doctor?" I asked.

"There's no great rush," she said. "If it is Alzheimer's, it's not reversible."

"God."

"What."

"How can you be so cold about this?"

"I'm just being practical," she said.

"Do you think he's worse?" I asked her.

"No. Maybe."

"God," I said again.

"What's the problem?" Heather said tersely.

"The problem is that you don't give a damn."

"That's not why you're so angry," she said.

I gathered the bags of corn husks furiously and took them out to the garbage.

The sun was setting, the sky pink and blue. I thought of a sunset I'd watched at fourteen, and how Dad had told me he'd seen it before. How would I care for my father?

I remembered a day in the park with Sarah, the spring when she'd just been starting to walk. She had led me gaily to the foot of some stone steps, and when we'd been halfway up them, I'd noticed an old woman and her nurse down below.

The nurse had been urging the woman onward.

"I don't want to!" the old woman had cried, and I had turned, horrified, to see her face as it crumpled with tears and panic.

The nurse had tried to lead her on, a patient hand at her elbow—she had, no doubt, heard many protests before—but I had been flatly unable to move, shocked by the woman's cries, so much like a baby's, so confused and lonely. Who was to say that that couldn't be my father's future? And who would be steering him by the arm? All right, I thought. I was jealous about Sarah. But why couldn't Heather see how vital these questions might turn out to be?

"I don't want to!" I heard the woman cry.

I ran back into the house to find Dad.

"Hi, hi," he said, looking up from a book.

"How are you, Dad?" I said.

"I'm fine."

I looked down at the floor.

"We want you to see a doctor when we get back to New York," I said.

"I just had a checkup. In May. No. In March."

"Which was it?"

"I don't remember."

"Dad. You've been forgetting things."

"What things?" he said.

"You forgot I was pregnant."

"No I didn't. When?"

"The other day."

"I didn't."

"Dad. You did," I said.

Out of the corner of my eye, I saw Heather creeping out from behind the kitchen counter.

"Is this the way you both feel?" Dad asked.

Heather wiped her hands on a dish towel.

"It wouldn't hurt to check it out," she said.

Our father put down his book and visibly tried to appear serene.

"You know," he said after a long pause, "there are plenty of times, I'll admit, when I'll see someone at the hospital and totally blank on his name. Or I'll find myself trying to remember the name of some actor in a movie. But I know enough about aging to know that it's fairly natural."

"That's not what we're talking about," I said.

His serenity started to fade. He stood up.

"I know people *half* my age," he said, "who have the same troubles, or worse."

I looked to Heather for help, and of course she was totally mute.

"Maybe *you're* forgetting," he said, more to me than to

Heather, "that I spent roughly thirty years in practice treating patients in their eighties and nineties."

"I know, Dad," I said.

"You think I don't know the signs? You think I wouldn't know if I was slipping? You think I can't take care of myself?"

"I just want you to look into it," I said quietly.

Richard and Jeffrey came in from outside.

"When's dinner?" they asked us together.

"Soon," Heather said.

"That's *Richard,* Heather's *husband,*" Dad said with brutal sarcasm. "That's *Jeffrey,* Heather's *son,*" Dad said. "*Sarah,* who is your *daughter,* is upstairs, being bathed by *Edgar,* your *husband.*"

Heather was smirking with Dad, enjoying his nasty precision.

"If you are all right," I said to him slowly, "then what possible harm could come from seeing someone in your own profession?"

"*Medicine,* right?" he said in mock triumph.

———

I was furious, and grateful. Who wouldn't rather feel anger than pity toward a father?

———

I was now almost ten weeks pregnant. I missed my daughter. Daily, it seemed, we had less to say to each other. I tried to get in on the dollhouse, offering to take her to the toy store in town to look for some dolls who might live there someday.

"We're not ready yet," she said, with more than a little of Heather's condescension.

"Watch that tone in your voice, young lady," I said.

"What tone?" she asked me nastily.

It was nearing the end of August. The lake was warm and soothing, and in the afternoons, Edgar and I went for swims, floating on our backs, side by side. The baby floated inside me.

———

The discretion that Richard and Heather had shown when Richard arrived had vanished. At night, we heard their arguments now: Richard, rational and pleading; Heather, cruel and dismissive. He wanted to move to the country, he said: He had seen lots of very nice houses, and he couldn't bear living where David had lived. Heather said her feelings counted too: What if it comforted her to be where David had been? What if she didn't want to run away scared? And—amazingly to me all over again—what if she wanted to be near her family?

Richard wanted Heather to have her tubes untied and to get pregnant again.

"It's *my* body!" she screamed at him.

"I know that, for Christ's sake!" he screamed at her.

Their voices rose and fell like the sounds of a storm.

"Go to hell!" Heather shouted Saturday night.

"Can't you think about me?" Richard shouted back at her.

"You don't even spend time with Jeffrey now! Why do you want another?"

———

They wrestled, and they compromised. He left on Sunday night. His plan was to spend the whole week looking for a house in the country. Heather said she would try her best to keep an open mind.

"How many rooms will there be, Uncle Richard?" Sarah asked him.

Richard looked past Sarah, to Heather. "I don't know, sweetheart," he told them both.

Sarah smiled to herself as if she knew something none of the rest of us did.

———

She came into our bed that night, awakened, it seemed, by another dream.

"What is it, sweetie?" I asked her.

She yawned. "David's going to come back," she said.

"What?"

"David. He says he's going to come back. He's going to be in Aunt Heather's belly. Then he's going to be borned."

At that moment, I realized I'd had enough. I may have occasionally talked to my dead mother, but my dead mother had never talked to me.

I sat up straight, wishing that Heather were here to make note of the clear, firm voice I intended to use.

"Look at me," I told Sarah.

She did.

"Sweetheart. David's dead. He is never going to come back. Never," I said.

"He is!" she said.

"He can't," I said.

"He is! He is!" She started crying.

"He can't," Edgar told her again, just as firmly.

For nearly an hour, we tried to console her. But when she had finally fallen asleep, her face was still slick with tears.

At nine o'clock in the morning, I woke, grateful that Edgar had let me sleep and impressed, as always, by the raucous effects that pregnancy had upon my body. Edgar and Sarah were both gone, so I made the bed and tidied things up and brought Heather's hairbrush into her bathroom. On her dresser I found a small notebook that I instinctively opened. Inside it were pages and pages of her maddening doctor's scrawl, but it took me only a moment to realize, with dread, what I was reading.

"When televisions die, they go into big television boxes and they sail away to television heaven. And when pictures die, the big ones go into big picture boxes and the little ones go into little picture boxes and the little ones are carried and the big ones sail away to picture heaven."

That was the first entry.

I was sitting to read the rest.

"Working on David's house," Heather had written. "I asked Sarah what songs David likes to sing now. She said, 'Edelweiss, because of bloom and grow forever.' Then she said: 'What does bloom and grow forever mean?' "

Another page:

"I asked her what happens at night there. She says David says he gets to sleep in heaven on huge pillows. Can she really be imagining all of this? And if she isn't scared by this, why should I be?"

It went on, entry after scribbled entry. A diary of death, dictated by my daughter, prompted and savored by my sister.

"Sarah asked: 'If you live to be a hundred, then you don't die?' "

"I asked her what David said about the accident. He said it didn't hurt to die."

I threw up in the bathroom.

———

"Heather!" I screamed at the top of my voice. I barreled down the stairs but found no one. I knocked on my father's bedroom door.

"Where is everyone?" I asked him.

"I don't know," he said. "Is there coffee?"

I ran down to the lake just as Edgar was pulling the rowboat up.

"No fish for breakfast," he said, smiling.

"Where's Sarah?"

His smile vanished. "I don't know," he said. "I'm sorry. She was gone when I woke up, so I figured she'd gone off early with Heather."

"I'm going to kill my sister," I said as Edgar and I raced back up, side by side, to the house. We walked in and heard a car in the driveway. Out the front door, we saw the empty place in Heather's car where Sarah both shouldn't and should have been.

"Where's Sarah?" Edgar and I screamed in panic.

"I don't know," Heather called back.

———

We searched the house first, but fruitlessly.

"Divide up," my father ordered us when we'd reassembled downstairs.

Edgar, I noticed, was pale and gray.

"Jeffrey," Dad barked. "You come with me to the lakefront. Edgar, you stay here in case she comes back. And Heather and Erica, go to the woods."

———•———

I would have preferred another search-party partner, but something in Dad's tone of voice had dictated complete obedience and immediate action. Heather and I jogged toward the woods.

"I found your book," I told her.

"You went through my things?"

"I found your book. You bitch. You're doing this to her!" I said.

"I'm not doing anything to her except listening," Heather said.

"There's listening and there's listening," I said, already out of breath from running.

Somehow, I had expected to find Sarah by the boulders where I'd always sought my own refuge, and when she wasn't there, I started to cry and to gasp for breath.

Under the old, familiar elms and oaks, Heather and I took turns screaming her name.

Nothing else was said. We covered the path that the years of our summers had worn, and then we turned around and ran back.

———•———

When I finally saw her—nearly smothered by Edgar's embrace, her nose and mouth flattened against his chest—I started to shake.

"Where *were* you?" I cried when Edgar finally let her go.

"I went for a walk around the lake," she said.

"You scared us," Heather said, and only then did I notice that Heather was also weeping.

"I'm sorry, Aunt Heather," Sarah said.

———

Her arms and her legs were covered with scratches, some of which were bleeding.

In the kitchen, Dad and Heather both reached, with old competitiveness, for the one clean dish towel.

"I'll do it, Dad," Heather said.

"No, I'll do it," he told her.

Reluctantly, but quickly, she stepped aside. Dad cleaned Sarah's cuts carefully with warm water. Already she'd started to calm down by now, her sobs tapering off like a long coda. The cuts weren't bad, and they'd almost stopped bleeding.

"You okay?" I asked her.

She nodded and sniffled. "I want a Band-Aid," she said with great dignity.

Edgar, still shaken, kept staring at her.

"Why did you do it?" he finally asked her.

"What could you have been thinking?" I asked her.

"Mommy told me he wasn't coming back," she said.

"Who's not coming back?" Heather asked.

"David," Sarah said. "Except he is. He told me. He's going to come back in your belly."

"Sarah," I said gently. "That's not possible."

"Yes it is," she said. "He said it is."

"You see," I said, "after Aunt Heather had David, she decided—the doctor told her—that she couldn't have any more
children."

"He could be wrong," Sarah said flatly.

"No—" I began.

"Yes," Heather said. "He could be wrong."

I stared at her, amazed that she would want to foster this
kind of hope.

"David says kids who die get to choose," Sarah said.

"Choose what?" Heather asked her.

"Choose what?" I asked.

"Choose where they want to come back," she said. "No one
else gets to. Not grown-ups. But David had Snack, and they
told him he could. So he's going to choose Aunt Heather and
Uncle Richard again."

She smiled, satisfied with her logic.

"And he's going to live in the country," she said.

A sense of exhaustion swept over me. Sarah pointed to the
dollhouse. "And this is going to be his house," she said.

———————

Edgar took me down to the lake.

"We've got to stop this!" he yelled at me.

"Edgar," I said.

"No, I mean it!" he said.

"How are we going to stop her?" I asked.

"We'll take her home."

"Oh, come on," I said.

"We're her *parents,* for Christ's sake. We'll tell her no."

I sat down.

"That'll only make her want it more," I said.

And want Heather more, I thought.

But I felt we had to talk to her. In the house, we found her perched on the kitchen counter, now proudly counting for Dad and Heather the cuts and scrapes that were covered with Band-Aids.

"She okay?" I asked Dad.

"She's fine," Heather said.

———

Edgar and I took her back down to the lakefront and sat with her on the dry, warm grass.

"Are you mad?" she asked me, squinting up against the sunlight and, no doubt, against my fiercer glare.

"Not exactly," I said.

"Are you happy?" she asked.

"No."

"I spy a wide flower," she said.

"Wildflower," I told her. "And don't try to butter me up."

"I'm sorry I ran away," she said.

"It's not just that," I told her.

"I won't do it again," she said.

She had one knee at her chest now and she was fitting the lace of her sneaker into one lace hole after another.

"Look at Mommy," Edgar said.

She looked up.

"I'm worried about you spending all your time making this dollhouse," I said.

"Why?"

"Because, for one thing, you're spending all your time indoors, and that's not good for you. And for another thing . . ."

I looked to Edgar.

"For another thing," he said, looking back at me.

"For another thing," I said, "we're worried about you thinking so much about David."

She considered this quite calmly, then said: "David thinks about me."

"Sweetheart," I said. "You know the difference between real and pretend, right?"

"Sure."

"Like Freedo, for example," I said. "Is Freedo a real bear or a pretend bear?"

She looked at me, no doubt, the way I was looking at her.

"Mommy!" she said, and let out a small, delicious giggle.

"Is Freedo a real bear or a pretend bear?" Edgar repeated.

She thought a long moment. "He's a real pretend bear," she said with exquisite accuracy.

"Can Freedo growl?" I asked, not ready to give up quite yet.

"Mommy!" she said again, this time with a squeal.

"Does Freedo eat or drink?" Edgar asked.

"No!"

"Can Freedo grow?" I asked.

"No!"

She was giggling hilariously now. Clearly, we'd discovered a great new game.

"Sarah, calm down," Edgar said sweetly.

"Sweetheart," I said. "Is Freedo alive?"

She stopped laughing.

"No."

"Is David alive?" I asked.

She looked at me bitterly, understanding how completely she'd been set up and trapped.

She stood up.

"Sarah," I said, taking her hand.

She yanked it away from mine.

"Sarah," I said. "Is David alive?"

"Well, *he* thinks he is!" she said, and ran off.

———•———

At night, Heather came down the road with me when I went to empty the garbage.

"I'm not doing anything bad," she said.

"You're not going to get a chance to," I said.

"What's that? A threat?"

"Heather," I said, near tears. "She's my daughter. I know you miss David—"

"Don't you see?" she said, and, amazingly, burst into tears. "Don't you see that she tells me about him?" she asked.

I touched her shoulder with my hand. She didn't pull away from my touch.

"Don't you see that she's trying to please you?" I said. "It can't help her, all this talk about him. It's too much. It's too strange. It's got to stop."

"But what if he's out there?" she yelled at me.

"Then find him yourself," I told her.

———•———

We took Sarah driving the next day. Just Edgar and Sarah and me in the car. Freedo came too, more my idea than Sarah's, and a fairly lame attempt to create a connection with something that I could see.

We played I Spy along the way.

I spy a windmill. I spy a kite. I spy a daughter who has no desire to play I Spy.

There was a goat farm and petting zoo about fifteen minutes away from the house, and there we watched Sarah become a child again. She fed great bunches of bright green grass to the goats; she laughed while a baby goat nibbled at her T-shirt; she counted the cats that prowled the roads.

"Maybe we should get her a pet," I whispered to Edgar.

He said: "You're kidding yourself."

But we were both warmed and buoyed by the sight of her seemingly so free and glad.

For lunch, we drove to Lee, a town over, and went to the old-fashioned drugstore there. We sat at the counter, three in a row, and ordered french fries and hamburgers and real malteds. Behind the counter were the signs of other attachments: 100 CUPS OF COFFEE FOR GARY FROM MARSHA; 50 CUPS OF COFFEE FOR ZEKE FROM LUCY.

"What are all those numbers?" Sarah asked, seeing me look at them.

"People here can give each other gift certificates of coffee," I said.

"Just coffee?" she asked.

"Or ice cream," I said. "Look."

I spun her stool around and helped her hop off onto the floor.

"Where?" she said.

I led her around the counter to the corner by the phone and pointed to a piece of faded paper. I read her the words: "Five ice cream sodas for Erica from Mommy."

"Is that *you?*" Sarah asked, wide-eyed, as if she'd just found out that I was famous.

"Yup," I said.

"And *your* mommy?" she asked.

"My mommy," I said.

She looked strangely uncomfortable.

"Do you need to use the bathroom?" I whispered.

"No."

She walked back to the counter.

"Is something wrong?" I asked her.

"No. It's just—"

"Just what?" I asked.

"Your mommy," she said.

"What about her?"

"She's not alive either," she said.

"That's right, darling," I said, thinking perhaps we were making some progress.

"But she helped take care of David in Arts and Crafts," she said.

I looked down, forlorn, at my chocolate malted.

"She was helping him learn how to make sweaters," she said.

Then despite everything, I heard myself saying, "Yes, she always loved to knit."

———

We returned late in the afternoon to find Heather sitting in an armchair, reading a medical journal.

"You know," I told her after Sarah had gone upstairs to wash up, "it's not like I never want you to play with Sarah. It's not like I don't appreciate all the time you spent doing that thing. It's not like I don't understand."

"Yes it is," she said simply. "It's exactly like all of that."

"I just don't think it's all that healthy," I said.

"I know what you think," she said.

"And you think it is?"

She sighed. "I think, first, that no one knows where David is. And I think, second, that different people, including children, have different ways of working things out. Play is a form of therapy, you know."

"Of course I know that," I said.

———

"Heather says we shouldn't worry about it," I told Edgar that night. "Play is a form of therapy."

"What else is she going to say?" Edgar said. "It's therapy for her too."

"She's a doctor."

"So?"

"Do you really think that if something was wrong with Sarah, she wouldn't admit it?"

"I don't think Heather's okay, either."

———

Sarah again had trouble sleeping that night. Several times, she called out for me. I went to her quickly, gave her a kiss, and asked her what was wrong.

"Mommy," she'd simply mumble to me, as if she was still asleep.

I would start to walk out of the room.

"Mommy!" she would call then, in a frightened voice.

"Are you awake, sweetheart?" I'd ask her.

"Mommy," she'd mumble again, and drift back into her dreams.

I lay awake for a long time, listening for sounds of her from the next room. It was a lot like the way it had been just after her birth, when every slight disturbance seemed like a warning of worse to come. This time, though, I listened for Heather too. I imagined Heather crouching at the bedroom door, waiting for the moment when she could waltz in and pounce on my daughter with vicious understanding.

I heard Sarah turn over her pillow, looking for comfort, no doubt, and rest. I fell asleep listening for nightmares. Then I dreamed myself. I dreamed that David was in Sarah's heaven, a place I recognized instantly by its high ice-cream-parlor chairs and paint-covered smocks.

"David," I said in my sleep.

"Hi, Aunt Erica," he said, with a brush in his hand. The brush had gobs of blue paint on it.

"That's going to drip," I told him. "Be careful."

"It's okay," he said. "It helps make the sky."

We stood side by side on a strange mesh fabric and watched as the paint dripped down and then through it. Slowly, it spread out below us, around large white clouds that were real.

"Hey, this is neat," I said. "Can I try some?"

He looked back over his shoulder as if he was listening to someone's instructions. He shook his head.

"No," he said. "Sorry, Aunt Erica."

"That's okay," I said. "It just looked like fun."

"It *is* fun," he said. "It's better than Chutes and Ladders."

"Do you have friends here?" I asked.

"Oh yes."

"Then why don't you leave Sarah alone?" I said.

"I miss her," he said.

"She misses you too. But leave her alone!"

"No way."

"Leave her alone!"

———•———

I woke with Sarah beside my bed, and Edgar, just waking up, on his elbow.

"What is it?" I asked, still groggy.

"Mommy," she said, "I think you were having a bad dream."

"You okay?" Edgar asked me.

"I'm fine," I said.

Sarah asked: "Did you see him?"

"Who?"

"David."

"Yes."

"Erica!" Edgar said.

"In my dream," I quickly added.

"Was he doing Arts and Crafts?" she asked.

"Yes."

"He likes Arts and Crafts," she said.

I nodded.

"It's good that you dreamed about him."

"Why?"

"Because if we ever forget him, he'll get weak, and then he'll really die. Didn't you know that?" she said.

I left them all in the house the next morning and walked down to the lake. I sat in the still-wet grass, watching the water ripple and shine, and felt in my belly the slight ache and stretch of the late part of early pregnancy.

Life, I thought, had a brilliance of unobvious dimensions: the meeting of cells, the replication of genes, the uncanny work involved in the making of a single finger. I had a totally improbable thing happening inside me that no one would have believed if the evidence of it were not so irrefutable. In the morning air, with the image of David painting the sky still in my head, I allowed myself to think about the chance of another wonder. Was it so bizarre to think that an afterlife was *more* improbable than life?

There was not a single culture or civilization I had studied that hadn't constructed a vision of heaven. The myths of an afterlife were, like all myths, designed to comfort and soothe. But myths had a different purpose as well, which was, in effect, to dispose of time. The action of myths took place out of time. Their very telling and retelling was a ritual designed to make their listeners partake of a timeless world, a world in which human beings were transient, and eternity was real.

I was as furious at Heather for helping Sarah build the dollhouse as I was for helping her build the myth of David. Both creations, I knew, would need to be dismantled at some point. But I had had enough of distance and jealousy, and I told this to Edgar later that morning.

"Now you want closeness and jealousy?" he said.

I decided that I had to try to keep up with Sarah, heaven and all.

No twin of mine was going to be better at fathoming myths than I was.

And I decided I had to try to judge how fickle Sarah's connection to reality really was. It would not be an easy assignment.

"My finger died," she'd announced to me, out of the blue, that morning.

"The hippo's mouth looks like a pepper," she'd told me the day before.

"Do you want some hot chocolate?" she asked me that afternoon while I was doing the laundry.

"Sure," I said, thinking she meant the real thing and wondering if we had any good cocoa in the house.

Sarah, meanwhile, took the soap-powder cup from my hands, picked up a twig from the laundry room floor, and positioned herself by the chair in the corner, where she stood, pretending to stir at a stove.

"Mix mix mix," she said. "Mix mix mix stir it with a spoon mix mix and get the cup and give it to Mommy do you think there are fishes in the lake?"

There seemed to be no punctuation, either in her sentences or in her thoughts.

That evening, she came upstairs with us and started drawing pictures of us: circles for the heads, circles for the eyes, diamonds for the mouths, rectangles for the bodies.

"It's a wig," she said, drawing spiky lines from the top of the head. "We're all wearing wigs no it's a spider with spider's legs no it's a sunshine I'll put you in a boat."

She drew a boat, and a face in it that represented me.

"That's you," she said, drawing my mouth and then a series of lines that obscured it. "I'll just do this so you won't be cold and you'll always be getting kisses. You know why you're in a boat? So we can all hold together and you can take us along with you."

———

The next morning, I stood with my arm around Sarah's waist, studying the dollhouse plans.

"So what's the next thing that you've got to do?" I asked her.

"The fireplace," she said. "It's going to have two sides. One in the living room and one in the dining room."

"A two-sided fireplace?" I asked her.

"Yes."

"Was that Heather's idea?"

"No," she said.

"When did you ever see a two-sided fireplace?"

I searched my memory for a picture book or a home she had seen that had had one.

"David told me about it," she said.

"And what's this?" I asked, unflinching.

"His bedroom. It's got its own bathroom."

"How nice."

The house had two bedrooms upstairs and one downstairs. It had a playroom in the basement, and an attic with a window.

"I want to help build it," I said.

Sarah looked at Heather.

"Fine," Heather said.

"But with Aunt Heather too," Sarah said.

Jeffrey sat on the couch with the stopwatch, intently clicking the stop and start button, timing God knows what: how long it took me to pick up a pencil, pick up a paintbrush, cut some paper?

Did he time the lengths of the loving looks Sarah gave to Heather, and Heather to her?

Did he time the lengths of my glances in their direction, or how long it took for them to notice that I was there at all?

———•———

Out in the driveway, I bent with Sarah for nearly an hour, trying to find the perfect pieces of gravel to make a stone fireplace. By afternoon, we had discovered a workable kind of mortar, but after watching my all-thumbs attempts with it, Heather bumped me out of the way and took over. Above Sarah's head, we both had to smile. We were actually playing together.

"Remember our butterfly wings?" she asked me.

"Mine were green, and yours were orange," I said.

She grinned with something like true fondness.

So we eased back into our old give-and-take, wordlessly helping and editing each other, losing track of the time.

———•———

Richard called that night, after Jeffrey and Sarah had gone up to bed.

Dad, Edgar, and I, as usual, were listening to Heather's side of the conversation.

"Really," she said. "Really. You went back? How many bedrooms again? Well, that's great, honey." She said it with barely concealed dread.

There was a lengthy silence, in which she did nothing except

listen and tap her foot on the hardwood floor. It hadn't occurred to me until that moment that she would seriously consider moving out of the city. I felt rage and loneliness, a
dangerous combination. But what about Heather? How dare
she, once again, need me less—and now, when she should have
needed me more?

I followed her into the kitchen after she'd hung up the telephone.

"Are you really going to move?" I asked.

Predictably, she shrugged.

"To the country? Where's the house?"

"Katonah."

"What about your practice?"

"I don't know," she said. "I guess I could commute. Or maybe
I'd start a practice out there."

"Just like that?" I asked.

"No. Not just like that. But what would you do if you were me?"

"I'd stay."

"And risk losing Richard?"

"You're not going to lose him."

"You want me to take that chance?"

It was the closest she'd come in ages to a declaration of grief.

"You never talk about David," I said.

"Yes I do."

"Not with me."

"With Sarah," she said.

———

In the middle of the night, I went to look at Sarah sleeping.
There were few sights that gave me so much peace. It had

something to do with the curve of her cheek, the arc of her lashes, the pace of her breaths. I thought about the day that David had died, when I'd watched while Sarah was sleeping and known that I'd have to tell her the news when she woke. She had seen David in her dreams that day. I had seen him in mine just the night before. Where was the difference, I wondered, between memories and heaven? If we were remembering David, I thought, might we literally be keeping him alive?

———

It was August thirty-first. Faint hints of cold air could be felt in the mornings and evenings now; we took our sweaters out. I realized that I was longing for true autumn. I realized I wanted the summer to end.

Edgar and I were due back at school on Monday, September tenth, and Sarah the Monday after that. We had planned to leave on September third, which now seemed, amazingly, too far away. But there was nothing to do but ride out the last days, trying to get as close to my daughter as she'd permit me to get.

———

"Looks like you could use some help there," Dad announced after lunch, as Heather and Sarah and I were just returning to our work.

"No, Dad, we're fine," Heather told him brusquely.

"Heather," I hissed.

"What?"

I waited till he had walked out of the room.

"He just wanted to help," I said.

"He's not a child," she informed me.

"I know, but—"

"He'll just get in the way."

Dad walked back in.

"Looks like you could use some help," he said.

Heather and I both started to laugh, then realized, with dread, that he wasn't joking.

"Dad," I said gently.

"What?"

"You just said that."

"Said what?"

"That it looked like we needed some help."

"Well, it does."

I glared at Heather. The unspoken words were: *Now* will you have some pity?

———

I had forgotten the grace of his doctor's hands. With infinite steadiness, they measured and taped the lines for the black-and-white-checked floor that Sarah had said should be in the hallway. Paintbrush finally in hand, he bent painstakingly over the pattern he'd made and began to fill in the white squares.

"You couldn't have had more carpeting?" he teased Sarah at one point.

"It's not carpeted," she said. "David says it's going to be black-and-white checks."

"Nonsense," Dad said, still bent over his work. "It can be whatever you want it to be."

"David wants it to be black and white," she said.

He looked up at me and put his brush down.

"How long are you going to let this go on?" he asked.

"This isn't the time to discuss it," I said.

"Discuss what?" Sarah said.

"Let's talk furniture," I told her. "What's going to go where?"

"We've got to finish the floors first," she said.

We worked all through that Friday, with Dad helping and Edgar fishing. I had never seen Sarah display such total concentration. She assigned us our tasks, took on her own, and never seemed to falter. She seemed utterly certain that she was doing something for David, building this house according to his instructions, as if his future depended on it.

Watching and listening to her, I began to understand how Heather had been so mesmerized. Part of the spell was, no doubt, simply the allure of creating something: When our mother died, I had learned to crochet, and I'd spent whole weekends doing little except adding row upon row to a blanket. It had been nearly mindless work, but therapeutic and, in its way, highly concrete. Making the dollhouse was like that. But there was more to it, of course. There was the distraction of entering into a myth, and at one point, I found myself asking her, "What does David say we should do for the kitchen walls?"

I wondered why it was so hard for me to make the leap—desperate, perhaps, but still loving—that Heather had managed to make. What was so bad about heaven, anyway? Was it so hard to believe in magic, or was I really upset only because Sarah was finding magic without me?

Late in the afternoon, it rained, and my father covered the white squares with tape and began to paint the black ones. I painted the kitchen walls white, the floor blue. Heather drew striped wallpaper onto the living room walls, and Sarah drew flowers for the walls in the master bedroom.

"Because he always liked the way your bedroom looked at home," she told Heather.

———

"You need to take her to a doctor," my father said to me that night.

"I know, Dad," I said.

"This thing is just not going away," he said.

"I know. And we're going to. But neither is yours."

"Neither is my what?"

"Neither is your thing going away."

"My thing is not a thing," he said.

"How can you be so rational about everyone else's health and so irrational about your own?"

"I'm not being irrational."

"I'll take Sarah to a doctor if I can take you to one, also."

"That's lunacy," he said, which of course it was.

"Tell me you'll let me make an appointment."

He sighed.

"Dad. Do it for me," I said.

"And what's your name again?" he asked me.

"That's not funny."

"I thought it was," he said.

"Will you let me find you a doctor?" I asked.

"I know who the best man is. It's Stanley Lane."

"Then we'll go, when we get back, to Stanley Lane."

He sighed. "I could never abide the man," he said, which I chose to hear as reluctant consent.

———

On Saturday morning, we painted the roof dark gray and let it dry in the sun. Nailing it on was all that was left. It was finally time to furnish the place.

Patiently, Sarah lined up all the things we had brought from the city so long before: the beds and dressers, the armchairs and couches, the tiny stove and the dining room table, the chairs and the desk and shelves. I could tell there would be no kibitzing now, and the three of us—Heather, Dad, and I—sat back in our chairs while Sarah went to work. As she leaned into the dollhouse, I saw only her back and her right arm as it appeared and disappeared, inserting first one piece, then another. She didn't stop to assess her work. It was as though she was putting a puzzle together that she'd put together countless times before.

She stopped only once to turn around.

"I've only got two armchairs," she said.

"You've got a couch too," I pointed out.

"There have to be three armchairs in the living room," she said.

"Why?"

"Because that's how it is."

"Well, how about two armchairs and a couch?" I asked.

"No, it has to be three armchairs," she said, her voice threatening some panic.

I didn't know what to say to her.

"Why don't you just cut out a chair from paper," Heather said, "and put it right down on the floor, in its place. When you're done, we can go into town and see if we can find a real one."

Sarah smiled sunnily. "Okay," she said.

Then she resumed her decorating.

We were all still sitting there, watching, when Richard arrived from the city. He had a blush of bright color on his cheeks, and an aura of well-being about him that I'd not witnessed since David's death. He hugged Heather and Jeffrey, shook Dad's hand and Edgar's, kissed my cheek, then froze when he saw the dollhouse.

"Richard. What is it?" Heather asked him.

Shaking, he pulled from his pocket an envelope in which a stack of Polaroid pictures revealed the house he had found in the country. It had two bedrooms upstairs and one below, a front hall floor covered in black-and-white tiles, and a two-sided living room fireplace, around which a couch and three armchairs were clustered.

Heather looked new in the same way that Richard had looked a few minutes before. What was new about her was hope.

"You told Sarah about the house?" Richard said.

Heather, smiling, shook her head no.

"She must have eavesdropped on our phone call, then."

"Sarah?" I asked, but she was studying the photographs.

Heather pointed out that most of the dollhouse had been constructed before Richard had even found the real one, so

David must have been able to see the future and must have described it to Sarah.

"Why would he get to see the future?" Richard asked Heather furiously.

"Because," she said, "it wouldn't make sense for time to exist in heaven."

On that point, I had to agree with her.

"It's just a coincidence," Richard said, though even he seemed shaken out of his usual, comfortable self.

"Coincidence," Heather repeated, derisive.

"It's not like the layout of either house is all that unusual," Richard said. "And the kitchen is in the wrong place. And the bedrooms are way too big."

"Maybe we just can't explain this," Heather told him, "except with heaven."

"I didn't realize how desperate you were," Richard told her.

"You're being an idiot," she told him.

"You're being pathetic," he said.

Dad said nothing to anyone and merely watched the volley of viewpoints with ever-mounting confusion. Next to Sarah, who seemed completely unfazed by the metaphysical turmoil into which she'd thrown the entire household, I suspected that Dad was the luckiest of us. He simply didn't remember the order in which everything had happened.

———•—•———

"And you?" I asked Edgar that night when the house was finally quiet.

"And me?"

"What do you think?" I asked him.

"I don't think it really matters," he said. "I don't think we're ever going to know. I think that we've got to get help for Sarah, and get her away from these people."

"You mean from my family."

"It's time to go home."

New Year's Eve, 1968

"You Should Have Been More Careful"

We're fifteen. We're so tan that we've already started to peel, but we have three more days of vacation left, three days to bake and fry beneath the rented Caribbean sun.

During the days, we lie side by side at the edge of a glimmering private pool. The water makes changing ovals of light—white and green patches in aqua blue. Above us, the fingers of palm leaves wave. Plates rattle in the kitchen, where the maid is making lunch.

"Can I have the suntan oil?" I ask Heather.

She turns a page in her mystery.

"Heather?" I say.

She does not respond.

"Heather?"

A few feet away from us, a thin black man in khaki shorts lowers a long net into the water and meditatively fishes for dead bugs and errant leaves.

"I'm talking to you," I say to Heather.

"What?"

"Hand me the suntan oil."

"Get it yourself," she says, and rolls over.

The pool man's bare feet move slowly one step forward and one step back, his toes over the side of the pool, his pink soles lifted. The smell is of chlorine, suntan oil, and jasmine. Newts and lizards dart up the trees.

"Want to go for a swim with me?" I ask.

"Go yourself," she tells me.

My parents, who are otherwise only slowly showing signs of life after the loss of their baby, keep asking me about her. They ask what's gotten into Heather as if she is subject to an unending series of demonic possessions.

"Are you mad at me?" I ask her. At fifteen, I view my forthrightness as the virtuous alternative to her secrecy.

"No," she says to her towel-covered chair.

———

At night, we read silently in our room and hear dogs barking down the road and island music drifting over the hills.

———

On New Year's Eve, we stand side by side in the bathroom mirror, looking into each other's reflections. We wear the silk pants and cotton halters we brought because Mom said they'd be just right. We're dressing as if we're going on dates. But down the hall in our rented villa, there's only Mom and Dad, who have spent the year nursing their sorrow and their anger and, occasionally, each other. Dad is enmeshed in his practice again, like a gear inside a clock. Mom worries about the strain on him, his restlessness, even with time off. I suspect that he needs the crises, and that the real strain comes when there's no one to save, no one to make him feel omnipotent.

Heather puts her forearm against my forearm.

"I'm darker," she says.

They're the first words she's spoken to me all day.

We learn it's midnight from a borrowed transistor radio that the maid rustled up in the afternoon. Dad tunes in a staticky station and insists on dancing with all three of us.

My mother goes first. I smile at them, watching, and wondering how bad they really feel. I sympathize like crazy but am furious that they've gone, in one year, from unbeatable to beaten.

When it's my turn, I cannot look up at Dad. I know he is not going to look at me.

When he puts his hand on Heather's back, she winces because of her sunburn.

"You should have been more careful," he tells her.

"So should you," she tells him.

It is unclear whether she's talking about the tiny thing he just did to her back or the big thing he did to Mom.

After the dancing, we play Scrabble. Mom and Dad and I want to play teams, but Heather wants every man for himself.

Mutts, cows, and goats can be heard outside. Inside are newts, salamanders, mosquitoes, and a brown moth the size of my hand. We could catalogue every form of tropical fauna while waiting for Heather to make her move.

"Someday we should play with a timer," Dad says.

I go to the kitchen to get some coffee. When I come back, Heather has still not moved.

Mom goes to the bathroom.

When Mom comes back, Heather has still not moved.

"Heather," Mom says, ten minutes later. "Come on, Heather. It's getting late."

I'm staring at my beige sandals, at the terra-cotta flooring, at the arms of the whirring ceiling fan.

Finally, Heather says, "Got it," and looks triumphant. She lays down the word D-O-O-B-I-E. She gets the D on the double-letter score, and the E on the triple-word score.

"What's *doobie*?" Dad asks.

"It's a word," Heather says.

"What's it mean?" Dad asks.

Heather says: "Three times two is six, and one is seven, eight, nine, ten, eleven times three is thirty-three."

"What's it mean?" Dad asks again.

"Challenge?" Heather asks.

Their eyes lock.

"Challenge," he says. "Where's the dictionary?"

"We didn't bring a dictionary," I say.

"It's a word, George," Mom says.

"Will somebody tell me what it means?"

"I think it has something to do with drugs," Mom says. "Doesn't it, Heather?"

Heather smiles, silent but victorious.

"Doesn't it, Erica?" Mom asks me.

"Yes, Mom," I say, suddenly exhausted.

"What's it mean?" Dad asks me.

"Joint," I say.

"Heather, are you on pot?" Mom asks.

"You don't say, '*on* pot,' Mom," Heather says. "You say, 'Do you *do* pot?' or 'Are you *on* drugs?' "

"Are you on drugs?" Mom asks her.

"No."

She is not on drugs. She is not doing pot. She has simply turned into a lunatic bitch.

"Because you know you can tell us if you are," Mom says.

"I'm not, Mom," Heather says.

Mom looks at Dad. Dad looks at Mom. They're trying to decide if they have the strength.

"So do I get my thirty-three points?" Heather asks.

I lift my tray of letters and let them cascade into the box.

"Erica!" she says, almost shocked.

———

Later on, I go to sleep with the exotic joy of knowing that for once in my life I want to be nowhere near the place where my twin sister is.

Autumn, 1990

"Why Don't You Try Growing Up?"

Edgar sang on the drive home from Lenox, producing a ceaselessly peppy accompaniment to Sarah's insipid traveling tapes: "Do the Hokey Pokey," "Rise and Shine," "If You're Happy and You Know It, Clap Your Hands."

He did.

He sang going over the Triborough Bridge. He sang as he parked the car.

"Daddy's happy," Sarah ventured.

"How can you tell?" I muttered beneath my breath. His sense of freedom was both extravagant and palpable, not at all like his usual back-to-work blues.

I could hardly blame him for delighting in the absence of my family. But he'd never had to love them, and now he didn't have to wish he could. So I seethed and felt sad and torn until the front door opened and I felt my own sense of liberty. Suddenly, there were *our* things, *our* furniture, *our* home. And even amid the odd constriction of city space after country space, I could feel the world expand.

Sarah, too, seemed delighted as she ran into her room to rediscover her toys, books, posters, rug, and bed. I wandered through the rooms with Edgar, turning on lights, opening windows, staring with true affection at the old bottles we'd found long ago and lined up on a living room shelf, with *our* books, *our* albums, the framed photographs of *our* wedding— and, best of all, *our* child.

For dinner, I made the mashed potatoes that Heather hated, with the fried chicken that was too fattening for Richard, and the asparagus that Jeffrey loathed. We sat at our table, ate from our plates, then opened our mail and stacked up our bills. Autonomy suddenly seemed to be an outstanding invention.

Sarah went off to bed and fell asleep without mentioning Heather or David, and though the dollhouse had come back to New York with us, carefully wrapped in a cardboard box, I had a hopeful thought that it might stay that way indefinitely.

Edgar and I sat up talking about the future, about the baby and where we would put the crib, and about how Sarah might make new friends at school. We made love in our bed, underneath our cool sheets, and lay together later, charged by our promise and thrilled by our privacy. Then I turned off our lights and listened to Edgar's breaths grow slow and even. I wondered how long it would take before the sentimental past, with its endless powers of regeneration, would once again outstrip the present. But I knew that I wouldn't call Heather or let her find her way back to Sarah. Or so I told myself.

———

Among the mail I'd opened was a package from Sarah's school. Mixed in with the usual calendars and schedules and the instructions for name tags and extra clothes was the "Tell Us About Your Child" questionnaire. This was the very document that, just a year before, I had filled out with infinite pride and excitement, relishing every question for the opportunity it gave me to explain and promote my child.

Now, while Sarah and Rosie were getting reacquainted the next day, I sat down at the living room desk, pen in hand and defenses ready.

I breezed through the checklists on motor, linguistic, and social skills. Did she know her colors? Check. Body parts? Check. Could she build a tower of five blocks? Check. Was she easily frustrated? No check. Could she hop on one foot? Check. (And what if she couldn't, I wondered, what then? A hurried conference at the principal's office: "It's come to our attention that young Sarah is having difficulty hopping on one foot"?)

But then came the essay question: "Anything else we should know?"

"As you're aware," I began in my best schoolteacher handwriting, "Sarah's cousin David died last February. In the months that have passed since then, she has—"

I stared at what I had written.

She has what, I asked myself. Has missed him painfully? Has been talking to him in heaven? Has become a little eccentric? Has gone stark raving mad?

"Has developed a bit of a problem," I wrote, guffawing inwardly.

"She has become convinced that she can talk to David in heaven," I continued. "I don't know whether she will bring this conviction into the classroom or not. But I wanted you to know about it. She seems quite fine in other ways."

From the next room, I heard the squeal and giggle of Sarah being tickled by Rosie, but I felt a sudden and altogether new preference for my unborn child. I longed for all the little problems that I'd tortured myself through with Sarah—the easy simplicity of feeding, sleeping, and diapers; the absence of tragedy; the absence of memory; the time of early mother-hood when stamina and anticipation are sufficient in them-selves.

"One other thing," I added to the questionnaire. "I'm ex-pecting another baby in March. I haven't told Sarah yet, and though I'm quite sure she already knows, I intend to have a real talk with her about it when I feel it's safe."

When would that be, I wondered.

———

I called Wilma to make an appointment.

"So," her receptionist said to me, "you got through your first trimester without telling us."

"Next time, I'll ask first," I said.

"Congratulations, honey," she said with genuine, and thus novel, warmth.

———

Rosie's reaction, too, made me realize what I had been missing. She hugged me emphatically, asked when the baby was due, announced that she wanted a boy, and said, "The Lord gives and the Lord takes away. But then sometimes the Lord gives back again."

———

The following Monday morning, Edgar and I got dressed in grown-up clothes and rode the bus together to school. I dropped him off at the history building, where we had a long, unflinching, back-on-campus kiss. I felt the leafy thrill of September renewal, one of the main reasons I knew I would always want to be a teacher.

My boss Bruno, of course, was another, and as I climbed the stairs to the Classics Department, I found myself running a hand through my hair.

"Again?" he asked when he saw me and my just noticeably pregnant profile.

"Again," I said.

"When's it due?" he asked.

"March."

"I assume I'll be arranging for a substitute in the spring."

"Yes."

We stared at each other with mutual but edgy fondness. I felt downright bouncy.

———————

Classes weren't beginning for another two weeks. In the meantime, there were a hundred administrative details to take care of. My office had been painted over the summer, so there were things to put up and put away. Bruno parceled out section leaders and teaching assistants, so there were schedules and lessons to plan and compare. I checked at the student bookstore to make sure the textbooks I'd ordered were all in stock. I posted my office hours on my door. Then I looked at my notes from the previous year and prepared an opening lecture that I hoped would pack the aisles.

On the home front, I felt similarly revived. I moved the summer clothes to the unreachable parts of our closets and brought the fall clothes forward. I bought new shoes, tights, and turtle-necks for Sarah, and, remembering the joy of the annual stationery store trip I'd made with my mother, a pencil case with three fat pencils and a bunny-shaped eraser.

Then I took her for her fall checkup.

"Seems great," Joe Worth told me after he'd examined her and I was helping her dress.

"Physically," I said.

We spoke in that telegraphic style that grown-ups so often use to talk about children when they are present.

"I know the rest," he said.

"Heather?"

He nodded.

"Think I should worry?" I asked him.

"Keep an eye out," he said.

"For what?" Sarah chimed in. "For David?"

———

"You know," I told Sarah that night in her bath, "they may not understand about David at school."

She shrugged a Heather shrug.

"Do you know what I mean, sweetie?" I asked her. "They may not understand what you say about how you can talk to him, and all that."

"He's still going to be in heaven, even if they don't think he's there," she said. "Can I wear my flowered pajamas tonight?"

———

It occurred to me that I might add a section on heaven to one of my courses.

"Why heaven?" Bruno asked me when I told him about it on Friday.

"Why not?" I said.

"It won't be in the course catalogue," he said.

"We can put it in next semester," I said. "Let me just play around with it."

"Why heaven?"

"I've been thinking about it a lot," I said.

"Your daughter," he said.

I nodded.

"So that's still going on," he said.

"She built a dollhouse for him this summer."

"A dollhouse?"

"According to his specifications. She says he told her what it should look like."

"Great imagination," he said.

"Bruno," I said. "She built this dollhouse, and it was like an exact model of the house my brother-in-law wants to live in, and she said she knew what it would look like because of what David said."

"So you believe in heaven now?" he asked, his gray eyes twinkling.

What remained of my once-intense crush on Bruno depended on his seeing me as unflappable. Seeing me, say, as Minerva, or as one of the lesser gods.

"Gee, Bruno," I said. "I don't know."

"Harps? Angels? Pearly gates?"

"There's more than one kind of afterlife, isn't there?"

"And that's what you want to teach about?"

"I just got interested, that's all," I said.

I regretted that I'd ever begun the conversation.

"Which course would you add it to?" he asked.

"What?"

"The heaven stuff."

"Creation, I guess."

"Well, let me see notes when you've got them," he said.

I hated it when he wasn't wise.

———

I was still feeling testy two hours later when I walked toward the subway to go downtown and see Wilma.

The bright breezes and sharp air that had signaled autumn when we were in Lenox hadn't yet cooled New York City. In the subway station, the air of a hundred scorched summer days seemed to hang still, trapped and unmoving. My clothes felt tight and my handbag heavy. I sat on a grimy bench to wait.

On the train, the air conditioning made a modest improvement, but four stops down, the subway lurched and then halted, and the lights went out. I closed my eyes in frustration. When I opened them, I saw the express train moving across the tracks, its cars, as it happened, numbered like years: 1962, 1844, 1973. I stared in fascination as our lights came back on and we started to move and we left the numbered past in our wake.

———

While Wilma examined me, I told her about the bleeding and the two sonograms. She asked me to set up another but said there was nothing to worry about.

She took out the special monitor, and I heard the beating

heart of my child, the pulse of a life, the tick of a new clock. My eyes filled with sudden tears.

"Your due date is March twenty-fifth," Wilma said.

"I know," I said.

"Maybe by then Heather will be pregnant too."

"Heather?" I asked her stupidly.

I watched her face grow tight.

"Have you seen Heather?" I asked her.

She looked away.

"Wilma," I said.

"I shouldn't have said anything," she said, sighing. "I just figured you had to know."

"She's going to try to get pregnant again?" I asked.

"Her surgery's scheduled."

"When?"

"For next month."

"And can you really reverse it?" I said.

"Nothing's impossible."

"You are a bitch!" I screamed into the phone that night.

Heather hung up on me.

Close to eleven, she called me back.

"I'm *sorry*," she said. But I knew she was smiling.

"When were you going to tell me?" I asked her. "On the day the kid was *born*?"

"I'm sorry. I've been busy," she said. "How's Edgar? How's Sarah?"

"Why didn't you tell me?" I asked her.

"I don't know. I guess I wanted to make you mad."

"And why did you want to make me mad?"

There was a lengthy silence.

"Heather? Why did you want to make me mad?"

"Because you've got something I want," she said.

I waited awhile myself before speaking.

"Sarah," I said.

"Yes. Sarah," she said.

Well, that's just too damned bad, I thought.

What I said was: "She's starting school on Monday. I want her to concentrate on that."

———

Sarah's new teachers were Terri and Elaine. On Monday morning, I searched their faces for signs of celestial understanding. Nothing was immediately apparent except an abundance of perkiness.

"The separation period is very hard for most of the children," Elaine whispered to me in a hurried aside. "We read what you wrote in your questionnaire, and we want to make sure that Sarah doesn't make it harder than it has to be."

"Harder?" I repeated stupidly.

"Because of her . . . problem," she said.

"Of course," I answered grimly, not knowing if I felt more anger or shame.

Inside the nursery school classroom was an extra set of tiny chairs, lined up for the parents to sit on so that, at least on the first day, our children would see that they'd not been abandoned.

The year before, I had watched the other mothers swapping

names and family histories as they'd searched for potential play dates in a strange maternal mating dance. Meanwhile, I had been sitting with Heather, ensconced in our smug self-sufficiency, outwardly griping about all the wasted hours, inwardly savoring our contact.

Now, of course, everything had changed. With no David and no Heather, I eyed the mothers hungrily, shook hands, and introduced myself. There were nine of them in all, and only one was familiar from the year before. As luck had it, she was Nancy Weiss, mother of the dreaded Judy, who'd squealed after Sarah's party.

That left eight—eight women who could never be Heather, whose children could never be David.

We would see one another every morning for a week, furtively comparing our children to one another's, finding things to envy and things to be grateful for. The year before, there had been one mother-and-daughter team in Sarah and David's class who had been placed there, I was convinced, solely to make the rest of us feel better by comparison. The daughter had been named Alexa, and the mother Alexis, and that had been just the tip of the iceberg. From virtually the first day of school till the last, Alexa had hit, bitten, scratched, and grabbed. She had whined constantly, and her mother had too, as she'd tried to explain the behavior and pleaded with the teachers to understand.

As the ten of us sat in our tiny chairs and looked out at our children painting pictures and getting to know the hamsters, I wondered what had become of Alexa, and which child would be the Alexa of this class. Then I saw that Sarah had painted a starry sky above a tall chair with long legs, and it dawned on me that this year's Alexa might very well be Sarah.

———

On the second day, the small chairs were moved out into the hall. By unspoken agreement, the mothers whose children were having the hardest time without them sat closest to the classroom door. On either side of this knot of nerves and embarrassment sat the rest of us, reading papers, doing needlepoint, sipping coffee, and trying not to look as if we felt superior. One mother paced the hallway, doing business on a cellular phone. Occasionally, she would stop at the open door, where her daughter would see her and try to come out. I made more clandestine spying excursions myself, and I realized angrily that I was worrying less about what Sarah thought of her teachers than about what they thought of her.

She seemed to be perfectly fine, if quiet. Already, signs of friendship seemed to be showing among some of the other children: tentative exchanges of blocks and trains, eager offers of make-believe pancakes. By contrast, Sarah glanced up in distracted confusion every time one of the others offered to share in something that she was doing. She wasn't mean or bratty, but she always, and sadly, shook her head no.

Nancy Weiss, whom I'd been cruelly happy to see in one of the trouble chairs next to the door, came my way to get some coffee.

We exchanged falsely pleasant greetings.

"I saw your sister at Judy's fall checkup," she said.

I nodded.

"She said Sarah's still convinced that she's talking to her cousin."

"Heather told you that?"

Nancy said: "I asked her."

"Well, it's true," I said. "It's still going on."

"That must be just dreadful for you," she exhaled.

"I think it's worse for Sarah," I said.

———

By Friday, the mothers had been freed to sit down the hall in the teachers' lounge, where we awaited further instructions.

We were sprung at ten o'clock and told we could leave the building briefly. A mother named Joanie Rothman asked if I wanted to go for coffee. The maternal equivalent of a pass.

We went to a coffee bar on Columbus Avenue and sat on high stools that reminded me of heaven but were a pleasure after the truncated nursery school furniture.

It turned out that Joanie had four children, of whom Sarah's new classmate, Leah, was the youngest. Joanie seemed calm, though, and nice enough. She had a wry, worn smile. She was older than I was by ten years, and I found that reassuring.

So we chatted about the school and ventured, first gently, then brazenly, into the more enjoyable arena of sizing up the other mothers and children.

"And I understand," Joanie said with a confidential nod, "that there's one child in the class who's basically having a nervous breakdown."

"What?" I said. "You're kidding. At four?"

She nodded. She looked around to make sure there were no spies.

"Apparently, this kid thinks she can talk to her dead cousin."
I smiled at her sympathetically.

"That's my kid," I said. "That's Sarah."

"Oh my God," she said, mortified.

"Sorry."

"Oh God, I'm embarrassed."

"That's okay."

"No."

"Really."

"I just didn't think—"

"You couldn't have known."

"I'm so sorry," Joanie said again.

"David was her best friend," I said. "My twin sister's son. They grew up together."

"How did it happen?" she asked, still aghast.

"A car hit him."

"Oh my God. When?"

"Last February," I said, amazed that it hadn't been longer ago.

"And she—"

"She started telling us that she could talk to him."

"What did you do?"

"I listened to her," I said, wishing that somehow I'd listened harder.

———

Walking back to the school with Joanie, I couldn't tell whether this conversation had forged an instant bond or an instant repulsion. I didn't have long to ponder this, though, because Sarah was not in the classroom when we returned to it.

I found her walking up and down the corridor with Terri.

Sarah was crying for me. I took her in my arms and held her tightly and kissed her neck.

"What happened?" I asked her.

"Judy was mean to me," she gasped between sobs.

I looked up at Terri, who seemed sympathetic but also stern.

"Sarah started talking about her cousin," Terri said. "And Judy was upset by that. So were some of the other children."

"So you sent her out of the *room*?" I asked, a bit too edgily.

"No," Terri said. "Sarah started missing you."

"I cried for you, Mommy," Sarah said.

"But you knew I'd come back, didn't you?" I said.

She shook her head and sniffled.

"We're just fifteen minutes from the end of the class anyway," Terri said. "Why don't you take her home today?"

———

On Monday, I gave my opening lecture, outwardly trying to inspire and attract, inwardly wondering the whole time what was going on with Sarah.

Rosie, though, reported no woe at the school pickup that afternoon. For the rest of the week, the morning drop-offs went seamlessly, almost sunnily. Sarah seemed eager to say good-bye, so by Friday my guard was totally down when I got a phone call from Terri.

"We'd like to talk to you and your husband," she said.

"You and Elaine?" I asked.

"Yes, Mrs. Ross. And the principal's planning to be there too."

———

They laid it out for us pretty straightforwardly: Sarah was a lovely child, and well-mannered. She showed interest in Play-Doh and building blocks. She poured her own juice at snack time. But throughout these first two weeks, she had been dropping in almost constant mentions of David and of heaven. The explosion with Judy was apparently only one in a series of such disruptions.

"What else has she done?" Edgar asked.

It was late Monday afternoon, the first of October, and Edgar and I were sitting in the classroom for this conference, five grown-ups at a play table, perched once again on tiny chairs. Tissue paper of many colors sat in a basket before us, along with paintbrushes and paper, already laid out for the next day's class. I conquered the urge to start a collage.

"Well, just today," Elaine said, "they were taking turns at the easel, and Sarah told a few of the children how in heaven children make the colors of the sunset by dripping their paints into the sky."

Arts and Crafts, I thought fondly, and remembered my dream of David.

"What's so harmful about that?" I asked.

Elaine raised an eyebrow.

Mrs. Murphy, the principal, cleared her throat. "Such fantasies can be very troubling," she said.

"We tell them about Santa Claus, don't we?" I asked.

"Some parents do."

"And we tell them about the Easter Bunny."

"I don't think those examples are quite germane," Mrs. Murphy said. "These are really quite morbid thoughts."

"They play dress-up here, don't they?" I asked, pointing to a trunk filled with cast-off clothes.

"Erica," Edgar said, putting a hand on my hand. I sensed in myself the possibility of an outburst so intense that we might spend the whole year trying to live it down.

"Mrs. Ross," the principal said. "We're simply saying your daughter may need some help."

———

Dr. Koenig was booked until the ninth of October.

"Where *are* all these messed-up kids?" I asked Edgar.

"Not in her classroom," he said darkly.

There, we had been told, the school psychologist would be joining Sarah's class as an observer.

"Looking for what?" I asked Mrs. Murphy over the phone Tuesday night.

"Looking for signs of her progress. And the class's progress," the principal said.

"And listening for complaints from other parents?" I asked, giving voice to the suspicion that I had hammered away at with Edgar all night.

"My concern," Mrs. Murphy said with grand and evasive certainty, "is the welfare of *all* the children."

———

Dad called that same evening to say that he didn't know what had happened between Heather and me but that he wanted us all together for his birthday, which was three days away.

"What happened," I told him, "is that Heather spent the whole damned summer encouraging Sarah to think she could talk to David."

Dad laughed lightheartedly, as if I'd just said something winsome.

"It's not funny, Dad," I said.

"But it's not really true, is it?" he asked.

"Dad. You were there," I told him.

"Yes."

"Didn't you see what she was doing? Didn't you hear what was going on?"

"What?"

"Dad! The dollhouse. That whole thing was meant for David. Heather did nothing to contradict her. She *helped* her," I said.

"Helped her what?"

"Helped her build the dollhouse. And believe she could talk to David." I made my voice acid. "Don't you remember?"

"Of course I remember," he said.

"Well?"

"Well," he said with ancient sternness. "Imagine how you'd feel if you'd lost Sarah and your marriage was on the rocks. I'd think you could show a little more tolerance, Erica, frankly."

———

Heather called a few minutes later. "What are we doing for Dad's birthday?" she asked.

"You never remember Dad's birthday," I said.

"Well, I remembered it this year. It's October fifth. Friday, right?"

"Right."

"So?"

"I don't know."

"Maybe we all should have dinner together," she said.

"Richard too?"

"Of course," she said.

"Are things—"

"Things are fine," she snapped, then instantly softened. "I think things are fine," she added.

"Well, I've got to ask Rosie if she can sit," I said.

"No," Heather said. "Let's not go out. How about here? Or at your house?"

"Why?"

"I don't know."

Of course she knew.

"He'd probably prefer to go out," I said.

"Then Jeffrey and Sarah won't get to see him," she said.

"And you won't get to see Sarah," I said.

"What's wrong with me wanting to see my niece?"

"You tell me," I told her.

"What do you think I'm going to do to her?"

"What do you think you've done to her?"

"What are you—like thirteen?" she asked me.

———·———

I told Sarah about the birthday plans later that night, expecting her to ask what kind of cake we were having, or perhaps if we could buy balloons. Silly me.

"Who's coming other than Grandpa?" she asked.

"Everyone."

"Is Aunt Heather coming?"

"Yes."

"I want to take out the dollhouse," she said.

"Not now," I said.

"I want to take out the dollhouse," she repeated, her voice dancing on the edge of a whine.

"Sarah," I said in my best warning tone.

"Pleeease," she said. A true whine now.

"No."

"Mommee!"

"Stop!" I shouted.

"I want it! Please! I want it!"

"Stop! That's it!" I said.

"I'm sorry, Mommy." Timid now.

"Go to your room."

"But—"

"Go to your room."

"But—"

"Go to your room this instant!" I bellowed, my anger scaring even me.

I had not lost my temper often with Sarah, partly because of her natural sweetness, partly because of my self-imposed sweetness—the unbending wish to be better and calmer at motherhood than Heather was.

Often before David's death, I had watched Heather go to extremes with the boys: her roaring voice, so much like Dad's; her Green Giant stance as she towered above them; their faces, with the smashed-up smiles that would have seemed no more smashed up by physical blows.

Often, seeing the look in my eye—no doubt a mixture of fear and rebuke—she had said, "Just wait. Wait till you have two." Or: "Wait till you have to deal with a boy."

I had loathed both these excuses of hers, and the imperious wall they had built around her. She had always had a reason for her job being harder than mine. That had made me only more set on being unflappable with Sarah; if possible, serene.

Now, hearing her cry in her bedroom, I recognized in myself a store of anger so deep that it made me shake.

I hated her at that moment, hated her damned dollhouse and the shape of her mourning. I hated how odd and abnormal she seemed, and the fact that her precious intelligence and sensitivity, which I had honored and loved so richly and so long, were now twisting her life up, and ours along with it.

"Mommeee!" I heard her call, a screeching, forlorn bird perched on the rock of her flowered bed.

"Quiet!" I shouted.

"Mommeee!"

I slammed my fist on the kitchen counter. I stormed into the laundry room, where the dollhouse, still in its cardboard box, had been stowed a month before. I picked up the box, marched to the back door, swung it open, and dumped the box outside.

"Mommeee!" my lonely, bizarre bird called. I heard her jump down from her bed and start walking.

"Don't you *dare* come in here!" I shouted.

Her footsteps stopped and then retreated. Along with them went my rage.

———•———

The box had a single, small dent in its side. I picked it up quickly and brought it back, returning it to its hiding place, where I believed, upon second and third thoughts, that its presence would cause less damage than its absence.

———·———

Heather called back later that night.

"What should we do for a cake?" she asked.

"Let me guess," I said. "You have an idea."

"How about if Sarah and I bake one?"

"Yeah? When?"

"I can get out of here by five on Friday," she said.

"I'll be stuck in a staff meeting," I said.

"All the more reason why you'll need my help."

"I don't know where Sarah will be," I said. "She may have a play date," I added, wishing fervently that this was the case.

"I'll set it up with Rosie," Heather said.

"I don't think we've got cake ingredients," I said, my last hope, and a fairly desperate one.

"Erica," she said. "We can shop, you know."

———·———

"Why'd you say yes?" Edgar asked that night when we were finally in bed.

"Edgar. She's my sister. It's my dad's birthday. What would you do?"

"You shouldn't have let her," he said, the last words I heard before falling asleep, and the perfect crowning touch to the day.

———·———

I came home Friday evening expecting the worst. But the doll-house was still concealed in the laundry room; a cake had been baked; the mess had been almost completely cleaned; the table had been set. A trio of sunny hellos greeted me as I walked in the door, and Sarah, Heather, and Jeffrey offered to let me lick the bowl. I tried not to watch Heather too hard, or to appear too suspicious, but as well as I knew her, I couldn't fathom what she felt or wanted. I stared at her too closely, braced for sudden moves. I felt as if we were playing out the old Marx Brothers routine: identical on either side of a large pretend mirror that was just open space. She wasn't me. I wasn't she. We moved in a seeming reflection. But I waited for the surprise.

"Make a wish!" Sarah and Jeffrey shouted at Dad when, at nine that night, Heather at last brought out the birthday cake.

Dad put his dry lips together and blew out the candle viciously.

"Why is there only one candle?" Sarah asked.

"Because," Dad told her, "I'm too damned old."

"David says in heaven you can be any age you want," Sarah said.

I expected him to dismiss her, but he turned toward her kindly instead.

"Is that so?" he asked her gently.

"You do it in Arts and Crafts," she said. "They give you beads to play with."

"Bees?"

"*Beads,* Grandpa," she said with a giggle.

His eyes grew merry. "What do they do with these bees?" he asked her.

"*Beads.* There's a separate room, just for the beads, and they're all in a big, low thing like a blow-up pool, only it's filled with beads, not water. They're all different colors, too, not just red and orange and yellow and blue and green, but there's gold and silver. And pink, too."

The way she said it made pink seem transcendent.

Again, my father surprised me. "I've missed this since Lenox," he said.

"You don't have to," I told him.

"Maybe I'll start coming Sundays again," he said.

"We'd love it," I told Dad, reaching an arm out to encircle Edgar's waist, which turned out to be halfway across the room.

Was it possible, I wondered, that Dad was finally figuring out that his grandchildren *were* his beloved future? Or was he actually starting to think Sarah knew a more direct path toward his immortality?

Dad turned back to Sarah with seemingly sincere interest. "So, tell me," he said to her. "What do you do with these beads?"

"You string them up into a necklace," she said, "so however many beads you put on the necklace, that's how old you get to be. How old would you want to be?"

"Your age," he said.

She giggled again. "That wouldn't be lots," she said.

Dad said: "Who wants to help me cut the cake?"

"I do!" Sarah shouted.

"I do!" Jeffrey said.

"Anyone for coffee?" Edgar asked from the door of the kitchen.

He got a duet of no thank yous.

———

Ten minutes later, Dad ambled into the kitchen, where Edgar and I were still cleaning up.

"What does a guy have to do to get a cup of coffee around here?" he asked.

"Dad, Edgar just asked you—" I began.

"No problem," Edgar quickly said.

————

I took Heather into the bedroom after I'd given Dad his coffee.

"What?" she said impatiently.

"He's not any better, Heather," I said.

"Who?"

"*Dad.*"

She sighed.

"Heather, he just asked me for coffee."

"So?"

"So two minutes ago, Edgar asked you two if you wanted any, and he said no, and now he's acting as if we never asked him in the first place."

"So make the appointment," she said. "Who's stopping you?"

"No one's stopping me," I said. "No one's helping me, either."

"This is a telephone," she said acidly, picking up the one on my night table and depositing it on the bedcovers.

"*Great,*" I said, my voice rising.

"Use it," she said.

"Why, when he has two children, am I the only one who's acting like—like—"

"A child?" she asked.

"Oh, screw you, Heather," I said.

"Shh," she said. "Sarah."

"What about Sarah?" I hissed.

"You don't want her to hear us fighting, do you?"

"Why not?"

"It would really upset her," she said.

"Why don't you worry a little more about your father, and a little less about my daughter?"

"Meaning?"

"Why don't you try remembering that she is my daughter, not yours?"

"Why don't you try growing up?"

"Oh, fuck you, Heather," I said, then grimly realized, by her triumphant expression, exactly who was standing behind me.

"Why are you shouting, Mommy?" the sweet voice said.

I turned to face her.

"Because I'm angry at Aunt Heather," I said.

"Why are you angry?"

"It's hard to explain."

"Your mommy is angry," Heather said with just the perfect ratio of sweetness to grief, "because she doesn't think I should spend as much time with you as I do."

"Heather!" I said, sincerely appalled.

Sarah looked to Heather and back to me, her eyes, instantly, as moist as a newborn's.

"That's not true, Sarah," I said.

"It is! It is true!" she shouted.

"Sarah."

"Why are you so mean to Aunt Heather?" she sobbed, and then ran out of the room.

Richard never showed. He called at ten o'clock from work to wish Dad a happy birthday and to tell Heather that their bid on the house had been accepted.

Hearing this, Sarah again burst into tears.

"What's wrong with her?" Dad asked, befuddled—almost insulted, it seemed—by her rapid transformation.

"What is it, Sarah?" I asked her.

She was walking in circles, crying.

"I don't want Aunt Heather to go!" she wailed.

"Come here, Sarah," Heather said, before I could get the words out myself.

Heather circled her with one arm from behind and started whispering to her. Sarah stood, listening, her eyes fixed on the carpet as if Heather's words were appearing there.

After a hesitant moment, Jeffrey kicked the rug, then looked on with unconcealed annoyance.

Mine wasn't much better hidden.

"Sarah," I said to her sternly. "Come on. It's time for bed."

———

Edgar and I woke the next morning to a Saturday that loomed large and long without playmates or play dates for Sarah.

"She's got to make some friends," I told Edgar.

"She will," he said.

Sarah stumbled in, sleepy, surprising us.

"Me?" she asked, climbing into our bed.

"You what?" I said, kissing the back of her neck.

"I will what?" she said.

"Make friends," I told her.

"I love Aunt Heather," she said.

We took her to the Children's Museum. There, in the basement, swarms of healthy children wrangled ceaselessly over
blocks in the block pile, and vegetables in the pretend market,
and buckets in the sand pile. Sarah surveyed the chaos and
opted to wait her turn for the wooden taxicab, the one spot in
the whole place where a child could be alone.

She turned the wheel and grinned happily.

"Oh, taxi!" Edgar shouted, waving his hand.

"Off duty," she said to him curtly, and pretended to drive on.

"Where are you heading?" he asked her.

"Aunt Heather's house."

In the cab going back home, Sarah pressed her small hand onto
the window and watched her fingerprints mark it, then fade. She
did this again and again. She didn't say anything, but I couldn't
helping thinking that she was baffled by the way those marks
disappeared. Like me, I thought, she was drawn to the question
of what could exist and then be forgotten. I watched her trying
to make the fingerprints stay. It didn't make sense when something one knew and had seen left no trace of its history.

"You know," she said to me while I was bathing her that night,
"Aunt Heather has to move."

"What do you mean?" I asked her.

"Aunt Heather has to move to the house, or else David won't
come back."

"So you're not upset about Heather leaving anymore?" I asked.

"It's the only way," she said.

I sighed.

"And we have to finish the dollhouse for him, or else he won't come back."

"What?" I said stupidly.

"Remember. You have to make something for the people so they can come back."

"You finished the dollhouse," I told her.

"No."

"You did. In Lenox. I helped."

"No, Mommy. He says it still needs more furniture. And lights. And flowers in the flower boxes."

"There are no flower boxes," I said.

"We have to build them, Mommy," she said.

"Tell me who's in your class at school."

Sarah's eyes narrowed just like Heather's. "Mommy," she said. "Don't you *want* David to come back?"

I didn't answer her, and I didn't try all that hard to keep the shampoo out of her eyes.

———

I dreamed that night that I was giving birth. A ring of white-gowned women made a necklace around me, with Edgar the clasp at the back of my neck.

I heard the voices I'd heard long ago: "Come on, Erica, come on, come on, come on, sweetheart, you can do it, hold it, hold it, hold it, don't let up, don't let up."

And then, from Wilma: "I see her."

And from the nurse: "She's got her aunt's hair."

I wanted to reach for the baby, but I couldn't move my arms or speak. I tried to turn around and tell Edgar, but I couldn't do that either.

Then I was standing next to the lake in Lenox, watching a figure swim toward me. I knew, in the dream, that this figure was my child. And I waded into the water to meet her. I met her, and she was David. In the water, I cradled him in my arms, where he turned from a child into an infant. Then I was kicking madly with my feet, trying to stay afloat in the water, with arms too full to steer us to safety. I woke drenched in sweat and relief.

Later, while I was helping Sarah dress, I told her that I was pregnant, that she would have a sister or brother.

"A sister," she said with cosmic wisdom, but then she put her right shoe on her left foot.

———

Monday morning, as I greeted the other mothers at the school drop-off, I sensed a stiff chill in the air.

"How's everybody?" I asked as we waited for the elevator to take us back down to the lobby.

They seemed to cluster closer together, taking refuge beneath the finger paintings as they let out a tepid chorus of fines and okays.

I scanned their eyes for possible warmth and zeroed in on Joanie.

"How's Leah?" I asked her.

"Oh, fine."

"Looking forward to Halloween?" I asked.

She nodded.

"What's she going as?"

Joanie looked around uncomfortably. I flashed an encouraging smile.

"She's going as a ghost," she said apologetically.

The elevator came. We stepped in. Two of the mothers were whispering. It was utterly plain to me that I was indeed now The Mother of *That* Child.

"Well, at least it's an easy costume to make," I said.

She smiled. The elevator doors opened, and as we stepped out, I touched her elbow.

"How about a play date for Leah and Sarah?" I asked her.

"Oh, that would be lovely," she said, smiling warmly at the bridge of my nose.

"When?" I asked, aiming for her eyes.

"You know what? I don't have my book today," she said.

"Well, I'll ask you tomorrow," I said with the lightest tone that I'd ever used to make a threat.

"Terrific," she said. "See you later," she said, and turned left as I turned right.

How could I expect making friends to be easy for Sarah when it was so hard for me?

———•———

Relief finally came the next day in the unlikely form of Dr. Rachel Koenig.

I took the subway downtown from school and walked into the apartment, where I found Rosie and Sarah in the midst of a game of hide-and-seek.

I had left a note for Rosie saying that I'd be taking Sarah to the doctor and not to take her to the park.

"She seems fine to me," Rosie said as I handed Sarah her jacket to leave.

"It's—it's not that kind of doctor," I told her.

She looked first confused, then mildly alarmed.

"Come on, sweetheart," I told Sarah.

In the elevator, she reached for my hand, a gesture I'd always found supremely touching.

"What kind of a doctor is it, Mommy?" she asked.

"A talking doctor," I said.

"A talking doctor?"

"A doctor you talk to."

"I talk to Dr. Worth," she said.

"I know you do," I said. "This is a different kind of talking."

"What kind of talking is it?"

"It's talking about whatever's on your mind. You'll see, when we get there," I said.

We were out on the street, and two blocks away, when she said, "I don't want to go there."

"Give it a chance," I said. "You may like it."

"What's his name?" she asked me suspiciously.

"This doctor is a woman," I said.

Her eyes brightened.

"Like Aunt Heather is a doctor?" she asked.

"Yes," I said. "Like Aunt Heather is a doctor."

———————

We sat together in the tiny, stifling anteroom where Edgar and I had waited to meet Dr. Koenig almost five months before. The door to her inner sanctum was closed now, but from behind it, I could hear occasional laughter and, at one point, what seemed like a shriek of delight. I looked encouragingly at Sarah, but she was captivated by a copy of *Highlights,* that magical staple of all children's doctors, the one in which things that were wrong with this picture were possible to see and to circle. In real life, I didn't know whether I would have put a circle around Sarah, or Heather, or me, or all three. But I was at last delighted by the prospect of handing the pen off to other, more practiced, hands.

Those hands, however, didn't open the office door until seven minutes past the hour, and then only to let a patient out. Then the door closed again, eclipsing a Cheshire cat–like smile. The patient, a ten- or eleven-year-old girl, sat down beside Sarah with total composure, presumably to wait for her grown-up. Sarah sidled over to me and whispered, "This is for *really* big kids."

"No, sweetie," I said. "It's for you too."

———

Five minutes later, Dr. Koenig opened the door again, revealing the full, dazzling force of her smile.

"Hello, Sarah," she said. "I'm Rachel Koenig."

"I have a friend at school named Rachel," Sarah said without hesitation, "except I don't know if she's really my friend or not."

If my daughter had just transformed herself into a troll—or, for that matter, an actual bridge—I would not have been more surprised.

"What makes you think she's not your friend?" Dr. Koenig

asked, and I didn't get to hear Sarah's answer, because the door closed in my face.

———

Embarrassed, I slid back into my seat. My view of the carpet was interrupted by the casual, rhythmic kicking of the ten-year-old's sneakered feet.

I looked up at her.

"I'm Carrie," she said. "I've been coming here for five years."

"Oh."

"Do you want to know why?"

"Do you want to tell me?"

"Because my parents use me to work out their conflicts with each other," she said.

My eyes must have looked as large as Sarah's.

"It's okay," Carrie continued, "because they're in therapy too."

"That's nice."

She smiled at me condescendingly.

"Is this her first time?" she asked.

"Yes."

"She's very young," Carrie said.

"I know."

"What's wrong with her?"

In light of Carrie's guilelessness, I decided that discretion would be unseemly. "Her cousin died," I said.

"That's rough."

I nodded.

"My mom's late," she noted.

I nodded again.

"I'm pretty sure that means something," she said.

"Maybe there's a lot of traffic," I suggested.

She shook her head, but sunnily. "She's usually late," she told me.

Her feet started to kick again.

"Tell me something, Carrie," I said. "Do your mom and dad know what you talk about with Dr. Koenig?"

She smiled with impish glee.

"Do they?" I asked again.

After another silence, she relented.

"Sometimes," she said. "But I usually don't tell them. But I think my mom used to listen at the door."

In the ensuing silence, I leaned toward the door but couldn't make out a single word.

Carrie leaned closer to me.

"There's a switch in the coat closet that controls the heater in here," she whispered.

I followed her glance in that direction.

"When it's on, you can't hear anything," she said. "When it's off, you can hear pretty much everything."

"And Dr. Koenig—" I began.

"I don't think she's figured it out," Carrie said.

The front office door finally opened, and Carrie's mother, looking harried, stepped in.

"Hello, sweetikins," she said, and kissed Carrie's head above unseen but rolling eyes.

———•———

Dr. Koenig called me in before the hour was up, and Sarah waited in the anteroom.

The doctor looked at me for what seemed like a too-long, too-analytical minute.

"Well?" I finally said.

"Well?" she repeated.

"Well, how did it go?" I asked her.

"Let's get a few ground rules straight," she said. "Of course I'll keep you apprised of Sarah's overall progress, but you have to understand that, even at Sarah's age, some semblance of doctor-patient confidentiality is essential."

"Why?"

"Because I have to be able to tell Sarah that she can trust me to tell me anything."

"But—"

"Even things about you."

I exhaled. "I see," I said. "Well, can you tell me how she is?"

I noticed for the first time that the carpet next to Dr. Koenig's desk was strewn with small toy figures and that behind them, near the windows, were two large, shallow wooden boxes—almost like drawers—with a number of dividing walls in them and numerous bits of dollhouse furniture.

"What are those?" I asked in horror, not waiting for her answer about Sarah.

"Those are our playacting environments," she said.

"They look like a dollhouse," I said.

"Exactly," she said. "The children use them to work out their feelings and—"

"But do you know about Sarah's dollhouse?" I asked.

She nodded.

"So—"

"Mrs. Ross," Dr. Koenig said.

"Erica."

"Erica," she said. "Your daughter is troubled."

"I know that."

"She needs help."

"I know that. That's why we're here. But one of her troubles is that she's spent her whole damned summer building a dollhouse with my sister for her dead cousin. To see another dollhouse here, it's just—"

Dr. Koenig smiled indulgently.

"Is it the fact she built a dollhouse that upsets you? Or the fact that she built it with your sister?"

"What do you mean?"

"What did *you* mean?" she said.

Oh, I thought. So *this* is therapy.

"I didn't think it was terribly healthy for Sarah's best friends to be a dead boy and his mother," I said.

"Have you and your sister always competed?" she asked. Her voice was warm, but her eyes were steel.

"Heather only seems to encourage her acting out all this stuff about David," I said.

"Acting out?" Dr. Koenig asked me.

"Yes."

"And what bothers you about that?"

"I think Heather's helping make it more real. I think Heather really believes it now too. Or at least I know she wants to. And my dad last week—even he started to act as if David might really be talking to her."

Dr. Koenig reached behind her chair, opened one of the cabinets, and pulled out two small dolls. She held them up.

"When we work here in therapy," she said, "acting things out is exactly what we do."

"I know that," I said.

"And we talk, too, sometimes, about imaginary friends."

"Yes. I know," I said.

"You need to be patient," Dr. Koenig told me with a patient smile.

"I know."

"And not take out your frustrations with your sister on Sarah."

"So you think it's all right if Sarah and Heather keep playing with the dollhouse?" I asked.

"What's bothering Sarah is not going to be solved simply by taking away the symptom," she said. "The dollhouse is a symptom. I think in general you can do more damage with a prohibition, especially if it's born of your desire to put your own feelings about your sister before Sarah's."

I felt mortified, and stung, but Dr. Koenig smiled again, as if she'd just told me I had a thread on my shirt.

She stood up.

"I have a thousand questions to ask you," I said, still sitting.

"Of course," she said, moving toward the door.

I stood up.

"But I have another patient waiting," she said. "Feel free to call me anytime. And I'll see you both next week."

She opened the door. Sarah was sitting exactly where we'd left her. No other patient was waiting beside her. She looked up brightly.

"Ready, Mommy?" she said.

"Good-bye, Sarah," Dr. Koenig said. "I'll see you next week, and we'll talk and play some more."

"Okay."

Sarah took my hand, which made me fiercely grateful, and seemed to steer me out the door.

———————

"So what did the doctor say to you?" Edgar asked that night after we'd put Sarah to bed.

"'Lighten up' would probably be a fair summary," I told him.

———————

My own turn in a doctor's office came two days later. The occasion was an amniocentesis. Edgar and I sat with three other couples and heard a lecture on genetics from a tall, jolly woman with too much lipstick and a snag in her stockings whose job it was to tell us about the nature of imperfection.

"Are you worried?" I whispered to Edgar as we waited between slides.

"No. Are you?"

"No."

He glanced at one of the other couples. The husband was clutching his wife's hand and stroking the hair on her bowed head.

"Maybe we should be," Edgar whispered.

I thought about that.

"Why aren't we?" Edgar asked me.

"Because," I said, surprising myself, "I feel like if there was something wrong, David would have told Sarah about it."

He looked at me, alarmed.

"This is the lightened-up version," I said.

I didn't watch the needle go in. I looked at the sonogram screen, where our child, as if on cue, stretched an arm out and brought a thumb mouthward to suck.

"Can you tell if it's a boy or a girl?" I asked the technician.

"No. Can you?" she asked brightly.

The baby's legs were crossed.

I had been told to take the afternoon off, and to drink a glass of wine.

I did not foresee a problem.

Sarah was still at school when Edgar dropped me at home, and Rosie would not be in until 3:30, when she brought Sarah back.

I stripped off my clothes, with their vestiges of sonogram conductivity jelly, and walked, pregnant and naked, to the kitchen. I made myself a grilled cheese sandwich and poured myself a tall glass of white wine.

October sunlight had already warmed the bed. I slid in between the sheets and did the most taboo thing I could think of: I ate and drank in bed and watched TV. I watched sitcoms. I watched soap operas. I watched the custody hearing for an adopted four-year-old boy whose biological parents were trying to reclaim him after a two-year absence. I watched, utterly riveted, a talk show called "My Sister Stole My Man."

After four months of abstaining, I found the wine as powerful as the solitude, and I became slightly drunk on both. I recalled that solitude was a state I'd occasionally enjoyed. Lying down with one child at school and another inside me, I allowed myself the illusion that I could still be alone.

Late in the afternoon, Sarah climbed into bed beside me.

She stroked the hair away from my forehead. I was thrilled by the sweetness of her touch and realized how much I was missing it.

"I'm making you pretty," she told me.

"Thanks."

"Why are you in bed, Mommy?"

"Because I had a test today to make sure the baby was healthy," I said. "And the doctor told me to rest."

"I want to go up to the roof," she said.

A stunning development, I thought: a desire to be outdoors, to do something healthy, to get fresh air. One part of our building's roof was decked with flowers and herbs and patio furniture. We'd gone up there a lot when Sarah was little: two parents in search of an urban backyard.

"Great," I told her. "I'll take you tomorrow."

"I need to go now," she said sternly.

"I can't take you now," I told her.

"But I need to go now. Because David says he'll have window boxes in his house."

"What?"

"I need to pick flowers for him," she said.

"Not now."

"But Mommy."

"Not now," I said. "You want the new baby to be healthy, don't you?"

She nodded unemphatically, and I fought down a somewhat tipsy urge to ask if she had any idea who this baby was going to be.

———·———

That night, I lay in bed, reading my calendar as if contemplating a rune. It was a week until I could start worrying about the amnio results. It was nine days until Heather and I turned thirty-seven. It was three weeks until Halloween. It was twenty-three weeks until my due date. What all this meant, I had no idea, except that for once I found myself certain that peace lay in the future.

———·———

Dad showed up on Sunday, as he'd promised to on his birthday, and arrived just in time to see the unveiling.

"Pretty good piece of work," he said as Heather and Sarah collapsed the cardboard box that had concealed the dollhouse. "Where are you going to put it, Erica?"

"Where?" I asked back glumly.

"Let's put it on the trunk," Sarah said.

"You mean where you play with your kitchen?" I asked her. She nodded.

I was about to say, But you love playing with that kitchen. I managed a "Fine" instead.

I watched her scurry back into her room and sweep the pots and dishes and cups and plastic fruit into a Lego box. Redundant, I watched further as Dad and Heather brought in the dollhouse, placed it ceremoniously on top of the trunk, and pulled up chairs around it.

———

"I cannot believe you are letting this happen," Edgar hissed at me in a kitchen conference.

"I told you Dr. Koenig said to lighten up."

"I thought that meant about Sarah," he said.

"It did. But it meant about Heather too."

"The doctor doesn't even know Heather," he said. "She doesn't know what she's capable of."

"My sister is not the Hound from Hell," I said without a whole lot of conviction.

Edgar raised an eyebrow.

———

Our misgivings seemed confirmed that night, when Sarah woke up screaming. Edgar and I rushed into her bedroom, to find her sitting straight up, her eyes wide open in seeming terror.

"Sarah," I said, lifting her up in my arms. Her hair was moist and matted with sweat. "Sarah," I said. "What is it?"

She had stopped crying, but she didn't answer.

Edgar said: "Honey, what happened?"

She looked at neither of us. She said: "I like the blue ones, with the gold dots and sparkles."

"Sarah," I said. I shook her.

She said: "The sparkles," and closed her eyes, and sighed, and fell back into sleep.

———

The next morning, as usual, I dropped her at school.

She hesitated at the doorway.

"What's wrong?" I asked.

"I'm sad," she said.

"Why are you sad?"

"Because," she said, "you're so mean to Aunt Heather."

"Aunt Heather was mean to me too," I said gently, but probably wrongly. Who knew anymore?

———

That night, it was the same thing: a shocked, lancing sound from Sarah, a surreal alarm in an empty night.

Again, Edgar and I ran in together.

This time, we found Sarah standing in the middle of the living room. At first, I of course thought that she was awake, but she stood completely motionless, and her eyes were again unseeing.

"Sarah," Edgar said the same way I had the night before.

"She's sleeping," I whispered.

He sighed sadly. He lifted her up and carried her gently back into her bedroom.

I kissed her on the forehead, which felt slightly clammy.

"Aunt Heather," she said.

"It's Mommy, sweetheart," I said, and shook her awake.

"What?" she said groggily.

"You were dreaming," I told her.

"I'm tired."

"Go back to sleep," I said.

"I'm tired," she whined. "I want to go with Aunt Heather."

Edgar reached down to tuck her in.

———

At Dr. Koenig's the next day, Carrie's mother picked Carrie up on time, so after they left, I had the full fifty minutes to ponder the ethics of turning off the heater and listening in at the door. I didn't last ten minutes. The controls were indeed in the closet: an elaborate system for cooling and heating. I turned the dial from ten to four, then slunk back to my chair. From a sitting position, I could now hear Dr. Koenig's voice but not Sarah's. I stood up, exhaled, and inched closer.

"Sometimes, I wish Aunt Heather could just live with us all the time," I heard my daughter saying.

I dove into the closet and cranked the heater back up to ten.

———

"How'd it go today?" I asked Sarah as lightly as I could while we were walking home.

"Okay, I guess," she said.

"Do you like Dr. Koenig?"

"Rachel," she said, correcting me.

"Rachel."

"I don't know. I guess."

"What do you do?" I said.

"Play with her dollhouse."

"Is it like your dollhouse?" I asked her.

"No, I made that one with Aunt Heather," she said.

"I know that, sweetheart."

"My dollhouse makes Aunt Heather happy," she said.

"You know you don't have to do it if it doesn't make you happy."

"I like to make her happy."

———

Back in my office that afternoon, I called Dr. Koenig and told her about Sarah's night.

"Dreams and sleepwalking are symptoms," she said.

"I know that."

"Sometimes they're a good sign," she said. "A sign that hidden things are finally coming to the surface."

"But she seemed so, so—"

"What worries you?" Dr. Koenig asked. "That she was having bad dreams, or that she was dreaming about your sister?"

This again, I thought.

"I did let them take out the dollhouse this weekend," I said a bit too defensively. "It's not like I think my sister's the Hound from Hell or something," I added.

"Erica," Dr. Koenig said, "you need to realize that even if David hadn't died, Sarah would still be in the midst of a very difficult developmental stage. She is four and a half years old."

"And?"

"And it's a perfectly normal age for pulling away from one's mother."

"Why?"

"Because of all the Oedipal conflicts. Because of the discoveries of birth and death. Because the imagination is so powerful, but the ability to tell dreams from reality is so weak. If nothing at all had happened to David, your daughter would still be trying to figure out where that baby you're carrying had come from, and why she can't make a baby, and why your husband sleeps with you instead of her, and whether you're going to destroy her if you find out that she wants you to disappear."

"Sarah wants me to disappear?" I asked.

"Heather is the mother without conflicts," Dr. Koenig said. "She's the mother who asks nothing of her, demands nothing of her, never gets angry at her, never punishes her. And never gets her feelings hurt, the way you do. Would you rather that your daughter had no one else to turn to?"

"I'd rather she turned to me," I said.

"If you think this is bad," she said with a laugh, "wait till you have to hold it all together for two whole *years* of her adolescence when she's telling you every day that she hates you."

"I can't wait," I said, and hung up feeling both more confused and more rejected than I had when I'd called.

———

Heather and I had learned envy early, wrangling and fussing over the single presents that foolish givers gave twins. She'd outpleaded me often and mercilessly, preying on my love of peace even while defeating my more childish longings. I could remember a teddy bear that I'd once given up amid equal amounts of tears and hope: tears that I'd lost the teddy bear; hope that when Heather had it, she would be happy and make us both happy.

Now I thought about what Dr. Koenig had said and about

how I'd overreacted. Perhaps, I thought, I'd just lost too many battles when we were children.

As I brooded about this on Thursday night, Heather called with perfectly timed kindness.

"Are you nervous about the amnio?" she asked me.

"A little," I said, amazed she'd remembered that the results were now due any day.

"You know the baby's healthy."

"Deep down, I guess."

"I know you don't want to hear this, but has it occurred to you that Sarah would have said something if the baby wasn't okay?"

"I thought that too," I said quietly.

"You did?"

"I did," I admitted. "But it's just superstition."

"*You* think so," she said.

This was the longest, most pleasant conversation I could remember us having had recently, and I didn't want to ruin it. I didn't answer her.

"What are we doing for our birthday?" she asked.

"I don't know."

"What do you want to do?"

"I don't care," I said. "How about you?"

"I don't care," she said. Stalemate.

———

"The baby's fine," Wilma's nurse told me Friday when she called with the test results.

"No problems?" I asked.

"None at all," she said.

"Boy or girl?"

"You want to know?"

"Of course I do," I said.

I could not imagine not wanting to know anything about my child that someone else knew.

"Wait a minute," she said. I could hear her turning pages. "Well?"

"It's another girl," she said.

So Sarah, I thought—or had it been David?—had been right all along.

—————

I called Edgar. I called Dad. I called Rosie. I called Heather.

Edgar said: "Oh, honey."

Dad said: "That's great, sweetheart."

Rosie said: "Sarah knew that, you know."

Heather said: "Fantastic!"

"I'm glad you're happy," I told her.

"Aren't you?" she said.

"Of course I am."

"Or did you want to have a boy?"

"I wanted a girl. I just didn't want to admit it."

"Sisters," Heather said.

"Sisters," I said.

"God help them."

"You said it."

"It's great."

"I know."

"My surgery's scheduled," she said.

"For when?"

"Next week."

"You'll be fine."

"What do you want for your birthday?" she asked me.

"I just got it. What do you want?"

"To spend time with you and Sarah."

I sighed, trying not to see in my mind a certain unique brown teddy bear as it passed from my hands to Heather's.

"Okay," I said. "See you tomorrow."

"With Sarah?"

"Happy birthday," I said.

———

We met at Dad's place. Heather and Richard and Jeffrey were already there when we showed up. Richard rattled the ice in his Bloody Mary as if he was rattling dice. Jeffrey sulked and pouted beneath a bouquet of pointless balloons.

Dad gave Heather and me matching copies of *Life* magazine from the year of our birth, 1953. I leafed through it over coffee and cake and found an ad for Kodak with the slogan "The children stay young in snapshots." There was a photograph of a mother getting her son ready for school. "Watch him turn his back on babyhood," the caption read. "Another chapter closes in the too-short book of childhood."

I had to wonder if my mother, with newborn twins, had ever had time to read this page, let alone to imagine that childhood would end.

That was thirty-seven years ago. In school, I remembered, you rounded thirty-six down to thirty-five, but you rounded thirty-seven up to forty. Forty loomed like a rock. And yet with

Dad looking foggy and ever more forgetful, I couldn't allow myself the normal dread. I knew that, for him, forty was a luscious and palmy past.

———

Heather had found a remarkable store on the East Side that sold only dollhouse things. It sold dollhouses themselves, of course, dollhouses you could make from kits or buy from the store already made: dollhouses of staggering size and detail—four rooms, five rooms, eight rooms and attic—dollhouses with gabled roofs, balustrades, columns, pillars, working doors. And then, of course, came the furniture: tiny worlds beckoning from behind display glass—Victorian wicker, Colonial wood, dressers with drawers that worked, working lights, pots and pans, miniature versions of soup cans and soap bars.

Confronted with so much magnificence, Sarah did what I wanted to do: She wept. She stood in a corner with Heather and cried her eyes out. Heather said: "Cookie, don't you like it?"

"Ye-es," Sarah managed to get out.

"She likes it all, Heather," I said darkly.

Sarah nodded, sniffling, overwhelmed.

"Well, that's no problem!" Heather said brightly. "It's my birthday. I can get anything we want."

———

On Monday, I took Dad to Dr. Lane's office and sensed in my father the same reluctant courage that I had often witnessed in Sarah when I took her to see Joe Worth.

Dr. Lane looked not a day younger than Dad, which I felt was a double injustice.

"Only five percent of the aged," he said after getting the briefest history from Dad and me, "will ever suffer from a major dementia."

He was smug and cogent and self-satisfied, and I could imagine him loving and counting every one of his healthy brain cells.

"Give me the test," Dad said.

Dr. Lane frowned at the interruption but then agreed. He took out a pristine typed form and began to read.

"I am going to say three words, and I would like you to try to remember them," he said. "The words are *chair, car,* and *tie.* What are the three words?"

Dad looked insulted. "Chair, car, and tie," he said tersely.

"I'll ask you to repeat them a little later," Dr. Lane, continued. "They are, again, *chair, car,* and *tie.*"

I hated him.

"Now," he went on. "What is your date of birth?"

A trick question. In Dad's best days, this could have stumped him. He had always been useless on all birthdays.

"September seventh, 1927," he said quickly.

He was bluffing. The right answer was October fifth, 1917.

Dr. Lane looked at me for confirmation. I wanted to lie but shook my head gently instead and winced when I saw him jot down a note.

"What month are we in right now?" he asked next.

"September. No. October," he said.

"What day of the week is it today?"

Dad scrunched up his face in concentration.

"Monday," he said.

"What is today's date?"

"Monday," he said, and closed his eyes. "October twenty-second."

"What year are we in?"

"It's 1990."

He was batting almost a thousand.

"Where are you right now?"

"I am in hell," he said.

Out of the twenty questions, he wound up missing four in addition to the one about his birthday. He could not count by sevens. He could not remember what he'd had for breakfast. He could not say how a cat and a mouse were alike. And when asked to repeat the three words again, he could remember only *chair.*

The good news: probably not Alzheimer's.

The bad news: probably a series of small strokes.

My lecture that afternoon was supposed to be about the tradition of oral history and the role of the mythic hero. Instead, I found myself speaking, with all-too-private emotion, about the importance of myth in our daily lives.

"In real life," I said, "mythic figures have been known to lose their mythic attributes and suddenly reveal themselves as having excruciatingly human dimensions. In your daily experience," I continued, "you may, for example, have seen your own parents or siblings as having mythic dimensions. You might have found yourself imbuing them with all the godlike attributes: wisdom, strength, courage, and the ability to protect you."

A field of baffled students rustled slightly beneath my expectant gaze.

"Myth, in this sense," I went on, bluffing madly now, "provides a state of perpetual childhood. It allows for childhood protection, and it is the answer to the monster beneath the bed. When a child grows up, she—or he—must forfeit the illusion of protectedness, and the mythic figure descends to earth."

Blank, unholy stares.

"And when a society loses its myths," I blustered on, "it, too, loses a kind of childhood, an innocence. Any questions?"

Four hands shot up like overfertilized plants.

I pointed to one of them.

"What does this have to do with the topic on the syllabus: 'The Tradition of Oral History, and the Role of—' "

"Oral history," I declared, "was an integral part of the most innocent, childlike societies in our recorded past. Where were the other questions?"

The three other plants had disappeared.

"Anyone?" I asked. "No one?"

———

That night, after Sarah had fallen asleep, Edgar closed her bedroom door and then ours, and then, to make sure that I'd gotten the message, he put a chair up against it.

"You have something in mind?" I asked him.

"What's on my mind is us," he said.

"Which us?"

"Exactly."

"I'm sorry."

"I know."

"I'm worried about my dad," I said.

"You're worried about why Heather hasn't called to ask about your dad," he said.

I smiled.

"What would you do if you were in my shoes?" I asked him.

"Take them off," he told me.

Jokingly, he leapt the three steps toward the bed and hurtled his body beside mine. He put a hand on my belly.

"I need to brush my teeth first," I said.

"Okay."

"And I need to get out of my work clothes."

"Okay."

"And I need to lose fifteen pounds."

"Sweetheart."

"I'm fat," I said.

"You're *pregnant*," he said.

"Don't get technical, Edgar," I told him.

I closed the door to the bathroom and brushed my teeth and washed my face and tried to remember what it had been like, in the old days, loving sex.

In the mirror, a mother was looking at me, wondering where the woman was.

In the bedroom, Edgar had created his favorite mood lighting, which consisted of a drastic dimming of the overhead lamp and the illumination of the vanilla-scented candle that I'd bought us seventeen lifetimes before but had still not managed to burn down.

"Come here," he said, and I obeyed.

We were still kissing when the phone rang.

"Don't answer it," Edgar told me as I picked up the receiver.

"How'd it go with Dad?" Heather asked me. "I'm sorry I didn't call earlier. I'm on call, and it's been nutty."

I could hear at least one baby, possibly more, screaming in her waiting room.

"That's okay," I said.

"How'd it go?" she asked.

"It went okay," I said. "More testing to come, if it gets worse."

"How'd Dad take it?" she asked me, and I sighed with relief and gratitude and the sense that I wasn't alone. So we talked about Dad a little bit, and then she said she was nervous about her surgery, which she was having the next day.

"Really?" I asked, impressed by this historic display of vulnerability.

Edgar, meanwhile, wrestled several pillows into a backrest, punching them up with impressive violence.

When at last I hung up, I saw a hideous look on his face.

I sank my head into his chest.

"I'm sorry," I said. "She was nervous about her surgery. It's tomorrow. She needed to talk to me."

"She wasn't nervous about her surgery. She's never nervous about anything," he said.

"So why did she call?"

"She just wants your attention. She just wants you to feel sorry for her so that you'll let her get closer to Sarah again."

I sighed and tried to compose myself. Finally, I said: "Remember right after David died how you wouldn't let Sarah out of your sight?"

"You're changing the subject."

"No I'm not. Remember? Remember how crazy you were?"

"That was different."

"I don't think so," I said. "I think you're still seeing danger where there isn't any."

It took at least a minute before his hand reluctantly stroked my back.

———•———

We watched a movie on television. I fell asleep halfway through it, guiltily grateful for that small, sweet, private wall that sleep can always build.

———•———

I dreamed that night that I lost the baby. I dreamed that I was in Lenox and that I woke up bleeding but that the bleeding didn't stop. I dreamed that I was in pain. I dreamed that Edgar walked in and found me lying on the bed, with blood all around me, and that he shouted, "Where's the baby? What did you do with our baby?"

"Where's the baby?" Wilma asked me.

"Where's the baby?" I said.

"Look at your stomach," Wilma said. "Your stomach's not pregnant anymore."

"Where's the baby?" Edgar asked me.

———•———

I woke up with his arms around me and the deepest sense of loss inside me that I had ever known.

"The baby's fine, darling," he said to me.

I burst into tears.

"God, poor Heather," I said.

"What?"

"Poor Heather."

"Why?"

"Because it's not even been a year yet, and you just asked me why."

The next day, I sat in my office, stitching a cat tail to a pink leotard. This would be Sarah's first Halloween without David, of course, and though she had not evinced much enthusiasm the night before, I'd managed to get her reluctant consent and her preference for being a kitten.

All day, I hovered close to the phone, remembering how Heather had called me when she'd been in labor with David, remembering how maddeningly calm she had been. I heard nothing, though, until three o'clock, when Richard finally called to say that everything was fine.

"Wilma says it worked," Heather said, sounding groggy, two hours later.

"That's great, Heather," I said. "Can she be sure?"

"Pretty sure. And anyway, David told me."

"David told you?" I said. "What the hell do you mean?"

"I mean told Sarah," she said hazily.

Well, that's better, I thought, and then couldn't believe I was capable of the thought.

On Saturday, Heather was still out of commission. I took Sarah up to the roof, where, with infinite delicacy and care, she plucked the tiny flowers that had so far survived the October chill.

"These flowers never die," Sarah said.

"Everything dies, sweetheart," I said. "Eventually, everything dies."

She shook her head tautly but emphatically. "These flowers never die," she said.

She stared out over the rooftops with a wistful, haunted look.

Behind her, a ladder led up to a shed that led to a large water tower and a maze of huge drainpipes and ducts. In their shadow, Sarah seemed for once as tiny and young and lost as she was.

———

On Sunday, Heather continued her recuperation, but Dad surprised me by coming over to hook up the dollhouse lights Heather had bought.

With Sarah watching and Edgar pacing, my father once more used his beautiful hands and made something magic happen. Heather had bought a lamp for each room, and a glowing fireplace, and one chandelier. Dad threaded small cables and concealed tiny wires, kneeling beside the house like a child, wordlessly absorbed, engaged.

By the time he was finished, it was nearly dusk, and he turned off the lights in the playroom and then with a flourish flipped on the tiny switch. The dollhouse lit up like the dream it was, and Sarah, exulting, was so thrilled that for once she forgot to be scared of my father and threw her arms around him.

"Now David can come at night," she said.

For the first time since before the summer, she took out her box of Playmobil people: the one in the red dress, which she loved the best; the man in the top hat; the children in green.

Sarah lined up her people outside the dollhouse.

"Don't you want them to go inside?" I asked her.

"Not yet," she said. "They're waiting."

The next night, she woke up crying again.

"Mommeee," came the wail of the flying, lost bird, soaring into my dream.

I was at the side of her bed in an instant. She grabbed my neck with her warm hands and pressed her cheek against my own and sobbed. For a full five minutes, she only said, "Mommy."

Finally, the back of her hand crept out to wipe the front of her nose.

"I'll get you a Kleenex," I said.

"No, don't go."

"You need to sleep," I told her.

"Will you keep me company?" she asked.

"Do you need me to?"

"I want you to."

"Put your head on your pillow," I told her, and I sat in the rocking chair.

It had been years, literally years, since I had taken this seat in darkness, waiting for sounds of even breathing and the chance to tiptoe out. The eyes of a dozen tired dolls and plushy animals stared out from the top of Sarah's bookshelf. My eyes watched her, looking for signs of sleep and peace. I rocked, remembering rocking when she was tiny in my arms.

I recalled Dr. Koenig saying that these nightmares might be a good sign. And it was true that throughout all the awful weeks right after David's death, the terrible time when she'd gone back to school, the newness and bleakness of spring without him, Sarah had not had a troubled night. It was as if David's durable presence had been so utterly real to her that the image of him never entered her dreams as hauntings or even nightmares.

Why hadn't she been frightened? Only now, sensing the faintest outlines of her dreams, did I realize what had been missing. Fear, I thought, might have kept things sane, or normal: fear of ghosts, spooks, specters, fear that Edgar or I—or she—might die too.

How had she put David in heaven? Where had that heaven come from? I'd never told her where I thought my mother was. And Edgar had never wanted to broach the subject—either with Sarah or with me. He had always seemed to feel that death and little girls simply didn't belong together. He had never read her *Little Red Riding Hood* or *Snow White*. And in his version of *Babar* (which I'd overheard at many a bedtime), the elephant's mother was never shot by hunters. Babar always just decided one day that he wanted to go to the city.

Maybe, I thought, if Sarah was having bad dreams now, it could mean that her view of heaven was finally collapsing upon itself.

———

We took her trick-or-treating on Halloween night. I dressed her in her kitten costume and painted a pink triangle on her nose and gave her a large plastic pumpkin.

We made the rounds in the building. She was the youngest

child by far, buffeted on every side by big kids ensconced in full face masks and fake blood and fake death. My little kitten, unsmiling, could barely reach the apartment doorbells.

"Trick or treat!" I shouted for her as Edgar and I tried to steer her, literally, through and past the monsters.

On the tenth floor, we passed two girls in sheets. To Edgar, I raised my eyebrows.

"What were they, Mommy?" Sarah asked me.

I laughed, then realized she was serious.

"Sweetie," I said. "They were ghosts."

"What's a ghost?"

I stared at her, disbelieving.

"You know what a ghost is, Sarah."

"But that's not what people are like when they come back," she said.

Exhausted, we returned to a dark apartment.

"Can I take my costume off now, Mommy?" she asked, which nearly broke my heart.

She was spent. Candy did not revive her. She asked to go to bed even before I could wash off her whiskers and nose.

At two o'clock in the morning, I woke up and went in to look at her.

The lights in her dollhouse were on, but I knew we had left her bedroom dark. The fake fire burned in the fake fireplace. The little lamps with the pink shades twinkled and glowed. I ran back into our room.

"Edgar," I said, waking him.

"What's wrong?"

"The lights in Sarah's dollhouse are on."

"So turn them off," he said thickly.

"They *were* off," I said.

"So she must have turned them back on," he said.

"But she was fast asleep," I said.

"So she must have gotten up," he said.

I went back in to her bedroom. This time, I saw that the dolls were in the dollhouse—the red-dressed woman and the green-dressed children and the man with the top hat. And sitting downstairs in the armchair, facing the fireplace, was the small blue doll that David had loved and had carried with him everywhere he'd gone.

———

"Where'd you find that doll?" I asked her in the morning.

"It's David's," she simply said.

———

The next day, the flowers she'd picked on the roof and painstakingly put in the window boxes had shriveled and died.

"They died," she said, staring, wounded, at them. "Why did they die?" she asked softly.

"Sweetheart. I told you. Everything dies."

———

She woke up with a fever in the middle of the night. Her hot, scratchy skin seemed baked and brittle. I held her and felt her shiver. I poured out the Tylenol. She wouldn't take it. I called for Edgar. He held her while I held the spoon. She lashed out an arm. The spoon hit the floor. The Tylenol seeped into the rug.

"Oh, Sarah," I said.

"I'm sorry, Mommy."

"You have to take your medicine."

"Why?"

"So that you'll get better."

"Why?" she said.

"So that you'll be healthy."

"Why?" she said. She was scaring me.

"Take this medicine. Now," I said.

She cried pitifully and shook her head. She said: "Mommy, I just want to go to sleep."

I found the thermometer in her drawer. I tucked it into her armpit and held her arm down tightly.

"Mommy!" she protested.

"Shh," I said as gently as I could.

She had 104°. She was burning.

"Call Joe," I told Edgar.

I heard him talking to the service.

"I'll put it in juice," I told Sarah.

"No."

"I'll put it in applesauce," I said.

"No!" she screamed.

"Okay," I said, rocking her.

She twisted and turned, hot and moist, in my arms.

"I spy Freedo," I whispered, and she looked up, just barely interested.

"I spy the moon," I said.

Finally, the phone rang, and I carried her into our bedroom and picked it up.

"Hello," I said.

"Hi," Heather said.

"Heather? What are you—"

"I'm on call tonight. What's wrong?"

"You're—"

"I'm on call, Dum. Get with the program. What's wrong with Sarah?"

"Fever," I said. "A hundred and four, and she won't let us near her with Tylenol."

"Can you force it?"

"I tried. It's on the rug."

"That'll never come out," she said.

"Fine. What do I do for her?"

"Put her on the phone."

"What?"

"You heard me."

I handed the phone to Sarah, who was lying across my lap, half-asleep.

"No!" she protested.

"It's your aunt Heather."

I held the phone for Sarah and let her listen while Heather talked.

I thought of our childhood Doctor game, where the patient had always grown sicker when the doctor had given the wrong medicine.

Sarah said: "Okay, Aunt Heather," and handed the phone back to me.

"She'll take it," Heather said. "If her fever spikes higher, wrap her in a wet sheet and call me back. I'm on call all night."

I poured out another spoonful of Tylenol.

Sarah took it without any complaint.

It was 104° again in the morning, so I took her in to see Dr. Worth. He found nothing amiss in her ears or her throat and declared that she had a virus.

"That's it?" I said.

He shrugged. "It's going around. Keep her fever down. Keep her warm and dry. Don't make her eat if she's not hungry."

"I'm hungry," she piped up, and we laughed. But her eyes were still dry, and her skin was still hot.

I was paying the bill, Sarah in my arms, when Joe came back and said: "Heather says wait."

"Why?" I said.

"She just said wait," he told me.

I frowned, but I sat down with Sarah. Together, we looked gloomily at the well-worn toys and well-thumbed books and the small slide that children played with when they were feeling up to it. It was a sign of just how ill Sarah felt that she didn't try to go down the slide. I remembered how I had steered her down it when she was an infant, and coaxed her down it when she was a timid toddler, and urged her to take turns on it with the younger kids when at last she'd become a big girl.

"I like the slide," she said, as if reading my thoughts.

"Want to go down it?" I asked her.

She shook her head no and pressed her face against my shoulder.

Heather finally emerged, wearing her white doctor's coat and her stethoscope. At her side was a middle-aged man with a beard, thinning hair, and twinkling eyes. In his arms was a boy of about Sarah's age with a pale face and a hideously crusty nose.

"I wanted you to meet someone," Heather said to me.

"I've got to get her home, Heather," I said.

"This is Frank Briggs," she said, ignoring me.

"Pleased to meet you," he said.

I tried to smile.

Simultaneously, we shifted our children up onto our shoulders and shook hands.

"Virus?" he asked sympathetically.

"Virus," I said.

I looked at Heather, utterly baffled.

She put her hand on Sarah's shoulder.

"Cookie," she said. "This is the man I told you about."

She roused herself. "Which man?" she said.

"You know," Heather said. "The one I told you we might go and see someday."

She said: "The one who can talk to David?"

"Excuse me," I said. "Could someone please tell me—"

"I can," Frank Briggs said. "I'm a channeler," he explained, smiling. "Here. I'll give you my card."

He shifted his son on his shoulder again and pulled out an elegant business card.

"Thanks again, Dr. Rosen," he told Heather, and with that he walked over to pay his bill.

By now, Sarah was half-asleep again, and a nurse was beckoning Heather into a room for her next patient.

"A channeler?" I hissed at her.

"He can talk to dead children. He's famous," she said. "He wrote a best-seller."

"And you told Sarah about him?"

She nodded. "She thought it was cool," she said.

———

Monday morning, Sarah stalled shamelessly before school. I thought perhaps she was still feeling sick. But her fever had been down for a whole day, and the night before she'd been perfectly sunny. Now socks mysteriously disappeared. Pants became mysteriously impossible to don. Teeth were not brushed.

"What's going on, sweetie?" I heard Edgar ask her while I was putting on my makeup.

"I don't want to go to school," she said.

"Not go to school!" he cried with that tone of fake surprise that we had both sunk to using from time to time.

"That's right, Daddy," she said, unfazed.

"But you love school," he said.

"No I don't."

She ran into our bathroom to stand beside me as I got ready.

"I want lipstick," she said.

"Sarah."

"Please, Mommy, I want lipstick. And perfume."

"No lipstick," I said.

"I want lipstick!"

"Little girls don't wear lipstick," I said.

"But I'm a big girl."

"Not that big," I said.

"Aunt Heather lets me wear *her* lipstick," she said.

Well, screw Aunt Heather, I wanted to say.

"Well, I'm your mother," is what I said.

———

At school, she clung to my leg in a way that she hadn't since the spring before, right after David had died.

We stood by the cubbies as the other children danced into class, and the other mothers looked condescending.

"Sarah," I said, disengaging her hands from my thigh and kneeling down beside her. "Tell me what the problem is."

"I don't want to go to school," she said.

"Why not?"

"Because I don't."

"Why don't you?"

"Because."

"Because why?"

"Just because."

It was the kind of dialogue that can make grown people weep.

"You know," I said, "all your friends are in there waiting for you."

"They're not my friends," she said.

"Your teachers are waiting," I said, "and don't tell me they're not your teachers."

I detected the faintest smile.

"Come on, sweetie. You know I'll see you at the end of the day."

Just then, Terri came to the classroom door.

"Sarah," she said, "there's something I want to show you."

"What?"

"Come on in, and I'll show you."

With that modest subterfuge, my daughter followed.

I waited for five minutes after she'd gone inside.

"Where's Mommy?" I heard her ask at least once. But no tears seemed to follow, so, confused but determined, I went to work.

Tuesday, Sarah said she didn't want to go see Dr. Koenig.

Once I had gotten her there, however, I turned off the heating system, and I listened, shamelessly, at the door.

"I love Aunt Heather," I heard Sarah say.

"Is that Aunt Heather?"

"Uh-huh," she said.

"And who's that, on the sofa?" Dr. Koenig asked.

"That's Mommy."

"What's she doing?"

"She's crying."

"Why?"

"I don't know," Sarah said.

I realized I wanted to break down the door.

"I don't love Mommy when she's sad," Sarah said. "But I always love Aunt Heather."

———

Wednesday, she said she didn't want to go to school.

"When I die," she told me on the way there, "I put on a rainbow dress and rainbow black shoes and rainbow tights and then I go outside and then I put on my wings and then I'm in heaven and I die but I'm not killed."

———

Thursday, Terri called me at the office to say that Sarah had spent the whole morning intermittently crying for me and sitting on the "meeting pillows" by herself, sucking her thumb.

"The whole morning?" I asked her, aghast.

"Well, yes, starting after you left."

"Why didn't you call me?" I asked.

"We wanted to see if she would work it out by herself," Terri said.

"What's she doing now?" I asked.

"When I left to come make this call, she was crying."

I looked at my watch. My noon lecture was forty minutes away.

"I'll call her sitter," I told Terri.

There was a ghastly, judgmental pause.

"Fine," Terri finally said.

I called Edgar instead.

"Can you get away?" I asked him.

"Can't you?"

"No. You know. I've got my noon lecture," I told him, as if his failure to recall that fact was proof of long-standing spite.

"I've got sections all morning," he told me. "What's wrong with Rosie?"

"I haven't called her yet."

"I think you should."

"But Sarah's really upset."

"She'll live," he said.

"She's crying," I said.

"She'll live."

"And what would you do if they'd called to say she'd broken two legs?" I asked him.

"I'd go."

"But crying is okay," I said, irrational and furious.

"If you don't think it is, then you go."

"I hate it when you're logical," I said.

"I hate it when you're not," he said.

———•———

I left a note on the door of the lecture room that said the lecture had been rescheduled for four o'clock, which was section-meeting time. I told the department secretary what I'd done, and to alert the section leaders. I flagged a cab and raced downtown. I ran up the front steps of the school and then up the stairs to Sarah's classroom. I arrived just in time to see Sarah calmly pouring apple juice into her classmates' plastic cups.

"Mommy," she said when she saw me. "What are *you* doing here?"

———

Excellent question, I thought as I rode, seething, back uptown in another taxi.

The amiable shrugs of Terri and Elaine were now burned into my memory.

But I got back in time to tell the secretary to cancel my cancellation with the section leaders. I tore the note I'd left off the auditorium door, and I delivered a woefully distracted lecture on the role of the hero in ancient and modern myth.

"The hero," I heard myself saying, "will usually sacrifice himself to a cause he deems larger than himself."

But rarely, I thought to myself, will the hero waste fifteen bucks on two taxis in an effort to see a child pouring juice.

———

On Sunday, it was unseasonably warm, a last hint of Indian summer and a perfect excuse, as I saw it, to get Sarah away from the dollhouse for once.

"Let's go to the park," I told her.

We went with Heather and Jeffrey, a compromise.

Heather and I sat side by side on the same park benches we'd sat on when Sarah and David were born. I wondered if she was remembering that, or if it was far too painful for her. I wondered if David still existed for her as the little boy he had really been, or whether he'd truly become some strange promise of a rebirth, a regeneration.

Jeffrey, with his water gun, ran in circles around and after his friends.

Sarah climbed the slide over and over and shushed her way down merrily. I was happy to see her do something so normal and so physical.

I watched Heather splitting her gaze between her son and my daughter.

At one point, Sarah ran over to me for juice, which I gave her contentedly.

She drank the whole thing down, wiped her mouth with her hand, and then looked up at the tallest slide in the playground, the one where the big boys usually ruled.

"Maybe next year," I told her, thinking I knew what she was thinking.

She shook her head.

"Gym comes after Snack, you know," she said.

"What?"

"And at the end of Gym, David gets to go on the highest slide," she said. "And that's how he comes back down."

"To here?" Heather asked.

She nodded.

"He gets to go on the highest slide, and he slides all the way back down from heaven."

—·—

I found it a guilty comfort to get back to school on Monday.

My lecture that day was the last one before Thanksgiving break. It was on the theme of the goddess, from Babylon to Canaan. I told my students about female deities giving birth to the earth, moon, and stars, and about the men who worshipped this fertility.

My belly and I got a lot of laughs.

For the next two days, I saw no students. I just sat, reading and grading their midterm papers and hiding myself.

—·—

But inevitably, the respite ended. Dad called me at school on the fifteenth.

"What's wrong?" I asked when I heard his voice.

"It's Sarah," he said.

"What?" I said, sagging.

"Something she said to me last weekend, when we were playing with the dollhouse."

"What?"

"Do you want to know what she said?"

"I guess."

"She told me about a fight I once had with your mother."

"What fight?" I asked.

"It was on New Year's Eve, I think," he said.

"Which one?"

"It was the year before Adam. You and Heather never knew this, of course, but your mother and I had a disagreement about—well, about the family."

"You wanted to have another baby," I told him. "And Mommy didn't."

"Sarah told you?" he asked.

"No, Dad," I said, laughing. "Heather and I were listening at the door."

"Well, did you ever tell Sarah about it? How could she have known?"

I tried to imagine a situation in which I would have sat Sarah down to tell her that her grandparents had had a baby who died.

"I guess I must have, Dad," I lied.

"Did you?"

"Well, how else would she have known?" I said.

"Your mother," he almost whispered.

"You think Sarah can talk to *Mom*?" I asked.

"I didn't know what to think," he said.

I knew I should have rejoiced in this historic acknowledgment of mystery. But at that moment, it seemed too much like the rest of the confusion in his mind—and in everyone else's.

"I must have told her, Dad," I said. "Or maybe Heather did."

"Yes. Heather," he said, somewhat mollified. "Would you ask her if she did?"

Oh sure, I thought.

"Sure," I said. "I'll let you know."

———

On Friday, Sarah told her classmates about David and Gym, and Judy Weiss, that pint-sized defender of the status quo, threw two wooden building blocks at Sarah's head, then jumped on her and pulled out her barrettes. The first wooden block made a huge and immediate bruise on Sarah's forehead. The second one bruised her shoulder. There were scratches too, one that bled, and the teachers, unable to reach either Edgar or me, called Rosie, who called Heather, who told Rosie to bring her in.

There, it was Heather who treated Sarah's cuts and bruises, made sure she did not have a concussion, and then, in a certain departure from her customary duties, sat with Sarah for nearly an hour as Edgar, finally reached at his office, rushed downtown to pick her up.

I learned all this two hours after the fact, when I returned to my office from a lunchtime that I'd spent blissfully browsing for baby clothes and ordering baby bedding.

At first, my concern for Sarah and my unspeakable anger at Judy Weiss outpaced my guilt, and my rage at Heather. Then, mollified by Sarah's own chipper mood, and by Terri's apologies on the phone ("It happened so fast"; "It couldn't be helped"; "Judy was taken home by her mother"), I started to brood about Heather.

Who was she to cancel an hour's work and come through with flying colors while I was out shopping? Shopping! Who was she to have the ready arms, and the soothing smile, and the medical certainty to boot?

Sarah's aunt, I told myself. She was Sarah's doting, lonely, still-maddening, and still-grieving aunt.

According to Shoshonean myth, Dzoavits was a giant ogre who stole the children of Dove. Eagle and Crane helped to rescue them, but Dzoavits kept after them, and they had to hide in Weasel's hole. Dzoavits was still not prepared to give up. He asked Badger where the children were hidden. Badger had dug another hole, into which he directed Dzoavits. When the ogre finally was lured in, Badger threw hot rocks and stones after him, then used another stone to plug up the hole for the rest of time.

———

The school psychologist, Edna Lear, called my office in the afternoon. She said she wanted to know how I thought Sarah was doing.

"How do *you* think she's doing?" I asked.

"Well, I gather she had a little fight today."

"A *little* fight?" I said. "I gather you weren't there."

"Actually, I had just stepped out when it happened," she said.

"It wasn't a little fight. That Judy Weiss practically bashed her head in."

"Judy does seem to be having a problem with Sarah."

"Have you talked to *her* mother?"

"Well, no, as a matter of fact."

"Were you planning to?" I asked.

"I don't feel that Judy is inherently troubled by aggressive feelings," Dr. Lear said.

"You're saying the only problem is Sarah?"

"Sarah is certainly the catalyst, Mrs. Ross," she said. Then: "Listen. I know you're upset about Sarah. I would be too."

I sighed.

"You know, it may be hard for you to believe this, but it's highly possible that Sarah isn't even going to remember any of this someday."

I laughed.

"All children have what's known as infantile amnesia," she said. "At a certain point in their childhoods, usually when they're resolving their early conflicts, they simply repress the past because so much of it is just too painful to bear."

"You mean that she'll just forget?" I asked, suddenly loving Dr. Edna Lear.

"Someday. Yes. She will," she said.

"So therapy?" I asked, hoping she'd tell me that I'd never have to look at Dr. Koenig again.

"Therapy may well help her resolve these problems," Dr. Lear said, "and certainly help her deal with the Judy Weisses of this world. But as far as the future goes, she's going to outgrow this anyway, on her own, and someday, she'll only remember David by the pictures she sees, and the way you talk about him. She's going to forget about heaven. Children do forget their fantasies. It's just part of growing up."

I felt, simultaneously, hopeful and sad. I didn't want Sarah to lose her myths. I just wanted to be sure that she was keeping them for her own sake, and not for anyone else's.

———————

Edgar and I had midterms to grade all weekend. On Sunday, we let Heather take Sarah to the park, though the weather wasn't nearly as warm as it had been the weekend before.

At two o'clock, I missed her.

At three o'clock, I started to worry.

I walked alone to the playground, passing the Upper West Side cafés, where young couples without children sat in smoky, ecstatic ignorance of what they had in store for them.

I scanned the playground: the swings, the tires, the jungle

gym, the ropes, the sandbox. I looked at the slide. Sarah was nowhere. And then I heard her voice.

"Look at me, Aunt Heather!"

My eyes shot heavenward.

She was standing on top of the highest slide, waving her arms in mad pride.

At the foot of the slide was my twin, a broad grin on her face as she waited to catch my daughter.

And sitting behind Heather, on a park bench, was Frank Briggs and his pale, thin son, who swung his feet as he drank chocolate milk, a bit of which dribbled onto his shirt. Frank Briggs took a napkin out and lovingly wiped his son's mouth and shirt. Just another father and son in the playground on Saturday, watching a small girl come down a huge slide.

———·———

I was so enraged when I reached Heather that I could barely frame a coherent question.

"Where do you get off—what do you—how do you—how could you think that Edgar and I would—what is he doing here?" I said.

"He brought his son to the park," she said.

"I don't want you taking Sarah to see him."

"I didn't think you did," she said.

"What's that supposed to mean?" I asked her.

"It's supposed to mean what it says," she said.

"Like I'm doing something bad by depriving my daughter of going to see some creepy fake?" I said.

"Shh," she said. "He'll hear you."

"I don't give a damn if he hears me."

"Hi, Mommy!" Sarah shouted. "Watch me!"

I did.

She slid down the slide like a shot but landed, miraculously, on both feet.

In the five seconds I had before she ran over, I leaned in close to Heather and said: "I'm telling you now. No bullshit. Keep him away from my daughter. You got that?"

"Message received," she said briskly, and then I had Sarah in my arms.

"I love Aunt Heather," she declared that night. I was bathing her at the time, trying to remove the whole day's worth of playground grime and an evening of dollhouse furniture painting, which she'd undertaken alone.

"I know you love her, honey," I said, reaching for her small pink piggy scrub brush.

"I *love* Aunt Heather," she said, as if I had tried to contradict her.

"I *know* you do, honey," I said. "Give me your hand, please. I need to get that dirt off."

Her hand fluttered up through the bath bubbles, and I caught it while she started to squirm. I brushed her knuckles and fingertips. I scrubbed them harder.

"I love Aunt Heather more than I love anyone else in the whole world," she said.

I brushed. I scrubbed.

"Mommy!" she yelped. "You're hurting me!"

"I've got to get this paint off," I said grimly.

"Mommy!"

She yanked her hand away.

"Give me the other one," I said.

"No."

"Sarah."

"It hurts."

Oh, you think *that* hurts, I thought.

"I'll try to be gentler this time," I said.

She sat back and produced her other hand, a five-fingered canvas of pink and maroon.

A dangerous silence ensued while I rubbed. I felt a hatred for Heather so deep that it made me feel sick to my stomach. I wanted to scream. I wanted to hit. I felt I was on the brink of a rupture more final than any that had come before.

"I do, you know," Sarah said, softly now. "I do love Aunt Heather the most. Better than Daddy. Better than you."

"Edgar!" I shouted, and he came running.

"What is it? What's happened?" he asked as he stood anxiously at the bathroom door.

I dropped Sarah's hand back into the tub.

"Your daughter," I told him, standing up, "has just informed me that she loves Aunt Heather more than you and more than me."

He blinked at me, looking for a cue.

I looked down at Sarah as if she were Heather.

"Don't ever say that to me again," I said, and stormed out of the bathroom, leaving Sarah's hands motionless in the tub, and the pink piggy circling around them.

Dad called later that night.

"You'll never believe what Heather did," I told him.

"You mean about Frank Briggs?" he asked.

I was startled.

"What do you know about it?"

"I know that Heather has found someone she thought might be able to help Sarah, and that you treated Heather as if she was some kind of criminal."

"You've got to be kidding," I said.

"I'm not kidding."

"Dad, do you have any idea what kind of person this is?"

"Do you?"

"I can't believe you're saying this."

"I think she's just trying to help."

"Oh you do."

"The man," said my father, the doctor, the rationalist, "apparently has this uncanny ability to speak directly to dead children. He's apparently written this book that's sold millions, and before that he'd never advertised himself or anything, but very quietly, over the last several decades, he's been helping a whole bunch of families actually talk to their children who've died."

"Dad," I began, feeling almost hysterical. "You can't possibly believe—"

"I'm just telling you what Heather told me," Dad said. "She wants to take Sarah to see him, and I thought I'd go along. I mean, what possible harm could it do, and let's say this guy does have some ability, and the rest of us could hear what David has to say, and maybe even talk to your mother, Erica, I mean, who knows, right? We don't have an answer for everything."

"Daddy," I said gently. "What's happening to you?"

There was a lengthy silence, filled only with his breathing.

"How do people do this thing?" he asked me softly. "How do they grow old?"

"Oh, Daddy."

"I just wish that I knew," he said.

"Daddy, you have to know Edgar and I would never let Heather take Sarah to someone like that."

———

"Have you ever thought about living somewhere else?" Edgar asked me late that night.

"Like where? The suburbs? No thanks," I said.

"No. I mean London. Or Paris. Or maybe Seattle," he said.

"Are you serious?"

"Absolutely."

"I couldn't do it," I told him.

"Why not?"

"Because I could never leave my family."

"Sarah and I are your family," he said.

"I can't leave my family," I said again.

"Hasn't your family left you?"

———

On Thanksgiving, they ganged up on me, a full family assault.

One by one, they made their case. Heather took me aside while we were mashing the potatoes. Dad took me aside while we were setting the table. Richard took me aside while he was sharpening a knife for the turkey. What was so bad about trying Frank Briggs?

We got through the meal somehow. We left. And at night, while Sarah was sleeping, Edgar and I talked about Paris.

In my classes, I had always tried to define the various meanings of myth: stories with legendary or historical figures; stories that explain natural phenomena; stories that are meant as mere entertainments. I also read my students a favorite definition, which is the third definition offered in Webster's: that myth is "an ill-founded belief held uncritically, especially by an interested group." Family myth, of course, falls under the last definition. I was the interested group, a group of one, and the extent to which my belief was ill-founded was becoming ever and ever more apparent to me.

It was two weeks later that I came home from doing errands with Edgar and found that Heather and Sarah and Dad were not at their usual dollhouse posts.

"Back soon," read a note from Heather that she'd pinned to the door of the dollhouse, as if she had written it on David's behalf.

An hour passed. And another ten minutes.

"She took her," Edgar shouted at me. "I knew it. I knew she was going to. She took her to that goddamned flake."

I shook my head. "She wouldn't have done that," I said, even as I knew that I would never be able to say it again.

There was no answer at Dad's or Heather's apartments. Heather didn't answer her pager.

"I'll kill her," Edgar told me.

"Don't say that," I said. "Are you more scared or angry?"

"She took my daughter," was all he said.

———

I found Frank Briggs's card in my purse, where it had been since the Saturday when I had met him at Heather's office.

I called, and a cool receptionist answered.

"He's in with a client," she said. "Can I have your name and number?"

"I'm trying to find out if that client is my child," I said. "Is she there? With Heather Rosen?"

"I'm afraid that's confidential," she said.

"What the hell do you mean, 'confidential'?" I said. "Is my child there or not?"

"Is it Sarah?" she asked.

I slammed the phone down.

"I'm coming with you," Edgar said.

"No. You've got to be here in case I miss them."

I grabbed my bag and ran out the door.

———

"There's a woman with a little boy," said Briggs. He was sitting in a large brown armchair in a totally unassuming office, surrounded by Heather, Sarah, Jeffrey, and Dad. I was watching them through a two-way mirror in an observation room. Beside me, Briggs's reluctant receptionist eyed me warily.

"The woman is an older woman," Briggs said. "She's an older presence. I hear the name Gloria."

I watched a ribbon of shock connect the members of my family.

"Does the name Gloria have meaning to you?"

"Yes," Heather finally said.

"She's with your son. She protects him. She is guiding him

through this time," he said. He paused, seeming to listen. "Was your son David?" he asked.

"Yes."

"I want to go home," Sarah said. No one seemed to hear her. And for the moment, I couldn't move.

"Was your son David Alan?" Briggs asked Heather.

"Yes," Heather told him quietly.

I wasn't sure I had remembered that.

"He tells me," Briggs said, "that he knows his mother and father feel that they are to blame."

Heather stiffened noticeably.

"He tells me to tell you it wasn't your fault. He has learned that it was his time to go. He is talking about a country house."

"That's the house!" Sarah shouted, jumping up from her seat.

"He is saying it wouldn't have made any difference where you had lived."

Briggs paused for a moment and seemed to listen.

"Are you afraid of having another child?" he asked Heather.

"Yes," she told him, startling me.

"He tells me to tell you that you mustn't be afraid. He says he's trying to come back to you. He says he will, if Sarah can let him go."

"Me?" Sarah asked.

"Sarah, David says he's trying to come back and join you. He says he thinks he sees a way. But he says he can't come back until you decide to let him move on."

"I want him back," Heather said, and started to weep. Sarah was wailing now and started to climb onto Heather's lap.

"I'm going in there," I told the receptionist.

"Wait," she said. "The link is so strong. Can't you tell?"

"He says he's going to come back," Briggs said.

"What does he say about Gloria?" my father asked.

"He says that she comforts him," Briggs said. "He says that she is preparing a place for George. Do you understand the name George?"

"Yes, it's my name," my father said.

"He says she has told him something about a walk—no, it's like walk."

"Waltz?" my father said.

"Yes. Waltz. Waltzing. Does that have meaning to you?"

I walked past the receptionist and flung open the door.

Four heads looked up at me in anger and surprise. Only Sarah smiled. She said, "Mommy!" as if we hadn't seen each other for months, then burst into tears and lunged into my arms.

Heather stood up, came over, and put a hand on Sarah's back.

"Take your hands off my child," I told her.

"Dum," she said. "You should have heard it. It was incredible. Just sit down—"

"I don't want to hear it. I don't want to hear you," I said.

Sarah was sobbing now, her sweet, hot tears falling, one by one, on my neck.

"But—" Heather began. She looked as if she'd been roused from a dream and was trying to find her way back into it.

"Keep the hell away from us," I said, and carried Sarah out the door without looking back, not wanting to see the pain and confusion in my father's face, or the stern loneliness of Heather.

———

Sarah cried all the way home in the taxi, but by the time we'd returned home to Edgar, she seemed to have calmed herself down completely.

She wanted to eat a hot dog for dinner. Again, the little pieces of life gave comfort. If she could want a hot dog, I asked myself, how bad could everything really be?

At nine o'clock, we put her to bed.

At ten o'clock, we heard her call out, and together we dashed into her room. She was sitting up in bed, looking confused.

"What about Aunt Heather?" she asked.

"We'll talk about it in the morning," I said.

"You told Aunt Heather to leave me alone."

"Yes."

"Why?" she asked me.

"Because I'd told Aunt Heather not to take you to see that man, and she took you anyway."

"Are you going to let her come back?" she asked me.

"Not for a long time," I said.

Sarah threw her warm arms around my neck.

"Will you keep me company?" she asked.

"Yes. Lie down. Put your head on your pillow."

Sarah started crying. Edgar and I both sat with her.

"Mommy, I'm scared," she said again and again. "Hold me, Mommy. Hold me."

Edgar stroked her hair and patted her back.

"Tell me," I said to her over and over, but she shook her head and kept crying. She clung to me, and finally, exhausted, she simply fell asleep.

I dreamed a memory, from two years before, a day in the dead of winter when Heather and I had taken David and Sarah to play in Central Park. The normal stale grays and browns of the park had been covered by snow the night before. Carrying our old double-length Flexible Flyer, Heather and I had searched for a hill that was not too steep or crowded for the kids.

In my dream, as in the past, I watched while David scrambled up a hill, leaving Sarah, timid and dumbfounded, behind him.

At the top of the hill, he turned, triumphant, his hat askew, his mittens dangling from his coat sleeves, his cheeks the color of ripe plums.

"Come, Sarah, come!" he shouted. "Come on!"

She clung nervously to my leg.

Heather followed David, starting up the hill with the sled.

"Go on, sweetie," I said. "Go with Aunt Heather. I'll catch you when you come down," I said.

At first reluctantly, then eagerly, she started up the hill behind Heather. An older boy on a sled was coming down.

"Come on, Sarah!" David shouted.

Heather was looking ahead, not behind.

The boy on the sled was coming toward Sarah.

"Sarah!" I shouted. "Sarah! Watch out!"

I woke thinking that I'd heard something and feeling a sense of unspeakable dread.

Sarah's bed was empty. Her room was empty. I screamed for Edgar. We searched the apartment. He called Dad. He called Heather. They didn't have her. We threw on some clothes.

"Stay here," he said, and ran out the door.

Frantic, I paced and tried to think. Then, quite suddenly, I knew where Sarah was.

———

The roof was dark and frigid, lit up only by a few small lights that were meant to display the garden. The door snapped closed behind me, and I felt a new sense of panic when I didn't see her in front of me.

"Oh God!" I screamed at the top of my lungs.

I heard a sound from behind me. I spun around. There was only the dark, still door. The sound came again. I stepped forward and turned around and there Sarah was. She had climbed up to the water tower and stood just above a wide-open pipe as if it were a playground slide.

"Sarah!" I screamed.

She didn't respond.

"Sarah!" I screamed again. "Sarah!"

It was exactly the way it had been with her dreams. She stared, not seeing the world before her. She didn't seem to hear me.

I started up the ladder of the small shed from which she had reached the tower.

"No, Mommy," she said, but I still didn't think she had seen me. "That's not how you get back down."

"Sarah?" I said.

She took a step forward, as if she was going to come down the slide.

I took a step up. She took a step forward. I stopped, and she stopped. I was frozen.

"Get down, Mommy," she said, though whether she was

speaking to me in a dream or in reality, I had no idea. I got back down.

"Sarah," I said. "Wake up, sweetheart."

"I'm sliding to earth," she said.

"You're already here, baby," I told her.

I heard the roof door swing open and saw Heather, frantic, appear in the dim stairway light.

"What are you doing here?" I said.

"You just called me, remember? Is she here?"

"Go back," I told her.

"What's she doing?" Heather asked. "Where is she?"

She followed my gaze to the top of the tower.

"Heather," I said. "I mean it. Go back."

She looked past me, up toward Sarah.

"You've got to come down, Cookie," Heather called to her. "We've got so much to do together. Think about the kitchen. It's barely finished. We haven't set up the plates or the dishes. We haven't painted the dining room table. We haven't put the rug in the bedroom."

Sarah just stared at the far distance.

"Shut up, Heather," I whispered.

"Cookie," she said again pointlessly.

Sarah took another step forward.

"He's coming back here, remember, Cookie?" Heather said. "You've got to be here when he comes."

"Shut up, Heather!" I nearly spat.

Sarah needed—as I had for so long as well—something to direct her to the here and now, the concrete, the real.

"Did you call her doctor?" Heather asked me.

I didn't answer.

"I spy Sarah," I finally called, and at last Sarah stopped staring, and I saw that her gaze shifted just perceptibly.

"Sarah," I said again. "I spy Sarah."

She turned, and for the first time in what seemed like hours,
I wasn't looking at a profile. I was looking at my daughter's
face: the full, the whole, beautiful Sarah face.

"Dum," Heather whispered.

"Shush," I hissed back.

I searched the rooftop desperately for something I could tell
her I spied. Beyond her, I saw a waning moon, and fading stars,
and a whole city. But I didn't want her to look up. Up was too
close to heaven.

"I spy a flower," I said, lying.

Then finally, I watched her face collapse. Her face crumpled
like a paper bag. Her mouth gaped into an open cry. Her dim
eyes brightened amid her tears, and she said: "Mommy! The
flower died!"

I started crying myself, perhaps because for the first time I
knew that she would be all right.

"Come down, Sarah," I said calmly.

"Mommy!" she cried. "It died!"

"I spy a different flower," I said.

Heather, I realized, was gripping my arm. I shook her off,
and I stepped forward.

"I'm coming to get you, Sarah," I said.

New Year's Eve, 1990

"Auld Lang Syne"

"**Y**ou've got to be there," Heather said when she called at nine on New Year's Eve in a last-ditch effort to get me to Dad's. It was the first time I'd talked to her since the night on the roof, three weeks before.

"No I don't," I told her. "I don't have to be there, and I'm not going to be there."

"Think about Dad."

"I've thought about Dad."

"Think about Sarah."

"I am," I said.

"You can't stay away forever," she said.

"I can stay away for as long as I want."

"It's been almost a month," she said.

"I know."

She paused, then finally said: "I've got news."

Secretly, I'd been expecting it.

"You're pregnant," I said.

"Very pregnant," she said.

"You can't be very pregnant yet."

"Think," she told me.

I did.

"It's twins," I said.

So she would have two, and get one back.

———•———

She called back ten minutes later.

"I'm going to have twins," she said.

"You told me," I said.

"Twins, Dum," she said.

"Well, let's hope they turn out better than we did."

"What do you mean?" she asked me. "We were best friends."

"When?" I said, and hung up the phone, appeals to the past notwithstanding.

———•———

Dad's was the last call, and the one I'd dreaded most. For years, I had been incapable of saying I blamed him for anything, so afraid had I been that he might die halfway through some silly argument. Now I had lived with that risk for almost a month and was bent on continuing to live with it. For now, I felt the recent past had proved, I couldn't have both my child and my father, and I wasn't about to lose Sarah again.

He didn't ask me, straight out, to change my mind. He asked if I knew who'd written "Auld Lang Syne."

"Why?" I said.

"Do you know?" he said.

"I think it was a poem by Robert Burns," I told him.

"Look it up for me, would you, darling?"

I hung up and went to the bookshelf. I found the book, then the poem, and then I called Dad back.

"It is Robert Burns," I told him.

"Will you read it to me?" he asked.

"Why?"

"Just do."

I read:

"*Should auld acquaintance be forgot,*
  And never brought to min'?
  Should auld acquaintance be forgot,
  And auld lang syne?

"*For auld lang syne, my dear,*
  For auld lang syne,
  We'll tak a cup o' kindness yet,
  For auld lang syne.

"*We twa hae run about the braes,*
  And pu'd the gowans fine;
  But we've wandered mony a weary foot
  Sin' auld lang syne.

"*We twa hae paidled i' the burn,*
  From morning sun till dine;
  But seas between us braid hae roared
  Sin' auld lang syne.

"*And there's a hand, my trusty fiere,*
  And gie's a hand o' thine:
  And we'll tak a right guid-willie waught,
  For auld lang syne.

"*And surely ye'll be your pint-stowp,*
  And surely I'll be mine;

And we'll tak a cup o' kindness yet
For auld lang syne."

"What does it mean?" he asked me.

I sighed.

"Dad."

"Do it for me."

I scanned the notes.

" 'Auld lang syne' basically means 'old long since,' like 'the good old days,' " I told him.

"And the rest?"

"There's a rough translation," I said. " 'We two once ran about the hills, and plucked the daisies fine, but we've wandered on many a weary foot since auld lang syne. We two once paddled in the stream, from morning sun till dinner, but broad seas before us both have roared since auld lang syne.' "

I paused to catch my breath.

"Go on," my father said.

" 'And here's a hand, my trusty friend, and give us a hand of thine, and we'll take a right good little drink for auld lang syne. And surely you'll be in your cups, and surely I'll be good for mine, and we'll take a cup of kindness yet, for auld lang syne.' "

"What else?"

"It says that Burns was inspired to write this poem by hearing an old man's singing."

"What old man sings?" he asked me.

We didn't go. Edgar and I decorated the dining room with balloons and streamers. While Sarah slept, we made a crown for

Freedo, and put on the music from *Mary Poppins,* and poured her a champagne flute filled to the top with ginger ale.

Just before midnight, we woke her up.

"Happy New Year, sweetheart," I said to her as I lifted her out of her bed and felt the heaviness of her sleep.

"Aren't we going to go?" she asked me.

"No. Not tonight."

"I miss Aunt Heather," she said. "I miss Grandpa."

Get used to it, I wanted to say.

Edgar danced with her on his shoulders.

I let her rummage through my drawers and my jewelry box for dress-up things.

At midnight, we listened to "Auld Lang Syne" and gave one another a three-way hug.

"Next year," I told Sarah, "you'll have a little sister to celebrate with."

"And next year," she said without hesitating, "I'll have David back, too."

Fifteen minutes later, she was back in her bed, asleep, and I was pacing around the living room, ranting about tradition, family, independence, freedom, regret, betrayal, health, and happiness. I was giddy with rancor, and getting drunk. I told Edgar that I hated Heather. I told him that I would hate her twins. I couldn't imagine ever wanting to be with the family again, I said. I said: "You're right. *This* is our family."

I kissed him ferociously. I said: "Let's not stop at two. Let's have three. Let's have four. Let's have as many as we can. We won't need anyone else."

"Happy New Year, darling," Edgar told me. "You won't feel this way forever."

Spring, 1991

"Do They Celebrate Birthdays in Heaven?"

"Today is David's birthday," Sarah said.

They were her waking words on the first day of March, and she was right, as usual.

"He would have been five today," I said.

"I'm going to be five next month too," she said.

"Do they celebrate birthdays in heaven?" I asked her.

"He isn't in heaven anymore."

"He isn't?"

"Can I have cupcakes for my birthday?"

———

The baby's dresser arrived the next day. With Edgar beside me, I contemplated the crowded geometry of Sarah's bedroom.

"Where's it going to go?" he said.

Sarah came up behind us.

"Put it where the dollhouse is," she said.

"Really?" he asked her.

"Sure."

"And where should we put the dollhouse?" he asked.

"I don't care," she said.

That night, while she was sleeping, we packed it away like a memory.

Emma was born two weeks later. She was small, she was pink, she was perfect, and she was unmarred by any history, or at least any history I could know.

Half-asleep, I nursed her in my hospital room an hour after her birth.

Edgar, exhausted, stared and smiled.

"Should I call your father and Heather and tell them?" he asked me.

"No," I said. "Call home."

Sarah held the baby four hours later: a big girl, sitting in a bedside chair, her feet not quite long enough to touch the ground, her hand not quite strong enough to hold up Emma's head, the head of her little sister.

Edgar stood beside them, contented and amazed. He watched the two of them. I watched the three of them. They were my family. I wept.

"Why are you crying, Mommy?" Sarah said.

"Because I'm so happy."

"I'm happy too."

"I know you are," I told her.

"You're a big sister now," Edgar said.

"Will she always be my sister, Mommy?"

"Of course," I said.

"Should I call them now?" Edgar asked me.

"No."

I dozed with Emma asleep at my breast. At some point, Edgar took Sarah home. Later, a nurse came to take Emma.

"You need your rest, honey," she told me.

All through the night, I woke and smiled.

I thought it was still the middle of the night, but my father was standing before me.

"Daddy," I said, and wondered if I was dreaming.

"Good morning," he said to me nervously.

"Did Edgar call you?"

He nodded. Then he leaned over to kiss my cheek.

"Are you okay?" he asked gently.

"Yes."

"Much pain?"

"It's not too bad yet," I said.

"And the baby?"

"Her name is Emma," I said. "She's great. Do you want to see her?"

"Of course."

I buzzed for the nurse.

"Are you still angry?" he asked me.

"Yes."

The nurse walked in.

"Can you bring her?" I asked.

She nodded, then walked noiselessly back out.

"And how is Sarah?" Dad asked quietly.

"She's doing much better," I told him.

"No talk of David?"

"Very little," I said. "She told me he's not in heaven now."

"Maybe that's because he's in Heather," Dad said.

"Do you really believe that, Daddy?" I said.

He looked into the distance, perhaps into his future.

"I don't even think Sarah believes it now," I said. "Do you really believe it?"

"I guess I'm not sure what I believe," he said. He sounded weary and sad.

"Why did you go with Heather?"

"Sometimes a little myth helps," he said. "I would think you'd understand that."

The nurse came in with Emma, and I held her in my arms.

"This is your granddaughter," I told Dad.

"What's her name?"

My eyes filled with tears for him.

"Her name is Emma, Daddy," I said.

———

At home, Sarah watched while Emma slept. Sarah watched me bathe her, nurse her, wrap her up in blankets.

Sarah sang to her, with her high, clear voice sweetly mangling the lyrics of childhood songs:

"Oh, Susanna,
  Oh don't you cry for me.
  For I come from Alabama
  with a bandage on my knee."

I could not recall a more beautiful sound than the sound of the sister singing.

New Year's Eve, 1958

"Look at Those Schnooks"

The big hand is on the six now, and the small hand is on the one. The champagne that's left in the glasses lost its bubbles long ago.

Heather still sleeps beside me on the couch, her mouth open, her orange nightgown tucked around her toes, her cardboard butterfly wings crumpled behind her.

I lie beside her, pretending that I am sleeping too. Through the tiniest squint of my eyes, I can see the ceiling, where the balloons overlap and combine to make other colors. I can see Mom and Dad by the fireplace, murmuring words that I can't hear.

Then Dad takes a step in our direction. I close my eyes.

"Think we should wake them up and get them to bed?" Dad asks Mom.

"Look at those schnooks," she says.

I smile because I love it when she calls me her schnook.

"I think," my father says, "that one of these schnooks is really awake."

I hear him walk closer to me.

I do not move a muscle. I try to breathe exactly the way that

Heather is breathing. My eyes are closed, but I know that Mom and Dad are standing over me.

Then suddenly, Dad grabs my foot and tickles it, and I start giggling and open my eyes.

"Off to bed with you," he says, pretending to be stern. "Come on," he says. "It's very late now."

"George," Mom says. "Pick Heather up, would you?"

I watch him hoist her over his shoulder, which makes me briefly envious. But of course she won't remember this, whereas I'm going to get the last good nights.

They put Heather in bed in her room and then come into my bedroom, lean over me, and kiss me good night. Then they stand together in my doorway for an instant that lasts forever.

"Good night, schnook," Mom says.

"Good night."

"Happy New Year, darling," Dad says.

"Happy New Year, Daddy," I say. My toes wriggle and reach down to the cool places in the sheets.

They turn off the light in the hallway. I lie awake, hearing their voices and the sounds of them cleaning up, and I fight off sleep for as long as I can, because I know if I sleep, then tomorrow will come.

New Year's Eve, 1991

"What Channel Is Guy Lombardo On?"

Edgar put Emma, nine months old, in a carrier, covered her with his overcoat, and let Sarah put a hat on her head. Hand in hand in the frigid air, we walked to Dad's apartment.

"Hi, hi!" he said, greeting us at the door.

There were ten of us now—six of them, four of us. I hugged Dad. Edgar hugged Heather. Jeffrey hugged Sarah. Richard hugged Emma. Edgar hugged Mark and Arthur, the twins.

"Hi, Grandpa," Sarah said, and gave him a hug and then, shyly, a kiss, and then she asked Edgar if she could hold Emma.

"Only on the couch," he told her.

The twins were three months old now and just waking, it seemed, from the slumber of birth. Heather spread out a quilt on the floor, and we watched them squirm and wiggle. Sarah was staring at Arthur with particular fascination.

Since their birth, I'd been wanting to ask a question.

"Do you know which one you think is David?" I finally said.

She looked at me with utter confusion.

"David died, Mommy," she said.

I looked at Heather, who looked back at me, betraying no emotion.

"Do *you* know?" I asked Heather.

"Know what?" she asked me.

"Know which one you think is David," I said.

"David's dead, Erica," she told me.

Dad looked on, rheumy and pleasant, cocooned in his own confusion. He still had, in his eyes, the hungry look of a man expecting the best. His champagne glasses still caught the light. But he, of course, had forgotten as well.

In Greek myth, there was the River Lethe, from which all the souls of the dead were forced to drink before they could come back to earth. Pope wrote:

> *Here, in a dusky vale where Lethe rolls*
> *Old Bavius sits, to dip poetic souls,*
> *And blunt the sense.*

No people were allowed back to earth until they had forgotten their lives. I did not know a myth of forgetting on earth, except, perhaps, the myth of time.

We were all together, on New Year's Eve, and everyone had forgotten—or perhaps simply willed things into the past. Of course they all knew that Heather and Richard had had a son named David, and when Sarah saw pictures of him, she knew she was looking at her cousin. But heaven was gone now, quietly vanished, and all the talks she had had with David were as lost and inconsequential as the talks and fights that they had inspired.

Heather took turns holding the twins throughout much of the evening, even when they slept. She eyed them with passionate pride and intensity, laced her arms through Jeffrey's and Richard's, and talked about having her four boys with her.

The fifth she would no doubt continue to bury and resurrect, resurrect and bury, and there would be no chance of knowing where she believed on heaven or earth he stood.

I mourned the myth despite myself, the exquisite magic of heaven and the promise of its timelessness. But the present tense seemed to have swept me up in a large, high rolling, wave, and though I knew it would someday crash again, on the shore of the stubborn past, I had learned it was best for everyone if I kept that to myself.

"What channel is Guy Lombardo on?" Dad asked.

Not an eyebrow was raised, not a glance exchanged.

"It's on four," Heather told him.

"Four," Richard said.

"Let's find out," I said.

The chimes of his clock struck early. He didn't notice, or mind. He waltzed with Sarah. He waltzed with Heather and me.

We turned on the TV at a quarter to twelve, and watched the ball drop and the confetti fall, and saw all the warm, mad, grateful embraces of another new year.

Acknowledgments

I would like to thank:

Dr. Patricia Nachman and Dr. Mary Sickles for their insights about child psychology.

Liz Darhansoff, Ann Patty, Suzie Bolotin, Betsy Carter, Michael Solomon, and the Grunwalds for their excellent help and advice.

My husband, Stephen Adler, for his unfailing wisdom, patience, and love.